Caught in a Bind

Also by Gayle Roper

Caught in the Middle
Caught in the Act

Caught in a Bind

Gayle Roper

book three

an amhearst mystery

ZondervanPublishingHouse
Grand Rapids, Michigan

A Division of HarperCollinsPublishers

Caught in a Bind
Copyright © 2000 by Gayle G. Roper

Requests for information should be addressed to:

ZondervanPublishingHouse
Grand Rapids, Michigan 49530

Library of Congress Cataloging-in-Publication Data

Roper, Gayle G.
    Caught in a bind / Gayle Roper.
      p.   cm.—(An Amhearst mystery ; bk. 3)
      ISBN: 0-310-21850-0 (softcover)
      1. Women journalists—Fiction.   I. Title.
PS3568.O68 C36 2000
813'.54—dc21
                                                    99-088547
                                                              CIP

Interior design by Jody DeNeef

Printed in the United States of America

00 01 02 03 04 /❖ DC/ 10 9 8 7 6 5 4 3 2 1

For Christine Tangvald with love

You are a woman of God who knows how to live godly in Christ Jesus. And you are fun! I wouldn't have missed all those writer's conferences and Disney World visits for anything.

Acknowledgments

Thanks to:

Pen and Angela Frey for their enthusiastic help and plot suggestions. Pen, you could sell an automobile to an Amishman!

Linda Ingham, director of Jesus Connection of Lancaster County, for her insights and encouragement. Linda, your work with the women at REST Ministries has been a true God-thing, blessed and powerful.

Dave Lambert, Lori VandenBosch, Sue Brower, Joyce Ondersma, and all the other wonderful folks at Zondervan. You guys are a delight to work with!

Chapter 1

This time the trouble I got myself into wasn't Jolene's fault. Not that she helped matters any, but at least she wasn't the cause. Edie was. Or rather, Edie's husband.

Edie Whatley is my coworker at *The News*: the voice of Amhearst and Chester County, where she is editor of the family page and a features writer. I'm a general reporter and features writer.

"Edie," I called across the aisle that separated my desk from her desk in the newsroom. "Are we doing a house this week for the Great Homes of Chester County series? Can I do the ironmonger's mansion at Hibernia Park?" I thought of the big orange-colored home set on the knoll above the gently sloping lawn. It would be fun to write about it and its history. Since I'd moved to eastern Pennsylvania several months ago, I'd found local facts and trivia fascinating.

There was no response from Edie. In fact, she didn't seem to hear me at all.

"Edie!" I all but shouted.

Still nothing.

I frowned at her. Edie was the kindest and most thoughtful of people. It wasn't like her not to answer, especially since she was doing nothing but stare at her CRT screen.

Then spoke Jolene, Queen of Tact, with her usual insight and understanding into the difficulties of life. "Edie, what in the world's the matter with you? You've been a mess all day. Get a grip, woman." She scowled at Edie, her beautiful face contorted with frustration.

"Jolene!" I was appalled not only at her words but her acid tone. Still, I had to admit that she got Edie's attention. Edie sat wide-eyed and blinking, skewered by Jolene's accusing gaze.

"Spill it," Jolene demanded. "We know something's wrong. What is it? Is it Randy?" Randy was Edie's fifteen-year-old son whose life journey kept all of us glued for the next painful installment. Talk about *As the World Turns*.

"Randy's fine," Edie said.

Jolene and I looked at each other, then back at Edie.

"He is?" I said with more disbelief than was probably good for our friendship.

"Well," she hedged. "Probably fine is too strong a word, but he's not bad."

"He's not?" Jolene's surprise was equally obvious.

Edie's face scrunched momentarily in pain as she understood what we had inadvertently revealed about our opinions of her son. Then she got huffy Edie-style. "I *said* he's fine."

"Well, if it's not Randy," Jolene continued to probe, unabashed at having hurt Edie, "then what's wrong? Is it Tom?"

Edie flinched and smiled brightly. "Tom?" False little laugh. "Of course not. He's fine. What could possibly be wrong with him?"

I frowned. A good question. What could possibly be wrong with Tom? He and Edie were the perfect couple. Being around them was instant tooth decay due to the sweetness of their relationship. I don't mean just lovey, which I happen to think is good, or considerate, which I happen to think is necessary. It was the touching, the patting, the unconscious back rubbing and collar adjusting. Quite simply, Tom and Edie doted on each other and didn't care who knew.

Tom was Edie's second husband, and therein lay part of Randy's problems. He didn't like his stepfather.

Not that Tom should take that lack of appreciation personally. Randy wouldn't have liked any stepfather. In fact, Randy didn't like any adults as far as I could see. He also didn't like many kids, and I strongly suspected he didn't care much for himself either.

But Tom took the brunt of all the boy's angst, anxiety, and anger. More than once, Edie had come to work teary-eyed, only to tell Jolene and me about Randy's latest verbal abuse and disobedience.

I'd seen a picture of Randy's original father once. He was a giant of a man, all muscles and good looks, broad shoulders and charming smiles. He was Hulk Hogan with short hair, an amiable manner, and a dress shirt, a Certified Financial Planner who over the years had made a mint in the stock market both for himself and his clients. Randy resembled his father in size and coloring, a fact that gave him immense pride.

Tom on the other hand was a slight man, five feet eight inches in his hiking boots, gentle, pleasant, and balding. Typical of a teen, Randy looked at Tom's unprepossessing appearance and refused to think of him as anything but a wimp.

"He's a car salesman!" Randy would mock, as if automotive retail was on a par with prostitution. "Give me a break!"

I looked at Randy's mother as she sagged at her desk. She did indeed look upset, unsettled in spite of Randy doing "not bad" and Tom being fine.

"Is Tom sick?" I asked Edie. Surely something like a major illness would explain her melancholy.

Edie shook her head. "Not that I know of."

Not yes or no. Not that I know of. What an unusual answer.

I nodded. "Good." I had another thought. "He didn't lose his job or anything, did he?"

Edie shook her head quickly, actually smiling at the thought of Tom losing his job. "Are you serious? Hamblin Motors would fall apart without him."

I reached out and pulled a discolored leaf from the philodendron that sat on the edge of my desk. I wagged it in front of Jolene to show her she'd missed it when she did her daily Gertie the Gardener check on all the office greenery. "That's true about Hamblin's," I agreed. Even I, the relative newcomer to Amhearst, knew that Tom was Hamblin's mainstay. Of course, my major source for this information was Edie, and I recognized that she was a wee bit prejudiced.

"He's the best salesman they have," Edie said, unconsciously straightening her back with pride. "He just won a trip for two to Hawaii because of his winter doldrums sales. Only ten prizes were awarded in the whole country, and he won one."

"Hawaii?" Jolene looked impressed. "When do you go?"

"In three weeks." Edie looked uncertain, then nodded. "In three weeks."

"Then what are you so upset about?" Jolene wouldn't let well enough alone. "I mean, Hawaii!"

"I'm not upset."

"And I'm not Eloise and Alvin Meister's little girl." Jolene's chin took on that stubborn set that meant she was taking no prisoners. Poor Edie was about to be slaughtered on the altar of Jolene's curiosity and need to know.

"Jo," I said quickly, "I think your plants need watering."

Jolene glanced around the newsroom at the lush greenery that threatened to make the place resemble a nursery. A giant grape ivy that had once tried to eat me alive sat on the soda machine. A huge jade plant graced the filing cabinet, and spectacularly healthy African violets sat in perpetually blooming splendor on the sill of the big picture window at the far end of the room.

She shook her head as she checked the soil of the spider plant on her desk. Baby spider plants erupted from the stems like little green and white explosions. "They're all fine. I watered them yesterday."

"But those little yellow daffodils and the tall white ones look like they're drooping." I pointed to a cluster of pots on top of the file cabinet where the poinsettias had been at Christmas. If anything would distract Jo from Edie, it would be her plants.

"They're not drooping. They're leaning toward the sun." She rose and went to them. "And those white daffodils are not daffodils but narcissi." She deftly twisted the pots until all were facing the room.

My plant ploy didn't work. Jo returned to her desk undeterred.

"Come on, Edie. Give. Something's wrong. I know it. Of all the people who work here, you're the most stable."

"What?" I turned to Jolene, wide-eyed and blinking myself, to say nothing of irritated.

Jolene saw my look of outrage and grinned. "We all know I'm an emotional wreck," she said conversationally. "Though you've got to admit I've been getting better in recent weeks."

She paused a minute, looking expectantly at Edie and me, waiting for us to agree. After a short pause, we realized what she expected.

"Right," Edie said hastily. "You're getting better."

I nodded agreement. "It's church," I offered. "You're listening to Pastor Hal."

Jolene shrugged. "Maybe. Maybe not." Church was new to her and still made her uncomfortable. She returned to her commentary on office personnel. "We all know our noble editor

Mac is so on edge over the buyout of the paper that he can't even sit still, let alone think straight."

Edie and I nodded. Mac was certainly acting strangely though I thought maybe Dawn Trauber, director of His House, had as much to do with his foul mood as the paper.

"And you, Merry," Jolene continued, "are so bemused over Curt that you're always on some far mental planet."

"I beg your pardon," I said, miffed. "I am very much in control, aware, and on top of things."

She gave her patented snort, the unfeminine sound always a surprise coming from someone as lovely as Jolene. "That control and awareness are why Mac has been waving at you for the past five minutes, I guess?"

"What?" I looked quickly over my shoulder toward the end of the room. Sure enough, Mac was staring at me, his scowl so intense that his eyebrows were one long line from temple to temple. It was a wonder I hadn't felt the laser beam of his frustration cutting between my shoulder blades.

"You could have told me," I muttered as I rose from my seat and made my way toward Mac. "And Edie, ignore her. You don't have to answer any of her questions."

"Right," Jolene agreed. "At least not until Merry gets back. She wants to hear what's got you in such a tizzy too."

"Jolene!" The woman would never quit.

Edie smiled weakly at me as I walked past her desk. "I'm okay," she said with all the independent spirit of a groveling puppy. I looked at her skeptically. "Really." She gave me a shaky smile. "I'm just fine."

Even if her eyes hadn't teared, I don't think I would have believed her. I might tend to be too accepting for my own good at times, but I'm not completely without perception. Unlike a certain gorgeous coworker I could mention.

Suddenly Mac's bellow tore through the newsroom.

"Edie, for Pete's sake. Get over here!"

I stopped and pivoted to return to my seat.

"Where are you going, Kramer?" Mac snarled.

"But you said Edie."

"I want you both."

I turned back to him and continued between the worn desks until I was standing in front of him. He sat beside the great picture window on the second floor of *The News* building, his desk at right angles to the window. He loved to sit back in his ergonomically correct chair and stare down on Main Street, feeling the power that went with the editor's position.

Or, acting editor.

Mac had been acting editor for the past several months while *The News* was for sale. Recently the paper had been purchased, and Mac was going slowly insane wondering whether he would have a job come next Monday when the new publisher, Jonathan Delaney Montgomery, took over officially. We all understood Mac's uncertainty and had been more than charming and forgiving of his grumps and harangues. After all, Mac was a grouch in the best of times.

Still, he was going overboard with his testiness, and at times like this, I found my teeth grinding with repressed spleen. As I saw it, the greatest danger in waiting for Mr. Montgomery to decide whether Mac had a job wasn't Mac's career. It was the incipient development of ulcers in everyone in the newsroom.

"Mac," I said as I looked across his cluttered desk at him. "Please be easy with Edie. She's upset about something, and if you yell at her, it won't be good."

"You mean she'll cry?" he asked in disgust.

"Could be."

Mac looked at me with barely concealed contempt, whether directed at me for interfering, or Edie for being a possible crier, I couldn't tell. "I am always considerate of my people," he barked as Edie approached the desk.

I bit my tongue and said nothing.

He turned from me to Edie. "Now, Whatley, I've got a great assignment for you. I want you to do an article on spousal abuse."

Edie shuddered and actually swayed. She put out a hand to steady herself, gripping Mac's desk hard enough to whiten her knuckles.

"Edie," I said, grabbing her elbow. "Are you all right? Do you feel dizzy? Sick?"

"And you, Kramer." Mac plowed on as if he hadn't noticed Edie's distress, and he probably hadn't. "You are to do a profile of Stephanie Bauer, director of that organization that helps abused wives. You know the one. It's down a couple of blocks on Main Street."

I kept hold of Edie while I turned back to Mac. "You mean Freedom House?"

"Yeah, that's it. Find out how the place works and see if you can interview some of the abused women. You know, tearjerker stuff like you did with those pregnant girls at Christmas."

I nodded. Not a bad assignment.

"You two are to work together on this thing." Mac looked from Edie to me and back. "Got that?"

I nodded. Edie just turned away, removing herself from my support.

"Edie!" Mac's voice was abrupt.

She turned a white face to him, but he didn't see. He was looking at something on his desk. "Yes?" Her voice was a whisper.

"Do you understand what I want?"

"Yes," she whispered again. She turned and began walking back to her desk. "But I hate it." The last was under her breath.

"What?" Mac barked.

"Nothing. Nothing at all."

I blinked and looked at Edie. She hated the assignment? It was a great assignment with lots of potential for a very interesting couple of articles.

I stopped halfway back to our desks and put my hand on Edie's arm. She stopped too and looked at me.

"What's wrong, Edie? And don't tell me nothing," I said as she opened her mouth to say just that. She even got the *noth* out.

I liked Edie. She was a genuinely nice lady, slightly plump but cute in a wholesome way. She wore all her clothes a size too small, not because she wanted to be sexy or provocative but because she always kept hoping she'd lose that ten to fifteen pounds. Her fine, light brown hair was cut shoulder length and hung straight, swaying when she turned her head. Her blue eyes were often sad, but if Randy were my son, I'm sure I'd look sad a lot too. I hated to see her so upset.

She looked at me for a minute, then looked at the floor.

"I just want to help," I said.

She shook her head. "Let it go, Merry." Then to my surprise, she patted my hand. "But thanks for caring." She turned abruptly and almost ran to the women's room, a one-person operation where she could find privacy.

I watched her go, and as I turned back to my desk, I saw Jolene watching too. "We've got to find out what's wrong," Jo said.

"No, Jo," I said. "If and when she wants to tell us about it, she will."

Jo looked at me in disgust. "You're no fun," she said, but when Edie finally returned red-eyed to her desk, Jo kept quiet.

I spent the balance of the day reading the clippings on Freedom House and talking to the director, Stephanie Bauer, on the phone. I learned that Freedom House was established five years ago and that Stephanie had been its only director. I learned that in addition to providing counseling and comfort to abused wives, Freedom House sponsored training workshops for churches who wanted to know how to help abused women in their congregations.

I studied the pictures of Ms. Bauer and saw a woman of about forty, very slim and attractive with great dark eyes and dark curly hair.

"I was an abused wife," she was quoted as saying in one article. "I know what these women are going through. I know their fear and desperation. I know their feelings of being powerless. I also know God can help them deal with the overwhelming helplessness. I know they can live again."

How did she learn to live again, I wondered. What specifics marked her flight from her husband to her position at Freedom House? Or had he reformed and she was still married to him?

"May I come interview you some day soon?" I asked Stephanie when I finally reached her.

"I'd love to talk with you," Stephanie said. "Tomorrow? I know it's Saturday, but my schedule is crazy what with the ministry, the Easter holidays, and my kids."

I checked my calendar. I had rehearsal with the bell choir tomorrow morning for the upcoming Easter services, but I was free Saturday afternoon. Curt was taking me to the reception tomorrow night that Mr. Montgomery was throwing for *The News* staff and invited guests—not, of course, the invited guests of *News* staffers but of Mr. Montgomery. The reception was being held in the Brennan Room at City Hall, a wonderful place with a huge chandelier, beautiful wood wainscoting and crown moldings, and atmosphere galore. I thought it was savvy of Mr. Montgomery to use one of Amhearst's prime places of pride for his welcoming reception. Endear himself to the local community and all that.

But first Freedom House.

"Is two o'clock all right?" I asked Stephanie.

"Will we be finished by three?" she asked. "I have an appointment with my daughter at three. We're going shopping. She 'needs' some spring clothes."

"We'll be finished by then," I promised. Then thinking it might fit into the article, I asked, "How old is your daughter?"

"Fifteen."

Just like Randy, I thought. Poor Stephanie.

"A teenager at the mall," I said, sarcasm dripping a bit too freely. "It ought to be an interesting afternoon for you."

"It will be interesting," Stephanie said, ignoring my tone. "I enjoy anything I get to do with Sherrie. We're both so busy! And Rob is no better."

"Rob's your—?"

"My son," Stephanie said. "He's eighteen. We've been filling out financial information for colleges all year, and the hardest part is finding a night when we're both home!"

When I hung up from my conversation with Stephanie, I glanced at Edie. Stephanie's relationship with her children seemed the polar opposite of Edie's with Randy. What made the difference? Both women had had hard times in their marriages, but one had fun with her kids and the other cried. I couldn't help but wonder why.

It was almost five o'clock when Jolene said, "Hey, Merry, Edie, let's go get dinner together."

"Not a bad idea," I said. I hadn't been looking forward to a lonely Friday night. Curt was away overnight on a men's retreat, and he'd talked Jo's husband into going along. Apparently Jo wasn't any more anxious to fritter the night away alone than I was.

"Thanks, but I can't," Edie said. "I need to get home."

"But Tom works on Friday nights, doesn't he?" Jolene asked.

"Well, yes," Edie admitted.

"And Randy's certainly big enough to feed himself."

I could tell Jolene had been thinking about this dinner for some time, probably all afternoon. She'd figured out all the angles, something for which she was justly famous.

"He won't be home for dinner," Edie said, then covered her mouth in dismay. She had just thrown away her best excuse to decline, which was obviously what she was trying to do without much success. Bucking Jolene was never easy.

With a sigh that was part pain and part capitulation, Edie shrugged and said, "Okay. I'll just call and leave a message for Randy telling him where I'm going."

I'm sure it wasn't the most gracious acceptance Jolene had ever received, but she seemed more than happy. After all, she'd now have Edie in close quarters for an hour. More than enough time to turn the screws.

Now you be good," I whispered to Jolene as we waited for a table to open up at Ferretti's, Amhearst's one and only decent restaurant. "Edie doesn't need you badgering her."

"Me? Badger?" Jolene looked at me aghast.

This time I was the one who snorted.

"I didn't know you could do that," Edie said as she came to stand in line beside me upon her return from the ladies' room. "Have you been taking lessons from Jolene? I've never met anyone who can snort as well as she can—and still look beautiful."

Jolene, about to protest Edie's jibe, mellowed immediately when she heard the "beautiful" comment. Edie might be upset about something, but she still knew her way around a back-handed compliment.

I grinned. "I'm afraid it comes naturally. But I've gotten much more expressive at it since I've gotten to know Jolene."

"Well, I like that," Jolene huffed as we followed Astrid, the hostess, to our booth.

"Eggplant parmigiana," Jo told our waitress. "Raspberry vinaigrette dressing on the salad. And lots of rolls."

"Spaghetti and meatballs," I said. "Parmesan peppercorn dressing and lots of rolls too." I looked at Jolene and grinned. "There's something to be said for not seeing the guys tonight."

"A cup of chicken noodle soup," Edie said. "And a roll."

"A salad?" asked the waitress.

Edie shook her head. "Just the soup."

"You're on a diet! How wonderful!" Jolene said with her usual diplomacy.

"I'm just not hungry," Edie said, tugging self-consciously at the gaping front on her shirt.

"You can tell Tom's coming home tonight," I said, winking at Jo. "No garlic bread."

And just like that, Edie began to cry.

Chapter 2

I'm sorry, I'm sorry." Edie brushed at her eyes and sniffed mightily. She grabbed her napkin and blew her nose. She took a couple of deep breaths. "I'll be all right. I will." And still the tears rolled down her face.

"Oh, Edie," I said, instantly distressed for her. "Oh, Edie." I leaned over and put my arm around her shoulder. She began to cry harder.

My problem is that, while I feel badly for people at the drop of a hat, I'm not always certain how to make things better. I had no idea what to do for Edie. I just knew that she couldn't keep crying in a public restaurant without people noticing. And when they noticed, she would become even more upset.

For once Jolene kept her mouth shut. Instead she grabbed my arm, looked at me over Edie's bent head, and mouthed very clearly, "Fix it."

I stared at her blankly. "How?" I mouthed back.

Jolene made a desperate face and gave a great shrug.

I grabbed my napkin and shoved it into Edie's hands. "Here. Blow again." I patted her shoulder some more.

I was surprised when she did as I said.

Jolene, watching the goings-on with a gimlet eye, smiled at me and nodded her approval like a queen bestowing royal approbation. I ignored her and continued to pat Edie like I knew what I was doing.

"I'm sorry," Edie said again. "I'm such a baby."

"No, you're not. Not at all," I said. "We don't mind the tears, do we, Jolene?"

There was no response. I stared across the table at her until she mumbled something that sounded like, "Mmmphmm." I rolled my eyes and said softly to Edie, "We just mind whatever is making them fall."

She smiled weakly at that.

Jolene took one look at that travesty of a smile and decided Edie was well on the way to recovery. It was time for her to step in.

She reached out and awkwardly patted Edie's hand. "Okay, that's enough. It's time to straighten that spine."

Once again I was appalled and once again Edie responded positively.

"You're right." She crumpled the paper napkins into a ball and stuffed them into her purse. She sat up straight and looked from Jolene to me. "No more."

Jolene nodded as if she expected nothing less. Queens are used to being obeyed. "It's Randy, isn't it? It's okay; you can tell us what's the trouble. We'll understand. What's he done? Gotten arrested? Failed a big test? Gotten kicked out of school?"

Edie shook her head. "It's not Randy, believe it or not." She fell silent and looked from Jolene to me and back, hesitating as if telling us more was painful beyond belief.

I frowned. "Then it's Tom?" There seemed no other choice. I patted Edie's hand yet again. When in doubt, pat.

Edie looked at her clenched hands. "It's Tom."

The anguish in her voice made my chest ache. I always hated it when a husband and a wife had trouble, but I especially hated it now because Curt and I were so happy. Not that we were husband and wife, but I knew it was just a matter of time. And I wanted everyone to be as happy as we were.

"What's he done, Edie?" Jolene leaned in, fire in her eyes. She was ready to hate Tom for Edie's sake.

"I don't know," Edie whispered.

"What do you mean, you don't know?" Jolene demanded.

I shot Jolene a look. "Easy."

She scowled at me but sat back, lowering the intensity level considerably.

"I don't know," Edie repeated, her voice again full of tears.

I grabbed Jolene's napkin and stuffed it in Edie's hand just to be prepared. "Then how do you know there's a problem?" I asked gently.

She took a deep breath and forced herself to look at us. "Tom didn't come home last night." Then she looked away immediately, embarrassed by what she had confessed. She became absolutely fascinated with her plain white paper place mat.

"Another woman," pronounced Jolene without hesitation. She slapped the table for emphasis.

"Jolene!" I kicked her under the table.

Edie paled. "No," she whispered. "Please, God, no." It was an anguished prayer.

"That can't be the problem," I said, as ever eager to comfort. "I've seen you and Tom together. If ever two people loved each other, Edie, it's you guys."

"I always thought so too." The words were a mere whisper. She spun her water glass in circles, watching it slide in the condensation that had collected on the table. She looked up with haunted eyes. "But what if I'm wrong? What if Jolene's right?"

Just then our waitress brought Jolene and me our salads. Edie lowered her head to hide her red eyes, but the waitress looked at her curiously anyway. Jolene stared at the waitress until she blinked, flushed, and went quickly toward the kitchen. I watched her retreat with satisfaction and smiled at Jolene. There are occasional benefits in having a brassy friend.

I looked at my salad with its creamy dressing, surprised at how unappetizing it looked. Stress always affects my appetite. Still, I thanked God silently for the food, begged for wisdom, and stabbed a cucumber. I crunched it between my teeth, but it might as well have been Styrofoam for all the taste it had.

"He wasn't in an accident or anything, was he?" I asked. "Maybe he was injured and couldn't contact you."

"Merry the Merciful." Acid etched Jolene's comment. "Always looking for the Pollyanna way out."

"It's better than always assuming the worst." I stabbed a poor, innocent cherry tomato that reacted to my ill humor by shooting across the table and beyond. It landed on the table of an elderly couple across the aisle. When they looked up in surprise at the incoming missile, I made believe it wasn't mine.

"I spoke to the hospital and the police," Edie said. "The hospital says he's not there, and the police say there was no accident involving bodily injury last night anywhere in the county."

"That's good," I said as I gently skewered another tomato. It shot a stream of red juice and seeds straight at my heart. I stared at the red stain on my new pink charmeuse blouse and sighed. That's what I got for not being brave enough to own up to the first cherry bomb.

Edie smiled weakly. "I can't decide whether it's good news or bad news."

I remembered the old line: If I have to choose between another woman's arms and mangled in the street, I'll take mangled in the street anytime.

"Well, it's only one night." Jolene buttered her roll and took a huge bite. "What's one night?"

I think she was trying to be encouraging, but it wasn't working. One night would be devastating to me if I were in Edie's shoes.

Edie shook her head. "We made a vow to each other when we got married. We'd never be separated for the night unless it was unavoidable. And then we'd always call."

"So he couldn't find a phone," I said. Even without Edie and Jolene's stares, I knew that was a foolish line in this day and age.

"Did he show up at work this morning?" Jolene stabbed a forkful of greens and ate them with pleasure. I knew from past experience that very little interfered with her appetite.

Edie shook her head. "They haven't seen him at the dealership since nine last night." Her eyes were large and worried. "It's like he's disappeared."

"Aliens," said a snide voice behind me. "Though why they'd want him is beyond me."

"Randy!" His mother spun and, with a mixture of surprise and hurt, looked at him looming behind her. "What are you doing here?"

"I got your message on the answering machine about going to dinner with the girls." Somehow he made those few words sound very much like an attack on Edie's affection for her husband—and her son. "I came to get some money." Which, he didn't need to say, was his due.

"How did you get here?" Edie asked.

"I rode my bike." He glanced out the window where we could see it chained to a parking meter. "Only four more months until I get my car." He all but rubbed his hands together in anticipation. "Then it's good-bye bike!"

He was getting a car for his sixteenth birthday? He bad-mouthed Tom and still expected a car? Talk about gall!

He proceeded to confirm yet again my opinion of him by extending his hand to Edie, palm up. "Money." It was a command.

"But I gave you your allowance the other night." Edie scrambled to sound forceful but failed. "You wanted it early because you and the guys were going out somewhere."

"Well, it's gone. I need more." He stared down at her, tall, handsome, and implacable.

I wanted to poke Randy hard, inflict a little pain. Edie just sighed and began rummaging in her purse.

"By the way, Mom." Randy's voice took on an edge that made my teeth ache. I could hear the nasty glee and knew he was going to say something that would hurt Edie. And he was glad. "The police were at the house."

"What?" Edie stared at her son. "Did they say anything about Tom? Is he hurt? Where is he?" She started to rise.

"Don't get all overheated, Mom." Randy put a hand on her shoulder and pushed her down. "They don't know where Tom-boy is. In fact, they're looking for him, just like you."

Edie blinked. "Are you sure they were looking for him? They weren't coming to tell me something had happened to him?"

"They were looking for him."

She looked helplessly at me. "Something's happened to him. I know it. That's the only possible reason that he's missing."

"Randy." I looked up at the blond man-child with the wicked glint in his eyes. "Exactly what did the police say?"

"They said," and he paused for effect, making believe he was thinking. "They said that they needed to talk with Tom."

"That was it?" I asked.

He nodded. He looked at his mother with a disdainful smirk. "Isn't that enough, Mom? I mean, the cops are after him!"

Jolene opened her mouth to retort when a sweet young voice called, "Hey, Randy."

Randy jerked like he had been hit with an electric cattle prod. He spun to look at the lovely girl passing us on her way to a table on the other side of the restaurant. Gone was the smart-mouthed kid who delighted in causing his mother distress and in his place was a self-conscious, thoroughly smitten young man who stared at the little ebony-haired beauty, his heart in his eyes.

"Sherrie," Randy managed to say. "Hey, yourself." He wandered after her like he couldn't do anything else.

"He'd better watch himself," Jolene muttered. "His tongue's hanging out so far he's going to step on it any moment."

The girl was with a woman who had to be her mother, their hair and eyes showing that relationship clearly. A young man took a seat at their table, probably a brother by the casual way he treated Sherrie. In fact, he watched Randy stare at Sherrie with a smirk and a raised eyebrow. When Randy, smiling and chatting, took the last seat at the table without waiting for an invitation, the young man looked at his mother and just shook his head.

"Look at him talking to them. He's being polite." Edie stared in wonder at her son. "He's even being nice to the mother."

"You know kids are always at their worst at home," Jolene said as she ate the last bite of the crusty rolls that Ferretti's was famous for.

And how do you know that, I wanted to ask our newest authority on child development, but I didn't. Instead I turned to Edie.

"You've done a good job as a mom, Edie. Maybe a better job than you realized." I smiled. "Be happy about that."

She grunted, unconvinced, and we all acknowledged silently that the jury was still out on Randy and on Edie's good mothering. We tackled our main courses silently.

None of us wanted dessert, so when the bill came we gathered our belongings and went to the cash register. Edie glanced toward Randy, but he was studiously avoiding us as he listened attentively to Sherrie's mother talk.

"I guess he'll just have to ride his bike home," she said. I applauded the touch of starch in her voice. "If he can't talk to me, I can't wait for him. Right?"

"Personally, I think you should take his bike and make him walk," Jolene said. "It'd teach him a bit about respect."

Edie giggled as she went through the door. "He never did get the money he wanted. He'll ruin any good impression he might be making when he pulls out an empty wallet and that poor girl's mother has to pay for his food."

"Serve him right," Jolene said succinctly.

We walked in the spring dusk to the parking lot behind *The News* and dispersed to our separate cars. I was just about to put the key in my ignition when a thought struck me. I climbed out of the car and walked to Edie, who sat staring out the windshield of her little red Escort.

I knocked on the side window. Edie jumped, then lowered the window.

"Edie, I don't think you should go home to an empty house. It's been too hard a day."

"Maybe it's not empty," she said.

I knew that was a comment born of hope, but I also knew Tom worked tonight—assuming he was around to work. He worked every Friday night. In fact, he worked every night except Saturday and Sunday.

"Tom won't be home for two to three hours. Let's stop for a video and watch it together until he gets home."

I watched Edie's shoulder sag in relief and knew she'd been afraid to go home. I resisted the urge to pat her, got in my car, and followed her to the video store. We argued gently over our choices of films and ended up with an old Cary Grant comedy and a new Harrison Ford adventure, both nicely escapist.

I had never been to Edie's house before. I followed her to the outskirts of town where she pulled into the driveway of a white and brick split level with maroon shutters and lots of uninspiring yew bushes. Clumps of daffodils nodded their heads among the yews, warm splashes of sunshine in the glow from the light beside the walk. A dogwood sat in the middle of the front lawn, now just gray branches, in a month or so sure to be a glorious burst of bloom. I wondered if its flowers would be white or pink.

Edie unlocked the front door, painted maroon to match the shutters, and we stepped into an entry hall. The first thing I saw was a beautiful cherry pedestal occasional table with a delftware bowl and a pair of matching candlesticks on it. Above it hung what could only be an original Curtis Carlyle.

"Hey, great painting." I shrugged out of my coat. "Great artist."

Edie actually smiled. "You're prejudiced."

I looked at Curt's lovely portrayal of a creek running beside a stone farmhouse. It was dawn, and the roses and golds of early morning turned the water into a shimmering mirror reflecting the lush greens of the towering evergreens beside the house. I felt restful and serene just looking at the scene. As always with one of Curt's paintings, the detailing was amazing and accurate, and in the lower right corner under his signature were the initials GTG. Glory to God.

I reached out and ran my fingers over the signature.

"You're smiling," Edie observed.

I smiled more broadly. "I'm not surprised."

"You love him."

"Very much."

Edie smiled ever so slightly and looked back at the picture. "I prize this painting. Tom gave it to me for our fifth anniversary last October." She blinked rapidly, turned, and led the way into the living room.

"I'll just be a minute, but I've got to check the answering machine."

"Of course you do. Go right ahead."

I turned and looked at the living room, really looked at it, and I felt my mouth drop open.

The living room was full of the softest robin's egg blue leather furniture I'd ever felt. It sat on the plushest of pastel floral carpets and was lit by Stiffel lamps in glowing brass. The end tables were cherry with a satin sheen, and the coffee table was a great glass and cherry rectangle that took up half the room. The drapes—no, they weren't drapes; they were window treatments—repeated the blue of the furniture and all the pastels of the rug. The walls were covered with more original watercolors including a Scullthorpe, a Gordinier, a Bollinger, and another Carlyle, this one with a dark and stormy sky of deepest purples and blues. As I looked at it, I could feel the heaviness of the storm, hear the crackle of lightning, smell the ozone.

But the thing that caught my eye was the marvelous ceramic vase on the mantel. I had gone to some art shows and antique shops with Curt, and he was teaching me about quality. This vase was quality with a capital Q. The cream background was circled with raised garlands of bluebells and pink roses amid soft celadon leaves and vines. Gilt rimmed the lip of the vase and bathed the base. Fine, soft cracks crazed the entire surface, testifying to its age.

Edie came into the room. "Nothing. Not a single message, let alone one from Tom."

I turned to tell Edie how sorry I was and how much I liked the vase when my eyes fell on the adjoining dining room. Again the furniture was magnificent. Too overwhelming for the size of the room, but magnificent. Cherry sideboard, table, and breakfront gleamed above an oriental rug of luminous crimsons and blues laced with cream. The drapes echoed the colors of the rug, as did the matching seats on the heavy chairs crowded about the table.

I thought of my apartment with its well-used furnishings, most taken from either my bedroom or my parents' attic when I left Pittsburgh and moved here to Amhearst near Philadelphia. I was slowly buying nice pieces, but it'd be years if not forever before I could afford the quality Edie had. Tom must really be doing well at the dealership.

When we slouched on the blue leather sofa to watch Cary Grant maintain his impeccable style even in a negligee with feather trim, I felt I'd slide right off the sofa and onto the floor. I pushed myself upright time after time, only to sink into the enveloping cushions and feel myself slip south, a victim of the smooth grain, featherbed softness, and gravity.

It was almost eleven when we finished watching Harrison Ford save the world, and Tom wasn't yet home. I rolled my head sideways on the sofa and looked at a troubled Edie. I doubted she could recount a single one of Harrison's exploits. Her mind was otherwise occupied.

"Would you like me to stay the night?" I asked.

She looked momentarily tempted. Then she shook her head. "No, thanks. Tom'll be home soon."

Neither of us added, "I hope, I hope, I hope," though I think we both felt like it. I know I did.

No sooner had we fought our way out of the sofa's warm embrace—no easy feat—than the doorbell rang.

Edie looked at me, then the front door. She looked frightened. I didn't blame her. Who rang your doorbell at eleven at night? Only people bringing bad news. The question was: Was the bad news about Tom or Randy?

She took a deep breath and forced herself to walk into the entry and look through the little peephole in the door.

I heard her quick intake of breath. "It's the police."

"Oh, no." It was the worst-case scenario come true. I came to stand with her as she reached for the door.

"It's William."

Somehow that made me feel better. We both knew Sergeant William Poole fairly well from our work at the paper. We were always in contact with the police about one story or another, and William was frequently our contact man, much preferred over Jeb Lammey, the official police PR man who sometimes got persnickety about sharing information and for no observable reasons.

But William was not here for PR now. Edie and I knew from his stance and his face that this was police business, unpleasant police business.

"William." Edie nodded, equally serious. "Come in."

William looked distinctly unhappy, his deeply furrowed face pulled into a great frown. I'd always thought that in spite of his relatively young age, William was the human equivalent of a shar-pei, those Chinese dogs who are all wrinkles. Tonight he appeared to have acquired a few more.

He stopped just inside the door and nodded his head in greeting. "Edie. Merry."

"Is it Randy?" Edie's voice was tight with fear. "Is he hurt? Has he done something wrong and gotten himself in trouble with the law?"

"Easy there." William patted Edie's shoulder. "I'm not here about Randy."

Edie exhaled in momentary relief. One fear defanged. One to go. She closed her eyes as if gathering herself, then took a deep breath.

"If it's not Randy, then it's Tom?" Her voice was a mere whisper.

William nodded. "I need to speak with him."

"What about?"

William shook his head. "I need to speak with *him*, Edie."

Edie's shoulders sagged. "I need to talk with him too."

"I know you spoke to dispatch about him last night." William's brow creased more deeply. "He's still not here?"

"No." It was obvious that confessing to his absence pained her deeply.

William reached into a pocket and pulled out a tablet and pen. "When did you last see him?"

"Yesterday morning about 7 when I left for work."

I watched William scribble *Th 7 AM*. "Did he act in any unusual way? Say anything that in retrospect seems significant?"

"No. It was a morning like every other. He leaves for work later than I do, so he walks me to the car and sees me off. He—" She broke off and looked embarrassed.

"What?" William said. "Tell me, Edie."

"It's nothing bad. It's just a little ritual we have. He presses me against the car and gives me a big hug and kiss. We started it when we were first married and Randy didn't like to see me kiss Tom. The garage is private."

I thought of having to go to the garage to kiss your husband. Sad. Another blot against good old Randy.

"Why are you looking for Tom?" Edie looked William in the eye. "I need to know. Randy told me you were here earlier looking for him. Why?"

William returned Edie's direct look and seemed to reach a decision. "Charges have been filed against him, and I need to question him."

Edie paled. "Charges? What do you mean, charges? What kind of charges?"

William glanced at me, and it was obvious that he was unhappy with what he was about to say.

"Twelve thousand five hundred dollars is missing at Hamblin Motors."

Edie stared at William, aghast. "And they think Tom took it?" Her voice ended in a squeak.

"It's missing and so is he."

Edie looked wild. "But William, that's circumstantial! No one saw him take it, did they? Huh? Did they? Of course not. This is Tom we're talking about."

"Then where is he, Edie? Let me talk to him."

"Believe me, I would if I could." Edie ran a shaking hand through her hair. "Then you'd know. Tell him, Merry. Tell him Tom would never do such a thing." She turned desperate eyes on me.

Oh, Lord! It was definitely arrow prayer time, a plea shot straight from my heart to God's ear. *What do I say?*

And an answer came.

I turned to William. "How did over twelve thousand dollars go missing? It's not like Tom walked up to a cash register and grabbed it, is it? Or held up the dealership like a bank robber does bank tellers? People buy cars on time. Papers get signed, down payment checks get written, but cash doesn't get exchanged."

William just looked at me.

Suddenly I was overcome with doubts. "It doesn't, does it?"

William took a deep breath, and I immediately knew we weren't going to like what he had to say. "It seems that Tom sold a car to an elderly couple Thursday night. The deal was concluded about 8:50." He paused. "This couple paid cash and drove the car off the lot at 9:05."

"Cash?" I was surprised. "They walked into the dealership with twelve thousand five hundred dollars on them?"

"In her purse. In fact, they had about five thousand dollars more because they weren't certain how much the car they finally decided on would cost."

"And you think Tom just kept this money?" Edie's voice shook with outrage.

William's craggy face reflected his unhappiness. "The register was closed for the evening by the time the deal was concluded. Policy in situations like this is to seal the money in an envelope, have it initialed by the salesman and the manager, and lock it in the cashier's drawer until morning when it can be entered into the record appropriately."

"And Tom didn't follow procedure?" I asked.

"He did," William said. "That's how we know about the money."

"You mean that if he hadn't had the manager initial the money, no one would have known?" I was intrigued. "He would have been able to walk off with the money?"

William nodded. "At least no one would have known until the monthly inventory of cars on the lot, and one was found to be missing. Or until the couple brought the car in for servicing and there was no record of the sale or the service warranty."

"But surely if Tom wanted to steal the money, he wouldn't have gone to the manager," I said. "He'd have pocketed the money and walked out the door."

William studied the bare space on the wall beside Curt's painting. "The manager says Tom didn't get the chance to just walk out because he was passing by as Tom took possession of the money. Together they prepared the envelope as soon as the couple left."

"So it's Bill Bond's word against Tom's." Edie eyed William. He nodded.

"Now there's a tough call." Edie was derisive. "Bill Bond is not the most stable of men."

"Why do you say that?" William asked.

"Tom's told me lots of Bill Bond stories. One day he's fine, the next he's not. One day he's your friend, the next he's out for your hide. He's difficult to work under, very egocentric. Not that he does anything illegal. He just likes to ride awfully close to the line. Obviously he has finally crossed it."

William said nothing.

"What?" Edie asked. "Don't you believe me?"

"Edie," William said gently. "Bill Bond is here to talk to. Tom isn't."

Chapter 3

I watched Edie as William made his pronouncement. Tears sprang to her eyes and her mouth twisted in pain. My heart went out to her, and next thing I knew, I was patting her shoulder.

When in doubt, pat.

"I'm sorry, Edie. I have to consider the facts, not feelings or instincts." William looked sad but stoic. Duty first, then maybe friendship, especially a superficial professional friendship. "Bill Bond may not be the world's most charming man, but he hasn't disappeared."

Edie looked resigned. "I know. It's just that Tom is such a good man! He'd never take twelve thousand five hundred dollars. It isn't even logical. Surely you can see that. Twelve thousand five hundred dollars isn't worth ruining your life over."

"What if he wanted to disappear? Twelve thousand five hundred dollars would be a good starting point."

"But why should he want to disappear?" Edie obviously found the idea incomprehensible.

"People disappear all the time. They want to get out of dead end jobs, dead end towns." He looked at her carefully. "Dead end relationships and marriages."

Edie's head jerked like William had slapped her. "Never! We have a wonderful marriage. And believe me, because of past experience, I know good when I see it."

William nodded noncommittally.

"It's true, William. It's true! Tell him, Merry."

"It sure looks like a good marriage to me," I said, glad that this time I could answer the question asked instead of changing the subject. "Edie and Tom enjoy each other and respect each other."

William listened politely to me, then turned back to Edie. "Tell me about Tom, please."

Edie took a deep breath. "He's wonderful, caring, encouraging. He's gentle—"

"Not character traits," William said. "His history, family background, things like that."

Edie became engrossed in studying her fingernails. I thought for a moment that she wasn't going to answer William. Of course, she didn't have to if she didn't want to, at least not without a lawyer present. I wondered briefly what old Mr. Grassley of Grassley, Jordan, and McGilpin would think about being called out in the middle of the night.

"It is no problem," he'd say in his quavery, formal voice. "I am always available to serve my clients."

Then Edie spoke, and Mr. Grassley was allowed to sleep.

"I really can't help you, William." She glanced up from her nails, her face grim. "All I know is that Tom didn't like to talk about his past. He said it was too painful."

Too painful? Was it really, or was Tom harboring secrets?

Edie studied her nails again, finding and picking at a piece of frayed cuticle. "I know about painful pasts, so I've never pushed him."

"You don't even know where he was born? Where he lived before he came to Amhearst?"

"He was born in Philadelphia and lived in Camden, New Jersey, before he moved here."

William smiled, the furrows of his face going through a seismic shift in the process. "See? You know things about him. When was he born?"

"He just celebrated his fortieth birthday on February 15."

I waited to see if William would ask for his Social Security number and his mother's maiden name. With that information, Tom's name, birthplace, and birth date, he could find out anything he wanted to know about Tom.

Then it occurred to me that Bill Bond could supply the Social Security number from the dealership's financial records and that he'd probably do so with great enthusiasm. He wanted that money back.

Immediately I felt guilty because I was assuming Tom had the money. I was forgetting *innocent until proven guilty*. I dared a glance at Edie to see if she had read any of my traitorous thoughts on my face, but she was still working on her nails, slowly and deliberately peeling the soft pink polish from each in turn. I sighed in relief and determined to remember that a reporter is supposed to be unbiased and a friend is supposed to believe.

"Has he always been a car salesman?" William asked.

"I don't know."

"When did he move to Amhearst?"

"I don't know."

"Where does his family live?"

"I don't know."

"Who are his friends?"

Edie's head came up and her shoulders straightened. "Me."

William looked at her for several ticks of the antique mantel clock. Edie held his stare. Then he gave a little smile, closed his notebook, and put it away.

"Thanks for talking with me, Edie. If Tom comes home, please have him contact me immediately." He handed her a card.

"*When* Tom comes home, he'll call you immediately."

After William was gone, Edie curled up in the corner of the blue sofa, hugging herself like she was trying to warm the chill inside.

"Where is he?" The tears she had controlled when William was here flowed down her cheeks unchecked. "Doesn't he know how scared I am?"

I watched Edie and struggled with what to do with the information we had just received from Sergeant Poole. The missing money definitely made the missing man a story. In fact, it made Tom a major story in a small town like Amhearst.

But Edie was my friend. How could I lay her pain before the whole county? But how could I not? I knew Mac would go with the story as soon as he was aware of it, and the fact that Edie was an employee of *The News* wouldn't make any difference. In fact, it couldn't be allowed to make a difference.

And wasn't it better that I write the story than—than who? There was Edie or me. Or Mac. Obviously this story wasn't one Edie could write. And it was definitely better that I write it than Mac. Given his major grouch these days, anyone was better than Mac.

"You know this is going to make *The News*."

Edie nodded in resignation. "I know. You'll write it, won't you?"

"Probably."

"Please. I want it to be you. I know you'll be fair. You'll make it clear that just because Tom is gone and the money is gone, they don't have to be together."

I nodded and sighed. "I'm sorry."

"Me too. I thought my days in the paper were over."

"What days?" I asked, intrigued.

She shook her head, and it was obvious that she regretted the slip of the tongue. She would say no more on that topic.

We sat in silence for a while. Then suddenly Edie started crying again. "Where is he?"

I had no answer, just useless sympathy. "Edie, why don't you go to bed? You can sleep the night away."

She shook her head. "Like I could sleep." She sniffed mightily and looked at me through puffy eyes. "But you go on home, Merry. There's no reason one of us can't have a good night's sleep."

I sat in the blue leather chair, my feet tucked beneath me so I wouldn't slide onto the floor. "I can't leave you like this." I was scandalized at the very idea.

"Pish-posh," Edie said. "I'll be fine."

"Pish-posh? Now where did that come from?" If you aren't patting, distracting is good.

Edie gave a weak smile. "My father always said that."

"What was he like?" I asked, pleased that distracting was working. Maybe I should ask Mac about doing an advice column.

"He was a professor at the University of Delaware, a charmer, a marvelous guy—when he wasn't drunk." She became very interested in the needlepoint pillow in her lap, picking at nonexistent loose threads. "He was a nasty drunk."

I made a distressed noise. So much for the efficacy of distracting.

"Don't let it worry you," she said. "He's dead now. And Mom and I survived."

I wondered at all that was involved in *survived*. "Where does your mother live now?"

"Still in Newark." She said it with the *ark* in Newark getting just as much emphasis as the *New*, unlike Newark, New Jersey, where the accent was definitely on the first syllable. "That's where I lived until I divorced Randolph."

"That's not too far away, is it?" My eastern Pennsylvania geography was still a bit weak.

"Just about an hour."

"Then Randy gets to see his father frequently. Wait. I'm assuming Randolph is still in Newark."

"He's still there, but Randy doesn't see him much."

"Really? I guess I just assumed he did because he's always ..." My voice trailed away because I couldn't find an inoffensive way to say that Randy was always comparing Tom to his dad and Tom came up short every time.

"Because he's always making our lives miserable?"

I felt myself flush. "Yes."

"Randolph's lack of interest is probably the main reason Randy fights with us all the time. A kid always wants what he can't have. Greener grass, I guess. It's an ego thing or a control thing or something. Or maybe it's just as simple as a broken heart. He can't do anything to make Randolph pay attention, so he takes out the pain on us because we're handy and won't turn him out."

I could just hear Jolene saying, "Maybe you *should* turn him out. It'd make a man out of him." I was glad she wasn't here.

"You guys are very good to him."

"Of course we are." Edie looked surprised that I'd find that fact worth commenting on. "I'm his mother."

And that said it all.

I watched Edie trace the pattern on the pillow she held. "So," I asked, "did you meet Tom in Newark or here? Or somewhere else?"

"Here. When I moved here, I lived in a tiny two-bedroom apartment and drove the oldest, most endangered car you've ever seen. Finally the car died, and I had no choice but to buy another even if I couldn't afford it. I went to Hamblin Motors and the rest, as they say, is history." She smiled softly to herself.

"Love at first sight?"

"At least serious like," she said. "He asked me out as soon as I signed the sales papers. I found out later that the price was so good because he didn't take his commission."

"Wow! That is indeed serious like."

"We were married in two months, and I've never regretted a day of it."

At least until last night, I thought, but I didn't say it.

The front door flew open and crashed into the hall wall.

Edie sat straight up. "Tom?" The hope in her voice broke my heart.

Randy stalked by the arch into the living room without so much as a glance in our direction. He continued down the hall to the back of the house. In a moment I heard him opening the refrigerator.

Edie checked her watch. "It's 1:05. No kid his age should be out this late, but, sheesh, tonight I'm just not up to the confrontation. All I can think about is Tom."

I nodded, thinking that Randy had been counting on and was taking advantage of her preoccupation. The kid was clever, a master strategist and champion manipulator. Usually that meant a keen intelligence. What a waste, I thought, to use your mind to wound and distress.

"I just hope he hasn't been with that adorable little Sherrie all this time. Too cute. Too many hormones." Edie shivered. "Imagination and projection—why mothers go gray. And I suffer from an abundance of both."

I could think of nothing to say except, "You're right. Too cute, too many hormones." But I didn't think that kind of identification would help, so I kept quiet.

Randy appeared in the doorway, a can of Mountain Dew in one hand and a bag of Chips Ahoy in the other. He had enough caffeine and sugar there to keep a small town awake for hours. He'd probably wolf it all down and fall immediately into a deep slumber.

"No word from Tom-boy?" he asked his mother.

She shook her head.

He smirked. "Aliens, Mom. Or else he's deserted you."

"Randy!" I couldn't help it. He was being so unkind.

He ignored me. "Just like you did Dad." His smirk deepened. "I guess you're finally getting what you deserve."

Edie sighed. "I'm not going to discuss why I left your father, Randy. You know that. He's your father, and I won't talk against him."

I watched Randy absorb his mother's comments without any perceptible change of expression or posture. I concluded that Edie's comments on this subject were familiar and frequent as, no doubt, were his barbs. He turned to me without even a blink.

"That your car in the drive?" he asked.

I nodded.

"I'm getting a car in a couple of months." He looked back at his mother and said, "My *father* is giving it to me."

"As in Randolph, senior?" I asked.

"He's the only father I've got."

"Oh." I nodded.

He looked nonplused as an idea flicked across his mind. "You weren't thinking of Tom as my father, were you? Little old wimpy Tom-boy?" He laughed. "He wouldn't get me a car if I was the last person on earth."

"And neither would I." Edie's eyes were unflinching as she looked at her son. "Things like cars and the trust to let you have one should be earned."

Randy shrugged. "I guess I'm lucky that Dad doesn't agree." He turned to me. "Want to see my car?"

I glanced at Edie, seeking permission. I didn't want to do anything that would put her and Randy any more at odds than they already were. She raised her hand in a be-my-guest motion. I turned to Randy. "Okay."

He put his Mountain Dew on the glorious occasional table in the hall, and I could see Edie bite her lip to keep from reprimanding him about it. All that condensation on that expensive wood. It didn't bear thinking about.

Randy opened the blue bag of cookies. He pulled out a handful to fortify himself while he showed me the picture of his dream car.

Only it wasn't a picture. It was the real thing.

"Come on," he said. "It's in the garage."

I glanced again at Edie.

"Randolph couldn't remember Randy's birth date," she said. "He thought it was sometime in the spring, so he sent the car ahead so he wouldn't be late."

Randy turned on his mother. "He knows my birthday! He wants me to have the fun of anticipation."

Edie shrugged. "If you say so."

"When is your birthday?" I asked.

"July 13." Randy scowled at me, daring me to make something of the midsummer date.

I merely nodded. "Well, show me."

Still scowling, Randy led me down a level, through the family room, to the connecting door to the garage. He went through first and flicked on the lights. I followed and blinked at what I saw. I knew then that Edie and Tom didn't have a chance.

There, gleaming softly under the harsh overhead light, sat a silver, ragtop Porsche convertible.

"It came three days ago." Randy ran his hand lovingly over the sleek curve of one fender. "Isn't it beautiful?"

"That it is." I began to circle the car. I didn't want to prick Randy's balloon, but all I could think of was how inappropriate I thought this expensive, classy, powerful car was for a novice driver. The potential for a serious accident was incredible!

I remembered my father's immortal words when he looked for a car that he felt appropriate for me and, eight years later, my brother when we first began to drive. "A heavy car. Lots of metal. And slow. Very slow. Why, my first car didn't even have third gear! And it backfired whenever I went over forty. My father loved that car."

And my father had loved the tanks he found for Sam and me despite the rust that threatened their passing inspection every year. But we were both whole and unmarked in spite of the usual new driver debacles.

My favorite accident occurred shortly after I got my license. As I turned a corner, I reached through the steering wheel to brush away a tiny spider. Because of the position of my arm, I couldn't return the wheel to its full and upright position. I ended up driving over the curb and into a giant sycamore. Aside from a broken headlight and a crumpled fender, the gallant old Oldsmobile, operative word *old*, was fine.

If Randy met a sycamore in this marvelous car, he would be in big trouble.

I bent down to peer inside. I might as well study the upholstery before it was drenched with Randy's blood.

Someone had beaten Randy to it.

Blood stained the passenger seat and floor, great quantities of blood, overwhelming quantities of blood. I knew there had to be very little if any left in the very dead man who slumped against the gray leather interior.

Chapter 4

I instinctively backed up and made a little noise halfway between a scream and a burp at the sight of the body. Or maybe it was the blood. I don't know. All I know is that my first thought was that Tom had finally come home.

"What's the matter with you?" Randy demanded, ever sympathetic to a woman in distress.

I couldn't find my voice, so I pointed. He bent and peered in. Next thing I knew he was retching in the corner. So much for perpetual cool.

I made myself look in the car again. I had to know if the corpse was indeed Tom. I didn't want to think about how Edie would react if it were.

It wasn't. First, the body looked too tall, even slumped. Tom was slight all over, and this man had wide shoulders and a paunch. Also, Tom wore his hair closely cropped, and this man had straggly hair that should have been cut weeks ago. Tom was a fastidious dresser who favored shirts crisply ironed, and this man wore a T-shirt with a hole high on his left shoulder where the ribbing of the collar band had begun to separate from the body of the shirt. And of course, this man had the wrong face with strong, broad features instead of the narrow, almost delicate ones that typified Tom.

I straightened from my quick second glance with a deep sigh of relief and turned to Randy, who by now was leaning weakly against the side of the car.

"Get off the car!" I all but shouted.

Randy jumped and obeyed. He looked dazed and green around the gills, much too shocked to react to my yelling at him.

"The car is a crime scene, Randy. We don't want to touch it and contaminate any evidence."

Randy nodded as he swayed, his large body as loose and unfocused as his eyes.

"Back into the house." I walked up to him and pushed. "We need to call 911."

"Sure. 911." He turned and stumbled into the house. I wasted no time following.

Edie took one look at Randy and surged to her feet. "What's wrong?" Her eyes were large with fear.

"There's a dead guy in my car!" Disbelief was the dominant emotion in his voice, now that he was away from the scene and in the safe environs of the living room. Feelings of outrage and violation would follow shortly. "And there's blood all over!"

Edie looked at me, seeking confirmation—or denial—of Randy's comments.

I nodded. "Where's the phone?"

They both pointed to the kitchen.

I called 911 and returned to the living room to find Edie and Randy gone. I hurried to the garage, my mind churning with thoughts of she-doesn't-need-this-right-now and please-don't-touch-anything and do-you-know-who-he-is? I was running across the family room just as Edie and Randy walked back in from the garage.

Edie was white-faced and too composed. She made me nervous. She clasped her hands together so tightly that the knuckles were white.

"Come on, Edie." I put an arm around her shoulders and led her to the sofa. "Lie down. Try and rest."

"I don't know who that is." She looked back toward the garage. "I never saw him before in my life." She spoke very precisely, like she had to concentrate completely on the words or she wouldn't remember them.

The police didn't recognize the corpse either, so he was still a John Doe when we went to press the next day, Saturday. He carried no wallet, no driver's license, no credit cards. His clothes were from Penney's, at least his underwear and T-shirt. His jeans were Levis, available countless places, his sneakers Reeboks, same thing.

The unknown victim was shot at close range after he was seated in the car. There were no signs of struggle. Police speculate that the victim knew his assailant.

Edith Whatley and her son, Randolph Mercer Jr., did not recognize the victim.

"I have no idea why our house, our garage, our car," Mrs. Whatley said.

Police are investigating to determine if there is a connection between the murder of John Doe and the disappearance of Tom Whatley who has been missing for two days.

"I was worried about my husband before," Mrs. Whatley said. "Now I'm terrified."

I had chosen not to mention the missing money in my story, and Mac had agreed. There was, after all, no definitive connection between the murder and the money.

I also chose not to quote Randy. Everything he had said, once he got over his shock, made him sound either selfish or nasty. Granted he was both, but the whole county didn't need to know this piece of information. Some day he might grow up and become a nice man who could live without everyone knowing he was a jerk as a kid.

"Who is he?" Randy demanded of anyone who'd listen, and that was usually me. "How'd he get here? And why in my car? My car!"

To all of which questions I answered, "I don't know."

"How long's he been dead?" he demanded of the police. "How did he die? And why in my car? My car!"

"Speaking of your car, son," William Poole said quietly. "When was the last time you looked into it?"

"Ah." Randy looked very wise. "You want to know when the body got there."

William nodded. "That's the idea."

"Well, I sat in it just before I left for dinner. I met Mom at Ferretti's, not that she invited me." He gave me a patented Randy dirty look, like it was my fault he wasn't invited. I felt like saying, "Blame Jolene. She's the one who suggested dinner," but I resisted the urge to lapse into adolescent defensiveness. *Did too, did not* seemed inappropriate under the circumstances.

"And there was nothing unusual about the car or the garage when you last saw it at what? About 5:30?" William asked.

Randy thought for a minute. "Yeah, about 5:30. And if by unusual you mean was a dead body lying around bleeding all over the place, no, there was nothing at all unusual. I just sat behind the wheel making believe I was driving." Randy's hands were in front of him, steering.

William adjusted his gun on his hip. "One piece of advice, son. Don't even think about taking that car onto the road before you have your license."

Randy blinked and flushed. "I'd never do something like that."

I could almost hear William's mental, *Right*.

"Besides," Randy continued, "Mom has the keys."

William nodded. "Good. Make certain you leave them in her care. If you break the law here, we can make it twenty-one before you can get a license."

Randy stared. "Twenty-one?"

"Twenty-one," William repeated. "But since you're not going to take her out early, there's no problem. Right?"

Randy nodded reluctantly. Busted by the cops before he even committed the crime!

"And when you do get your license," William continued, "don't see how fast she can go."

Randy held up his hand, palm out, in the traditional stop sign. "That's two pieces of advice. You said one. Two's one too many."

Sheesh, the kid was mouthy. Disrespectful, too.

William shrugged and moved on to other people, other business. Randy resumed pacing, cursing and muttering under his breath.

I suspected, however, that it wasn't the death of the unknown man that upset him. Beneath the distress and excitement he was experiencing at being part of an official murder investigation, he was livid about the blood spilled all over his new upholstery.

This suspicion of mine was confirmed when he sidled up to me as the police talked with his mother about when she and I had come home. He leaned over and whispered to me out of the side of his mouth like a gangster in a B movie, "How do you get blood out of things?"

I was tempted to say, "Wash it thoroughly in cold water" and offer him the hose. However he was just being fifteen and Randy.

Edie had become wracked with fear ever since the discovery of the body. I must say that I didn't blame her for being distraught. A dead man in the garage upped the ante considerably on the importance and scariness of Tom's disappearance. Visions of danger and foul play were no longer the sole fear and concern of the wife.

It was both comforting and disconcerting to have the police now take Tom's absence seriously. The big question was, if they no longer saw Tom as a husband jumping his matrimonial ship, did they see him as another potential victim like the man in the garage, or did they see him as a thief and a murderer?

I looked at William's shuttered expression and knew he wouldn't easily tell. Edie and I were not only media, but potential accomplices. At least Edie was. Who knew how far she would go to protect her husband, even if he were guilty of some crime.

"And you've never seen this man before?" William asked Edie again, referring to the corpse.

"Like I told you a million times before, William, no." She was lying on her sofa under a blanket that I'd pilfered from the upstairs linen closet and placed over her. Still she shivered as with a terrible chill. Her eyes were closed and her words were barely audible.

"I know this is hard, Edie," William said. "But you know the drill."

She nodded. "I've never seen him," she repeated.

William was unfailingly polite, but as I watched him, I thought I detected a subtle skepticism. Not a happy observation.

After the police, the coroner, and the body left, Randy disappeared in the general direction of upstairs and, I presumed, his bed. I knew he would have preferred to begin clean-up operations on his car, but it was off limits as part of a crime scene. With any luck, the police would impound it until his twenty-first birthday, saving themselves a few years of dealing with him as a green and clueless driver.

We turned out the lights and silence fell. Edie slept restlessly on the sofa, muttering occasionally in her sleep, at other times sighing as though in despair. I took catnaps in my cushy chair.

I pulled myself awake at seven, feeling as alert as any drunk the morning after. I took my burning eyes and sour mouth into the guest bath and did my best to transform myself. It was about as hopeless as turning coffee dregs into fresh brew. Still, when I pulled up to the window at McDonald's and ordered an Egg McMuffin, the sleepy teen who took my order and money understood what I said.

I wrote the story on Edie's mysterious body, turned it in to Mac, and left *The News* quickly before he thought of anything else I should do. I made it to bell choir practice with one minute to spare.

The good thing about bell choir is that it takes every ounce of my concentration not to mess things up, so every other worry gets put aside for the duration. It's the only real benefit I have found to being a marginal musician. Smiling to myself, I lined my bells up, C-sharp, C, B, and B-flat, glad to put Edie, Tom, Randy, and the corpse aside for a while.

The difficult rhythm on the first piece we played continually tripped me up. When we played the arrangement for the third time and I actually got it right, I was euphoric.

"Maddie, did you hear that?" I turned an excited face to my best friend who stood next to me and played the D and E bells. "I got it right!"

"You're wonderful," she said. "Talented and beautiful and ..." She peered at me. "And you've got dark circles under your eyes that rival mine. I know it wasn't a late night with Curt because he's on the retreat with Doug and the rest of the men. And you can't blame it on a baby like I can. What gives?"

"Covering a story," I said. "Read about it in *The News*." I didn't want to shatter the respite of bell choir by reviewing the crime. To divert her, I quickly asked, "How's Holly?"

Maddie's smile lit up her whole face. "Merry, I can't begin to tell you. Even after a sleepless night like last night, I wouldn't trade her for anything. She's wonderful." She turned toward her pocketbook resting on the floor behind her. "I've got pictures."

In the few short months since her birth, I had seen more pictures of Holly than I'd ever seen of any other single human being in my life, including the president. The child's every breath was being recorded for posterity, whoever that was.

"All right, people," said Ned, our director, arresting Maddie mid-search.

"Later," she whispered as she straightened. "You should see the ones of her in the bath."

I was tempted to ask how they differed from last week's pictures of Holly in the bath, but I was afraid Maddie would tell me. "See? She's got a bigger smile. And that's a boat floating there, not the rubber ducky. And her hair is a sixteenth of an inch longer! And look at that sweet, pudgy knee. Did you ever see anything so adorable?"

How about the same pudgy knee last week?

Enjoy her while you can, Maddie, I felt like saying. She'll grow up to be fifteen someday.

"You may remember," Ned said, "that we will be accompanying the kids' choir on Easter morning. We won't actually practice with all the kids until next Saturday, but today we're going to practice with the soloist, Sherrie Bauer."

As he spoke a familiar raven-haired beauty walked in. She had music in one hand and dangled a backpack from the other.

I half expected to see Randy trailing after her, tongue lolling. I smiled at her, feeling like I knew her even though she hadn't the vaguest idea who I was.

Sherrie Bauer had a wonderful voice, very full and controlled for someone as young as she. For her solo, we traded our bells for chimes which made a much softer sound and didn't drown out her voice. They also didn't amplify my mistakes as clearly as the bells.

As I listened to Sherrie and concentrated on my notes, I thought that Ned might have inadvertently given me the perfect combination of things to get Edie and Randy and hopefully Tom (fully restored to his family from wherever he was) to church. Thus far Edie'd always turned me down whenever I asked, in spite of the vast improvement in Jolene since she'd started coming.

But Easter and Sherrie. Sounded like an unbeatable combination to me.

When rehearsal finally ended and we'd put the bells into their velvet-lined cases and folded up the tables and stashed the foam cushions that sat on the tables, I managed to escape before Maddie remembered Holly's pix. I felt like a lousy friend, but I was just too exhausted to wax enthusiastic. All I wanted to do was collapse and sleep for hours, but I couldn't. I had an interview ahead with just enough time for lunch and a shower first, but nothing more.

Whiskers met me at the door of my apartment with several gruff meows and a strong cuff about the ankles. He couldn't decide whether to be glad to see me or mad at me for being away so long. For a time he stalked around the living room, tail held high. Then he butted my shins until I picked him up. I petted him until he purred like a formula car awaiting the green flag at the Indy 500. By the time I set him down, we were friends again. When I filled his food dish and gave him fresh water, he wrapped himself about my ankles as only a cat can, so fluid and supple you'd swear he hadn't a bone in his body.

While he ate, I listened to the messages on my answering machine.

Jolene: *So what happened when you went home with Edie last night? Terminal boring, I'll bet. Sort of like my night without Reilly.*

Wait until she read the paper. That'd teach her to shirk doing good deeds.

Maddie: *When you come to bell choir, will you please bring that recipe for chicken divan you fed us last Friday when we came to dinner? It was so good Doug wants me to make it.*

Oops. Too late. Well, I could take it to church tomorrow. Fortunately Doug was with the men on the retreat and couldn't eat it tonight, unless for some reason he was coming home early like Curt and Reilly.

Curt: *Where are you, darlin' girl? Out carousing with the girls, I bet.* Sigh. *I miss your sweet voice, Merry. Not that the machine message isn't charming, but it isn't you. I remember when a weekend with the boys was at the top of my list of fun things to do. Not anymore. I'll see you tomorrow evening at 7:30—if I last that long.*

I smiled, delighted that I had replaced the boys in his life. He'd certainly replaced everyone else in mine. In fact, I could no longer imagine a life without Curt.

I glanced at the clock. 1 P.M. An hour before I had to meet Stephanie Bauer at Freedom House. I smothered a yawn as I headed for the bathroom. I certainly hoped a shower would do something to stimulate my brain cells. They were acutely aware of missing their beauty rest last night.

I drove to Freedom House somewhat revived, though I suspected it was more the excitement of the coming interview than the shower. I loved interviewing people. Each person was fascinating in his or her own way, and I loved learning about them all, looking for what made them tick, what drove them, what mattered to them. The trick of a really good interview was to find the personal quirk or passion of the individuals and to get them to talk naturally about it, to step out of their public personae and into the real *them*.

I parked in front of a large Victorian house in what used to be the elite section of Amhearst. In fact the whole street was full of once-great homes that were now medical and dental suites, photography studios, and offices for financial planners, psychologists, and ministries. Some of the homes still had their pride intact with their well-tended lawns and shrubs, their fresh paint, their gilt signs and electric candles in each sparkling window. Some were showing their age, all wrinkles and creaky joints, peeling paint and sagging shutters.

Freedom House, one of the latter, was gray with white and rose trim; it desperately needed painting before the rose became grayer than the gray. The wooden steps were somewhat soft underfoot, and the wraparound porch rippled like a lake under a strong breeze. The rhododendron and azaleas across the front needed trimming, and there were two spindles missing from the porch railing. The rose-going-to-gray shutters looked like they had a bad case of psoriasis.

No financial resources to speak of, I guessed. The perennial problem of ministries.

Stephanie Bauer met me in the front hall, and I immediately recognized her as the mother of Randy's true love. She was Sherrie in twenty years.

"Hi," I said. "I think I saw you last night at Ferretti's."

Stephanie nodded. "I was there with my son and daughter."

"I was there with the mother of the tall kid who crashed your family party."

"Randy." Stephanie laughed. "What a delightful, funny guy."

Randy? Wow! He sure had them fooled. I toyed with the idea of telling her to lock Sherrie in her room for several years to protect her from Randy. Nah, I thought. Jolene might be right. Maybe he was much better in public than at home.

"I'm also in the bell choir." I smiled. "I heard Sherrie sing this morning. She's wonderful."

Stephanie beamed. Nothing like a proud mama. "She does sing well, but I'm proudest of her for her commitment to the Lord."

What a refreshing thing to hear a mother say about her child. "It's probably from watching you and Freedom House."

Stephanie grimaced. "I haven't always been the best example of a healthy Christian woman."

She didn't expand on that thought, and I didn't press her. Maybe later.

"How about your son?" I asked.

"He's a great kid too. I think he's going to go into the ministry, but he's not certain yet. I keep telling him not to do it unless he feels he has no choice, that God has called him and there's no getting away from it." She smiled at me. "Ministry is hard. He's seen that enough with Freedom House and takes the importance of his decision seriously."

She stopped abruptly and smiled. "You know, you shouldn't ask me about my kids unless you want long answers. They're my great joys." She turned toward the back of the house. "My office is in the old dining room. Follow me."

On the way we had to step around considerable clutter in the entry hall.

"We're getting ready to open a secondhand clothing shop," Stephanie explained. "We're collecting both clothes and supplies in preparation." She waved her hand at a couple of clothing racks, a slightly dirty, well-used counter, and several bags of clothing shoved into a corner. "We want to use the store as a training facility so that the women we counsel can get jobs if they need to. Too many women stay in abusive situations because they are financially dependent."

"When will the store open?"

"In a couple of months. We're going to call it Like New. That's what the women are when they find Christ and learn that with his help, they can control their lives." She grinned. "We just signed the lease for a store in the center of town. Talk about a leap of faith. I have no idea where the monthly rent is going to come from. As you undoubtedly noticed, we can't even afford to paint this place. If the store succeeds, it's all of God."

She spoke as if trusting God this way were commonplace, and I thought that for her, it probably was.

I peered into the living room as we walked past. It was filled with chairs of all sizes, colors, and fabrics.

"A motley mess, isn't it?" Stephanie said cheerfully. "But we don't have the luxury of being choosy. If someone offers us a chair, we take it. As long as it'll hold a woman up safely, we don't complain about the looks."

We settled on a dirty, well-used sofa and chair in a corner of Stephanie's office. I checked my little tape recorder to make certain it was working properly. Satisfied, I leaned back.

Stephanie patted her chair, and thousands of dust motes burst free, sailing through the air like seeds from an exploding pod. "A mission in Allentown was going out of business and they offered us first dibs on their furniture. Isn't it comfortable?" She was clearly delighted.

"It is," I agreed, though I had just been thinking that I wouldn't give the ratty stuff house room. I swallowed, feeling shallow and materialistic.

"How did you get involved in Freedom House?" I asked. I knew the short answer to this question from my research, but it was still a good place to begin.

Stephanie looked away from me for a minute, staring out the window.

"It always amazes me when I have to admit that I was an abused wife. Not that I'm ashamed or feel guilty. I'm just amazed. How did I let myself get trapped like that?"

"How did you?" I asked, marveling that someone as strong and assured as Stephanie was now had once been the victim of domestic abuse.

"I got trapped for two reasons. I wanted to please. And no one had ever taught me the power of choice. After all, I was only eighteen when I married."

"So young," I said. "Is marrying at a young age typical of abusive situations?"

She nodded. "Often, though not always. In our case it was too many stresses before we had the ability to handle them. And I was so naïve. When I married Wes, I was in a romantic fantasy. I saw him as strong and knowing, my knight to protect me from the world. I knew everything would be perfect for us because we loved each other. I would be the best wife a man could ever have, and he wouldn't lose his temper at me anymore because I'd make him so happy."

She looked into space, I suspect seeing herself at eighteen, twenty, twenty-five. "I bent over backwards to please him. When he got angry, I knew it was my fault because I hadn't tried hard enough. When he hit me, I knew I deserved it. When he heaped verbal abuse on me, I knew I was all those terrible things he called me. After all, he'd never say them if they weren't true."

"But you're an intelligent woman," I protested.

She nodded. "But he was incredibly clever, a master manipulator. And he always begged for forgiveness with tears in his eyes. 'I'm sorry! I didn't mean to hurt you. You just made me so mad. Let's agree that you'll never do that again. Then I won't have to hurt you again.'"

"That sounds like an apology that's no apology at all."

Stephanie nodded. "I know that now, but then I only heard the I'm-sorry part, not the it-was-Stephanie's-fault part."

"How long were you married?"

"Nine years. Nine long years."

"What led you to leave him?"

"Deep inside I knew it was wrong to hit people, even stupid wives who deserved it. I just couldn't admit it out loud. But I started reading things about abuse after a nurse talked to me the time Wes gave me a concussion and broke my arm."

"How?" I cut in.

She frowned. "How what?"

"How did he break your arm?"

"He threw me down the stairs for not making the bed with the sheets he wanted."

I blinked. "You're kidding."

She shrugged. "At least that's what he said. In reality he was about to lose another job and was taking it out on me. You see, if it was my fault he hit me, then it couldn't be his. He was still the good guy. I was the evil woman." She smiled grimly. "It took me years to figure that out."

I looked at this calm, competent woman and had trouble thinking of her as so unhealthy, so dependent. It must have shown in my face, and she sought to explain.

"When you're in an abusive marriage, it's like you're addicted. You are totally dependent. There's this intimacy and these soul ties from the sex, often violent or demeaning. You think you can't live without him even as he's killing you. You think it's normal to live with this tension, this pain. And you know everything will be all right if you can just love him enough.

"For him the issue is absolute authority. Total control. That's the goal of every abuser. On some level he recognizes your shame and despair and dependency and plays on it."

"The puppeteer pulling the strings," I said.

"That's too kind an image, but it definitely gives the idea."

"How were the kids during this time?"

Stephanie smiled. "They were the one bright spot in my life. But as they grew and became louder and misbehaved as all kids do, I began to fear that Wes would beat them too."

I thought of vivacious Sherrie and felt sick at the thought of someone hitting her. "Did he?"

She shook her head. "I thank God daily that Wes never laid a hand on them."

"What made you finally leave? Something must have forced you to take that huge step."

Stephanie took a deep breath. "One day I was outside in the garden when I heard Sherrie begin to cry. She was about five years old. I rushed inside and found her and Rob in the living room. Rob was yelling at her like Wes yelled at me. He was calling her the same names that Wes called me. And on her cheek was a red handprint from where he had hit her. 'She didn't do what I asked,' Rob said. 'I told her to get me something to drink and she didn't.' 'I didn't, Mom,' Sherrie said, hanging her head. 'I'm sorry.'

"I thought my heart would break. 'You can't just hit her like that, Rob. It's not right.' He looked at me, all confused. 'Why not? Daddy hits you.'"

Stephanie looked at me. "That's when I knew I had to leave. I couldn't let my children become Wes and me. I just couldn't."

"What did you do?" I asked. "Did you have any money? A place to live? A job?"

"I called that nurse and asked her for help. She sent me to a safe house. The kids and I lived there for two months. I couldn't go to my regular job because Wes could find me there, but I found another one in another town nearby. And for some reason I began to go to church."

She turned and pointed to the photo of a little white building that looked more like a VFW hall than a church. It hung on the wall beside this year's school pictures of Sherrie and Rob.

"What I learned in that building changed my life. The safe house gave me protection when I needed it and helped restore order to our lives, but it was at church that I met Jesus. There I found healing for my soul. There I met Absolute Authority and learned he wasn't abusive but loving and consistent. There I learned the power of choosing God's way. That's when I determined to offer women everything the safe house had offered me plus the power of God to redeem broken lives."

"And Freedom House is the result?" I asked.

Stephanie nodded. "We only make a small dent in a very large problem, but we can do that."

"Did you ever see your husband after you left?"

"I saw him in court when I fought for sole custody of the kids." Stephanie smiled. "I won. After all, I had all those medical records of my various injuries. And a judge who understood the issues at stake."

The phone rang.

"Excuse me." Stephanie went to her desk. "I'm on a twenty-four-hour page because of the nature of Freedom House."

I thought about all the things Stephanie had just told me. I thought of my father, who was an absolutely wonderful husband and father. I thought of Curt, so kind and loving, all any woman could dream of in a husband and eventual father, certainly all I could ever want.

I was suddenly ashamed for all I'd taken for granted.

"Tina!" The command in Stephanie's voice drew me. "Tina! Now listen to me."

Stephanie leaned forward in her seat, her face intense. "No, you aren't listening, Tina. You're doing what comes naturally to you. Don't let yourself do that. You've got to choose to do the right thing, not the known thing. Now tell me again your plan of action for when your husband becomes abusive."

Stephanie listened for a moment. "Good. Good. Your purse and the kids are absolutely necessary. What will you do next?"

Stephanie stared out the window at a bare trellis resting against the side of the house next door.

"Which sister are you going to?" she asked. "Marie? Okay. Where does she live and how are you getting there without a car?"

Tina talked some more, and Stephanie's concentration was total. In a minute, she sat back in her seat and smiled.

"You've got it, girl. I'm proud of you. You're sure you have the taxi fare safely hidden? Why not give your sister a call and tell her you might be coming over?"

The phone rumbled gently as Tina talked some more.

"Tina, a bad morning at work doesn't give him the right to unload on you. Just remember: it's your choice whether you stay and take it or whether you leave for safety's sake. Your choice." She listened for a minute. "I know it's scary. It's terrifying. Oh, Lord, please give Tina your strength and your courage. Help her make wise choices for her children's sakes. And protect all of them, Father. Protect all of them."

I listened to Stephanie's prayer and wondered how many women she'd prayed with through the years, either over the phone or in person. How many women now lived without fear because of Freedom House?

Stephanie hung up and sat quietly for a minute or two with her eyes closed. Then she looked at me.

"One of the things we do for women who want to escape and are willing to take that risk is plan an exit path. What to take and where to go. Some, like Tina, have been under their husbands' thumbs so long that we have to begin with things as elementary as getting their purse and the kids. And some like Tina need time to save the taxi fare."

"Do they live here if they bolt?" I asked.

She shook her head. "Once in a while someone stays here if there's no other option. But I don't take people in often for two reasons. My family and I live here, and I don't want to endanger my kids. Also, we're too public to be a safe house. A true safe house is a closely guarded location."

"If this isn't a residential facility, what do you do besides plan escape routes?"

Stephanie stood and walked back to the easy chair across from me. "We're basically a training ministry. We teach women all about the power and freedom of choice. We teach them they can make good choices or bad choices. Bad choices are like Eve way back in the Garden of Eden when she chose to believe the words of the serpent rather than the words of God. And we all know what happened because of that poor choice."

I nodded. "How about the children of Israel when they chose to believe the words of the spies who said the Promised Land was too well fortified, instead of the words of Moses who promised victory in the Lord. They all ended up in the wilderness for forty years."

She grinned. "You've got it. And on the good side, there's Joshua who said, 'Choose who you're going to serve. As for me and my house, we're going to serve the Lord.'"

"Or Mary at the Annunciation when she told the angel, 'Be it to me as God wills.' And Christ was born."

Stephanie spread her hands. "It sounds so obvious, this choosing well, when we say it to each other, doesn't it? But it's a new truth to many women. I'm not exactly dumb, but it took me years to learn it. Choices about my life are mine to make. Choices about your life are yours to make. And of course we teach the women that the greatest power and freedom of all come from choosing to believe in Christ."

"So how do you teach this? What specific programs do you have?"

"I have a staff, mostly volunteers, who work with me. We teach Bible studies. We have support groups. We counsel. These programs might not sound like much, but they represent hours and hours of work each week."

I didn't doubt that for a minute. "May I come to one of the Bible studies?"

She looked at me carefully. "I need to know that you'll respect the privacy of these women. It's crucial to protect them. Their lives are literally at risk."

"Believe me," I said, hastening to reassure her, "I understand that. I promise to protect them."

She nodded. "Okay then." She relaxed back into her chair. "We also go into the prison each week and lead chapels in the women's wing. We spend time with inmates who want to escape their old lives when they get out, basically preparing them for the choices they're going to have to make. And for variety, today two of our staff are teaching seminars at a pair of churches who want to learn how to help the hurting women in their congregations."

A knock sounded on the door of the office. Stephanie and I both looked over and saw Sherrie grinning at us.

"Hey, honey," Stephanie said. "Come on in. Is it three already?" She glanced at the clock. "Just about."

Sherrie came in and sat on the sofa across from her mother. Her eyes sparkled with life and good humor.

"This is Merry Kramer," Stephanie said. "She's a reporter at *The News*. She's going to write an article about Freedom House."

Sherrie looked at me. "Hey, that's great. Somebody needs to write about Mom and all the great stuff she does."

The phone rang again, and Stephanie went back to her desk to take the call.

"You're proud of your mother, aren't you?" I asked Sherrie.

The girl nodded. "She makes a difference."

I was listening to the girl with half an ear, not wanting to be impolite but trying to hear what Stephanie was saying at the same time. It sounded like she was talking to Tina again.

Sherrie leaned toward me. "Can I be in the Freedom House article? I've got stuff I want to say, stuff I think kids need to hear."

Suddenly she had my full attention. "What do you mean?"

"Well, I've lived here for a long time now, and I watch the women." Her young face was serious, her brow furrowed. "I listen to Mom when she talks to them. I even go to some of the Bible studies. I've reached some conclusions about domestic abuse, things that might help girls not get into marriages with the wrong guy. Sort of preventative stuff."

I smiled broadly. "I think I'd like to talk with you."

She grinned happily.

"You understand," I cautioned, "that I can't guarantee that everything you say will be in the article. I can't even guarantee that anything you say will make it."

She nodded. "I understand that. I'm okay with it."

I could hear a high-pitched, desperate voice weeping through the phone. This time both Sherrie and I were drawn to Stephanie's conversation, though we tried for propriety's sake to make believe we weren't.

"Easy, Tina," Stephanie said calmly. "We'll work something out. If your sister's not home, what's your second place to go?"

"Poor Tina." Sherrie shook her head. "She's a nice person, but she's a waffler."

"A waffler?"

"She can't decide whether to get out or not. One minute she's leaving him, the next she's going back because he loves her." Sherrie snorted. "He doesn't love her. He likes to control her."

I looked at Sherrie with interest. "Can you stop at the newsroom Monday on your way home from school? We could talk there."

Tina's terrified voice cut across the room again, the desperation clear even if the words were not.

"How far away does your mom live?" Stephanie said into the phone.

I was now openly listening, and I was tickled to see Sherrie was as avid to hear as I was. The saga of Tina, properly disguised for her protection of course, would elevate the Freedom House story to a whole new level. Three prongs to each story, my mentor had taught me back when I was a new reporter at home in Pittsburgh. I had Stephanie's personal story. I had the facts about Freedom House and the services provided. I might even have a sidebar article from Sherrie aimed at kids. But an interview with an abused wife! And right in the middle of a crisis! Wow.

I leaned toward Stephanie. "Can I help Tina? Drive her somewhere?"

Stephanie looked at me thoughtfully. "Just a minute, Tina. I need to check something."

"I mean it," I said. "I'll be glad to help."

"She's not just fodder for an article," Stephanie said bluntly.

I flushed, caught. "I know that."

"Promise you won't write about her without her permission and promise you'll flatten her story so she can't be identified."

As if Stephanie's stare wasn't convicting enough, I knew Sherrie was watching me too. I sighed inside. It had seemed a good idea. "I promise."

Stephanie nodded, satisfied. "She needs a ride to Phoenixville. Public transportation isn't a possibility. And for financial reasons neither's a cab."

"Phoenixville's not that far. About a half hour up Route 113."

"It'll be very messy emotionally," Stephanie warned. "And that's the best possible scenario."

"That doesn't bother me." Anything for story color. "Has her husband come home? Is that why the sudden panic?"

"He called from work and is full of fury. Apparently things have gone badly there, and she's about to bear the brunt of his frustration if we don't get her out. She's terrified."

"Where does she live?"

Stephanie returned to the phone. "Tina, I have someone here who can take you to your mother's. I want you to talk to her and tell her how to get to your house."

I took the phone. "Hi, Tina. I'm Merry. I'll be glad to drive you where you need to go."

"I'm scared," she said, her voice a mere whisper.

"I know. Now tell me how to get to your house."

She gave me directions hesitantly, pausing several times to yell at a crying child who responded by wailing louder.

"I'll be there in about ten minutes. Don't worry. Okay?"

She sniffed. "The kids and I will be waiting. And please, please hurry!"

Chapter 5

Tina lived in a very attractive brick bungalow on a cozy, tree-lined street. It looked like the perfect neighborhood, a Norman Rockwell setting made for raising happy, well-adjusted children. I wondered what secrets lived in the other houses.

A new red sports car sat in the driveway of Tina's home, its sticker still on the window. I glanced at the price as I walked past it and flinched. He might be having trouble at work, but obviously he made a good income. Too bad Tom Whatley hadn't been at Hamblin's to make the sale. There had to have been a very nice commission on this one.

As I stood on the front step, I could hear raised voices inside, first deep and masculine, then shrill and feminine. Then I distinctly heard a slap and a cry of pain. A loud crash sounded, followed by a scream.

Suddenly getting a good bite for my story seemed very unimportant, very selfish, the least of the issues present. A woman's very life might well be at stake, and journalism faded to insignificance. I put my shaking finger firmly on the bell.

All noise within ceased. It was like everyone held their breath, me included. I heard a robin chirp in the maple by the curb and a car rev its engine as it waited at the stop sign down the street. A kid across the street yelled, "Coming, Mom." And then the woman inside this house began to cry.

I rang again.

The door opened and a floridly handsome man stood glowering at me from the other side of the storm door. He wore a dress shirt with the sleeves rolled to the elbows, revealing strong arms and wrists. Did he develop those muscles with exercises other than beating on Tina? His tie was pulled down and knocked to one side, its cheery pattern a great contrast to his thundercloud face.

"Hi." I smiled brightly, stoically ignoring the turmoil in my stomach. Not only did I have the long tradition of Nellie Bly and Brenda Starr to uphold, I had right on my side.

"We don't want any," he snarled. "I gave at the office. Go away."

I grabbed the storm door and pulled, praying it wasn't locked. It wasn't. The door opened wide. He blinked in surprise at my audacity.

"You must be Tina's husband. I'm Merry." I held out my hand and stepped into the house. He was forced to either collide with me or step back. He stepped back. He did not shake my hand.

"Hey, Tina, I'm here," I called gaily.

She appeared over her husband's shoulder, a red handprint clearly visible on her cheek. Her eyes were wide and full of fear, her face wet with tears, but her chin was held at a determined angle.

"How can I help?" I asked.

"Help?" He sputtered like an outboard motor that was misfiring. "Help? What's going on here?" He glared first at Tina, then at me.

Tina and I ignored him. She turned and disappeared.

I've lost her! "Tina?"

She reappeared with two small children, a boy about six and a girl about three. They looked more frightened than children should ever have to look. The girl had obviously been crying, her face mottled, her nose running. Each carried a little backpack.

Tina's husband turned to her with a roar and grabbed her by the upper arm. She winced at the pressure he exerted, and I knew she'd find a bruise there in a short time.

"Go," she whispered to the kids. "Out to the car."

"Mommy?" the boy asked, trying not to cry.

"Aren't you coming?" The girl looked at Tina with huge eyes dripping tears.

"I'm coming," Tina said. With her free hand she shooed the children. "Go."

"Don't you dare!" At his voice, both children froze halfway down the steps.

I turned to them and smiled, hoping my own fear wasn't making my lips quiver too much for my smile to be reassuring. "Why don't you two climb in the backseat and buckle yourselves in?" I suggested quietly. "Your mom and I will be right there."

The boy seemed to think for a second. He looked at his father, at his mother, at me. He apparently came to a decision because he grabbed his sister's hand.

"Come on, Lacey."

Together they ran to the car. He pulled the rear door open, and I almost smiled as he helped her in and tried to buckle the seat belt around her.

"You can leave if you want," Tina's husband told her in a steely voice, "but I'll find you, you know. You're mine. You can't escape. Ever."

There was about him an overwhelming power, an aura of command that he focused intensely on Tina. How could she possibly stand up to him? How could she simply walk to my car and drive away from someone who absolutely vibrated with the necessity to bend her to his will?

For a long minute she said nothing, just stared at him like a trapped rabbit. I feared she'd stay here simply because she felt she had no option.

"Tina," I said. "Look at me. Look at me!"

"You stay out of this," he hissed, his eyes never leaving Tina. "This is between my wife and me."

"Tina!"

She pulled her gaze from her husband's.

"It's your choice." I tried to remember what Stephanie had said. "Remember: the power of choice."

When she responded, her voice was only a whisper and she talked to the floor, but she made her choice. "Let go of me. I'm going with Merry." She wrenched her arm from his grasp, probably as much because he was so startled at her audacity that he had loosened his grip as because she was suddenly strong.

He swore. "That's what you think." He grabbed for her. "You're not going anywhere!"

I stepped quickly out the door onto the porch, though I kept the storm door open. I looked at the empty yard next door and called, "Hi, how are you doing today?" I even gave a little wave.

The idea that there was someone watching what was happening caused Tina's husband to check for a minute. She took advantage and darted past him, ducking as he slapped at her. She and I hurried toward the car.

I stopped halfway down the walk and turned back to the house. He stood on the front steps, his face red with fury, his hands clenched in fists I knew he wanted to use on us.

"There's something you should know before you lay a hand on your wife again." I was so angry my voice shook. "I write for *The*

News and I'd be delighted to write about you by name. I'm sure they'd like to know at work just what kind of a man you are."

He stared at me for a moment, clearly surprised. Then he shouted, "You wouldn't dare! I'd sue you for all you're worth! You have no proof." He looked at his wife who was climbing into my car. "And who in their right mind would ever believe her?" The contempt in his voice gave me the chills.

"How about me?" And I turned my back.

It was seven before I got back from delivering Tina and her kids to her parents.

"Finally," her father had said with tears in his eyes. "And this time you're staying here."

Tina burrowed into his arms as he patted her awkwardly on the shoulder.

"Come on, Lacey, Jess," her mother said, taking a small hand in each of hers and walking toward the kitchen. "I bet I can find some ice cream in the freezer."

"Don't let them eat all mine," their grandfather said in an attempt to lighten the moment.

"It's okay, Grandpop." Lacey stopped in the doorway, trying to swallow her disappointment. "We don't have to have any."

With a very sad smile, the man said, "Honey, I was teasing. You eat as much as you want."

Lacey looked at him hesitantly.

"I mean it," he said. "It's all yours."

"It's okay, Lacey," Jess said. "Isn't it, Mommy? It's okay here."

"It's okay here," Tina repeated and began to weep.

If I had been weary before I went to see Stephanie, the emotions of helping Tina had wiped me out completely. All I wanted to do was sleep. Instead I plugged in my hot rollers and washed my face and tried to make myself feel some semblance of enthusiasm for tonight's black-tie reception.

I wanted to look extra nice tonight for a couple of reasons. I'd be meeting my new superboss for the first time. It would be nice to favorably impress him. And I hadn't seen Curt for two whole days. I wanted to knock his socks off, make him drool, froth at the mouth, and go weak at the knees. Typical guy stuff. I grinned at the absurd thought. As if I, Frizz Head Kramer, could do that. But maybe I could make him whistle.

I was standing in front of the bathroom mirror in my under-wear, one eye made up, my hair in hot rollers, when I realized that my dress, fresh from the cleaners, was still hanging in the car. I shuddered when I thought of its condition after sharing a backseat with Lacey and Jess, but it was the only truly fancy dress I owned—unless you counted four bridesmaid dresses, including one from Jolene and Reilly's wedding. Of course I wouldn't be caught dead in any of them outside a church.

This dress was one of those rare it's-exactly-right dresses. Its sapphire blue silk top was covered with hundreds of sequins so that I shimmered like the Caribbean Sea awash in sun jew-els, and its soft silk skirt fell in graceful folds. It made me feel like a million dollars every time I put it on, even though I only paid thirty dollars for it at a secondhand clothing store.

I glanced at the clock. Ten minutes before Curt arrived. I went out of my bathroom by its living room door—it also had a door into the bedroom and neither door had a lock, always interesting when I had company—and grabbed my new red coat. I threw it on over my undies and ran out the front door. I was halfway across the porch when I heard the door not only slam closed but snap in the way that meant only one thing: locked.

I exhaled in frustration, then searched my pockets, even though I knew I wouldn't find the keys there. They were in my purse on the sofa.

I stared at my front door. A couple of months ago someone had broken into my apartment by shattering one of the small panes of glass in the door. From that point on, I hadn't felt safe, so I'd asked the landlord for a new, all-wooden door. He hadn't been happy with the idea, but when I offered to share the cost with him, he'd agreed. My new, solid door with the peephole was impregnable, unless you happened to be carrying an axe in your coat pocket.

I had ten minutes, no, probably about eight by now, to get back inside before Curt arrived and found me in my rollers, underwear, half-made up face, and slippers with the Winnie the Pooh heads on them. I began a frantic circling of the apartment.

I was behind the yew hedge by the front window, trying in vain to make it open, when I heard a deep voice say, "It's a cinch that no one at the reception will hold a candle to you tonight."

For once the voice that usually thrilled me to my toes didn't.

Taking a deep breath, I turned to face him. He looked absolutely gorgeous with his black curly hair, dark eyes behind his new brown wire-rimmed glasses, and a tux. A tux! And I was wearing a coat and underwear!

He looked at me closely, his eyes moving from my one eye to the other. "Hmm." He was obviously trying not to laugh. "I'm glad you're ready and waiting."

"Very funny." I stalked out from behind the bushes, clutching my coat to me. "I'm locked out."

"Ah." Then he saw my feet. "Hey! Maybe I can get a pair of Tiggers! We could be a matched set."

"Go away." I scowled at him, trying to figure out how to tuck my feet behind me and still stand.

Instead he leaned over and kissed my cheek, getting poked in the eye with a roller in the process. He straightened quickly.

He looked at the front door. "You're sure it's locked?"

"I wouldn't be trying a spot of breaking and entering if I weren't." Unsweetened lemonade had nothing on my tartness.

"Well." He retraced the route I had just taken, trying all the windows I had just tried. I was perversely pleased to see that he had no more luck than I. The only change was that Whiskers greeted us from the windowsill of the front window this time around.

"Who's got a key?" Curt asked.

"Jolene."

"Let's give her a call then."

There was a daunting thought, calling Jolene when she was in the middle of either welcoming Reilly home or preparing to go out for the evening. But what choice was there?

"Do you have your cell phone?" I asked Curt.

He shook his head.

Just then we heard mine ring inside. Sometimes I could live without irony.

"Let's try your neighbors." Curt began hammering on the door of the other first-floor apartment where Mrs. Sousa lived.

"She's gone away for the weekend with a vanful of retirees. I saw them leave. They had enough canes and walkers among them to start their own medical supplies store. And Miss Wainwright, upstairs over me, actually went on a date with a computer geek who came to her school and taught the teachers how to teach the kids. Apparently Miss Wainwright 'has the knack,' although what that means I haven't the vaguest idea, though she seems delighted. And the Bobbsey Twins above Mrs. Sousa have gone to Philadelphia to a rock concert to further damage their hearing." The Bobbsey Twins were a pair of married teenagers who looked alike with their braces and zits, and whose sole interest in life seemed to be being groupies.

"So you really are out in the cold," Curt observed.

I nodded. "And I'm getting colder. It's breezy under here."

"What?"

"Nothing," I said quickly. "Just break a window and get me in!"

He stood quietly in thought while I fidgeted. Then he shrugged. "I guess there's no alternative. But let's make certain it's absolutely necessary first." And so saying, he pulled open the storm door of my apartment and tried the front door.

It opened obediently.

I stared at the open door, feeling betrayed. "But it clicked!"

"Yeah. That was probably the storm door."

I wanted to gnash my teeth.

I was in the bedroom after finishing my second eye when I realized that my dress was still in the car. I grabbed my red coat out from under Whiskers who had decided that if it was dumped on my bed, it could be his bed. He glared at me and I glared back as I opened the bedroom door and went once again to my traitorous front door.

"Well, your eyes match," Curt said as he looked up from the magazine he was reading. *Today's Christian Woman*. I bet he was enjoying that. "But something tells me you're not ready yet."

"My dress is still in the car."

"I'll get it," he offered. "At least I'm decent." And he grinned.

I looked down and saw that while I clutched my coat closed above the waist, below the waist the left side had caught behind me when I swung it on. The only thing I can say is that it wasn't quite as bad as if I'd caught my skirt in my pantyhose.

When I finally got myself together and emerged from the bedroom in one piece, Curt took a look and let out a low wolf whistle.

Suddenly the evening looked enchanted.

I chatted happily as we drove across town, telling Curt all about Edie's troubles. "And Tom's still missing," I concluded.

At a stoplight, Curt looked at me and raised an eyebrow. "Missing?"

I nodded, grinning happily at him.

"I can tell by your smile that you're very concerned."

I blinked. "Of course I'm concerned," I said defensively. Then I leaned toward him and smiled again, full wattage. "I'm smiling because I'm with you," I all but purred.

This time he blinked.

City Hall was a beautiful old stone mansion that had once belonged to one of Amhearst's first families. The Ruggles, like so many, had slowly died off. The last Ruggle, Miss Miriam, had deeded Refuge to the town. The town in turn had moved in.

I loved the grounds with the gracious beech whose branches swept the ground like the skirts of a great lady, the towering oak that stood tall and proud as a sentinel watching over the lady, and the glorious magnolias whose waxen, white petals even now promised spring as they dared a frost to wither their beauty.

Curt and I stepped into the Brennan Room, tonight alive with the strange combination of anticipation and concern. Jonathan Delaney Montgomery had done a masterful job of keeping his plans for his new newspaper a secret. *The News* was but one of the papers, now numbering twenty-five, that he owned, all small dailies, making him a mini-Rupert Murdoch. The concern was that he had, in fact, bought more than twenty-five papers, many more. The others had ceased to exist shortly after Montgomery's purchase.

We waited with trepidation to see which side of the ledger *The News* ended up on.

"Well, it's about time you showed up!"

Curt and I watched as a thoroughly disgruntled Mac Carnuccio bulled his way through the crowd to us. His tux almost fit him, and if he'd smiled, he'd have looked quite handsome.

"And a pleasant good evening to you, too, Mac." I smiled sweetly.

Mac looked at me for a long minute, then turned to Curt. "How do you stand her? She's so stinking saccharine she gives toothaches on sight."

Curt looked at me and grinned. "I don't know, Mac. I think her smile's kind of cute." He put his arm around my shoulders and gave a gentle squeeze.

I rested my head on his shoulder for a brief moment, reveling in the fact that this man, this marvelous, talented man, loved me.

"That pain in your jaw's not from me anyway," I said. "It's from clenching your teeth for the past three months waiting to hear the word from on high. Relax. Enjoy." I smiled again, knowing it would drive him crazy. It did.

"Ditch her, Curt, while there's time. Save yourself from contracting diabetes by association. It's deadly."

"Is it quick?" Curt asked. "I don't want to go quickly. I want years with her."

I glowed while Mac glowered.

"No date tonight?" I asked Mac innocently. If he could jab at me, I could jab at him.

Mac snarled. "Now there's a case of terminal sweet if I ever saw one." He scowled at his own reflection in a window made a mirror by the dark night outside and the bright light inside. Mac astonished me with the depth of his affection for Dawn Trauber.

"You're right. She's a sweetie," I agreed.

"I got stood up for some girl who's having a baby. Can you believe that? One of the most crucial nights of my life, and she's at the hospital going, 'Breathe deeply. Now pant, two, three, four.'"

Dawn Trauber, the object of Mac's frustration, was the director of His House, a home for girls in trouble, most of whom were having babies without benefit of marriage. Frequently Dawn was the birth coach for one of the girls, and apparently tonight was a command performance.

I laid a gentle hand on Mac's arm. "You know she'd be here if she could."

Mac looked unconvinced.

"She's crediting you with the courage and class to get through tonight. She knew the girl having the baby couldn't make it, given her age and situation, but she knew you could."

"You're saying I should feel honored that I've been stood up for a squalling baby?"

I nodded. "And I'm sure it won't be the last time." I smiled sweetly again.

Mac looked at Curt again. "It's your life, but I'm telling you, tooth decay and mind rot. She figures angles for everything! Before you know it, you won't have a decent gripe to your name. She'll Pollyanna them all away."

"You're just jealous because my girl's here and yours isn't," Curt said, snagging a canapé from the tray going by.

Mac shrugged his eyebrows and changed the subject. "I'm so nervous I can barely stand it."

I opened my mouth to make a wiseacre retort when I saw his eyes. Poor Mac.

"Have you been through the receiving line yet?" I asked.

Mac shook his head. "I haven't had the nerve."

"Then come with us." I slipped a hand through both Curt and Mac's arms and led the way to where Jonathan Montgomery was standing, royalty giving his beneficent nod to his adoring public.

We fell in line behind the mayor and her husband and two of the local councilmen. The politicians were delighted to meet Amhearst's newest minimogul, and everyone had a great time glad-handing. While we waited, I looked at Mac.

"Do you think you could work up a smile for the man?" I asked, not unkindly. "You do want him to retain you, don't you?"

He looked at me like I was daft.

"Then smile, for Pete's sake. Be pleasant. You may hate that he's kept you on a string ever since he purchased the paper, but it is his right."

"Yeah, yeah. I know. Dawn's been reading me the same riot act for days. And she's praying." He looked confounded by the idea. "She's praying!"

"Of course she is," I said. "I've been praying too."

Mac looked at Curt. "Does prayer make you saccharine or does being saccharine make you pray?"

"That may be akin to asking which came first, the chicken or the egg." Curt leaned toward Mac. "But you need to know that I've been praying too."

"Aaugh! I don't know if I can stand this." Mac ran a distracted hand through his already rumpled hair. "I'm not used to religion that's every day."

"That's why we're praying," Curt said.

Mac just stared.

"Hello. I'm Jonathan Delaney Montgomery." A hand reached for Mac who blinked, then rubbed his right hand quickly against his trousers. With his best smile pasted into place, he shook hands with the man who would decide his future.

"Mac Carnuccio, acting editor of *The News*. It's a pleasure to meet you, sir."

"Oh, yes, Mr. Carnuccio. I've been reading your editorials as well as studying your paper."

We all waited but the man offered no opinion, positive or negative, about Mac's work. While Mac sputtered something about loving his job, I studied Mr. Montgomery. A control freak, I decided. He wanted to keep Mac squirming as long as he could. Not only was it unkind; it was also unconscionably egotistical.

And then Mac was dismissed and it was my turn. I held out my hand, prepared to introduce myself.

"Mr. Montgomery." Curt reached around me. "Good to see you again, sir."

"Well, Curt, my boy. You're looking well."

While I was assimilating the fact that the love of my life knew my new boss and had neglected to mention that little fact, Curt said, "I'd like you to meet a special friend of mine, Merrileigh Kramer."

Mr. Montgomery beamed at me. "Miss Kramer, I'm pleased to meet you. Any friend of Curt's is more than welcome at this reception." He took my hand and patted it benevolently. Then he proceeded to ignore me.

"So tell me, Curt. How's the artist doing?"

"Fine, fine."

"Delia's been telling me the same thing. You took a risk giving up your teaching, son, but it seems to be paying off."

"I do not regret my decision one bit."

"And does your little lady approve?"

With a jolt I realized he was talking about me. Little lady? What century was he born in?

Curt smiled at me. "She does."

"Has she met Delia yet?"

"Not yet. There's been no occasion."

"You'd better warn her, boy."

"When I think there's something to warn her about, Mr. Montgomery, I will."

"Don't be a fool, Curt."

Curt looked at me while I stared wide-eyed, trying to decipher the conversation. "I think I'm already a fool, sir, for beautiful eyes, mismatched or not." His smile melted my bones.

Mr. Montgomery glanced at me again to see if he'd missed something. Apparently he decided he hadn't because he looked at Curt without understanding. Then his gaze slid over Curt's shoulder and he broke into a wide grin.

"Ah. Here she comes."

Curt's head swung in the direction of Mr. Montgomery's look. In fact, the head of every man in the room swung in that direction, and a few of the women's heads too.

I turned and my blood chilled.

A blond with the most perfect features I'd ever seen glided up to us, her eyes fixed on Curt. I'd seen lionesses look less predatory as they circled a wildebeest in a nature film on public TV. She was dressed in black from the tiny straps of her slip dress to the toes of her high-heeled sandals. She looked sleek and sophisticated and perfect.

Suddenly I felt every one of the thirty dollars I'd paid for my dress.

"Dad," she said in a husky warm voice. She stood on tiptoe as her father leaned down to receive her kiss on the cheek. "Quite a crowd. A success, aren't we?"

Then her eyes were on Curt in a proprietary way that made me most annoyed. I was the only one allowed to look at him like that.

"And Curt." She leaned up and gave him a kiss on the cheek, leaving a perfect petal pink imprint on his skin. She tucked her arm in his, her perfectly manicured, utterly synthetic nails resting lightly on his jacket sleeve. "How wonderful to see you again," she all but purred. "I've missed you since yesterday."

Curt smiled fatuously into her big, blue eyes. After an eternity, he blinked and recalled where he was and who he'd come to the dance with.

"Delia, I'd like you to meet—"

"Curt," Delia interrupted. "I need something to drink. It was a long drive from Philadelphia, and I had to hurry to make it for Dad's special night. I even closed the gallery early. It's all made me quite thirsty." She smiled up at him. "To say nothing of hungry. Help me out here?"

Before he knew what hit him, he was halfway across the room. Some small semblance of sanity must have remained because he looked back over his shoulder at me and made a face that was supposed to convey *what-was-I-to-do?* I felt like making a return face that said *drop dead*. The trouble was that I wanted to make it at Delia, and she was too busy fawning over Curt to deign to glance my way.

"Well, if it isn't Delia Big Deal-ia Montgomery," said an acid voice in my ear.

"Jolene!" I spun around, nearly poking Reilly in the stomach with my elbow as I did. "You know her?"

"Sure," Jolene said. "Everyone knows Delia."

Reilly nodded. "Can't say they all like her," he said, smiling indulgently at his wife who looked gorgeous in a vivid red sequin-and-chiffon number. "That homecoming queen crown was a prized treasure, you know."

"She cheated, Reilly! You know she did!" Jolene was even more passionate than usual—and that was quite a sight. Her eyes flashed and her cheeks flushed. Reilly smiled appreciatively. "She got people to vote three and four times. I mean, nobody liked her. She had to buy her votes!"

"I suspect she did, Jo, my sweet. But it was eight years ago or something like that. I think it's probably time to let go of the anger, don't you?"

"Sure you do." Jolene made a face at her husband. "It wasn't you she beat."

"No," he said. "But it was me who won. I got you." And he gave his wife a kiss right in front of everyone.

For once Jolene was speechless.

Grinning at his success, Reilly turned to me. "Can I get you something to drink?"

I never got to answer him because just then I spotted Edie coming in the front door. My heart sank as I took in her appearance. She was pale, not quite put together, and plastered.

Jo, Reilly, and Mac heard my indrawn breath and followed my line of vision.

Mac swore softly. Reilly sighed. And Jo took off across the room so fast that I practically had to run to keep up with her. We got to Edie just before she took her place in the receiving line.

"Ladies' room," Jo said as she grabbed Edie's right arm.

"Right." I grabbed her left.

"Hey," Edie said, not quite certain what was going on. "Let me go. I have to meet Mishter Mon'gomery."

"That's what we're afraid of," I muttered.

We got Edie into the ladies' room without incident, and once in there we claimed the sofa in the anteroom. Jo and I sat alertly on the edge of the sofa on either side of the slumping Edie.

"I take it Tom hasn't come home," Jo said.

"Or called," I added.

Two big tears rolled out of Edie's eyes in answer, sliding neatly down the pathway made on either cheek by previously melted mascara.

"Ranny tole me to stay home," she announced.

"For once, Randy was right." I patted her hand. When in doubt . . .

"But I need to meet the new boss." She pronounced it *bosh*.

"I think not," Jo said. "You want your job come Monday, don't you?"

Two more tears. "I don't care." She sniffed. She was deeply into self-pity. "I just came for Mac. I want him to have his job."

"That was very thoughtful," I said, trying to imagine how a drunk Edie would help Mac keep his job.

"Thoughtful, schmoughtful." Jolene stood and stared down at Edie. "If Mr. Montgomery saw you now, he'd fire Mac for hiring incompetents."

Edie drew herself up, quite a feat when you're slouching on a sofa. "I'm not incompetent."

"You couldn't prove it tonight." Jolene stalked to the sinks and grabbed a fistful of paper towels. She stuck them under the cold water. Then she walked purposefully to Edie.

Poor Edie. She never saw it coming.

Jolene was just finishing her forceful washing of Edie's face with Edie batting ineffectually when the door opened and Delia glided in.

Everyone froze for a moment. Then my stomach dropped and my hands turned cold. Of all the people who shouldn't see Edie, it was Delia.

She smiled nastily at Edie, who was too miserable to notice. "I see you still know how to pick your friends, Jolene Marie."

"Nice to see you, too, Delia." Jolene smiled regally, as if bathing snockered friends was the posh thing to do. Caring for the masses and all that bully stuff.

I watched Delia as she walked to the mirror and checked her perfect makeup. She pulled out a lip pencil and colored her already perfectly colored mouth. With a little finger she daintily brushed the corners of her lips to be certain things were perfect.

As she pulled the door open to leave, Delia looked at us and gave a silent sniff. Contempt oozed from every glamorous pore.

"Did you hear that?" I demanded as the door shut behind her.

"What?" Jo asked, staring daggers in Delia's direction.

"That silent sniff! I never heard anything like it. Jolene, how did she do it?"

"Don't ask me. I only make loud ones. They're much more unladylike. Besides, who hears silent ones?"

"I did."

"I did too," Edie said. "She doesn't like us."

"Well, I didn't hear anything. Silent sniff. Puh-lease."

Edie lay her head on the back of the sofa. "Where is he?" she moaned.

Neither of us answered. There was nothing to say.

Jolene reached into her little silver evening bag and pulled out a lipstick. She rubbed some on her index finger and then rubbed her finger over Edie's pallid cheek. She did this several times until Edie looked healthy again. Then she carefully put some on Edie's lips.

She studied Edie critically. "I don't have any mascara with me, but we can't risk her crying it all over herself again anyway."

I reached in my little black bag and pulled out a tiny metal bristled brush. "Sit up, Edie. It's hair time."

While I brushed, Jo went to the door and peered out. "Do you think there's coffee out there anywhere?"

"Probably not." I pulled Edie to her feet. She barely swayed. I smoothed her green dress over her hips and tugged at the hem to get it to lie smoothly. It was a bit snug, but not as snug as the skirts she usually wore to work.

Jolene left the door and circled Edie. She nodded approval. "If one of us is always holding her elbow, I think we'll be okay. Just don't let her near Mr. Montgomery."

"Mr. Montgomery," Edie repeated. "I have to meet him."

"Not now," Jo said. "Maybe later. Now's not a good time. He wouldn't be happy to be interrupted. He might get mad at Mac."

"We don't want him to get mad at Mac," Edie said. "We want Mac."

"Shoulders back, Edie." I took her elbow. "Here we go."

We walked back to the Brennan Room, and no one but Mac and Reilly even knew we had been gone. I snagged a Perrier with a twist of lime and handed it to Edie. She took it eagerly until she realized it was Perrier and not champagne or some such thing.

Once when we were standing near one of the floor-to-ceiling windows, I thought I saw a shadow outside. I frowned as I tried to decipher what I saw through the reflected glare, but the impression was nebulous at best. I could have sworn I saw a man and a bicycle staring in. I guess we did look like we were having fun.

Occasionally as the interminable evening wore on, I saw Curt in the distance, always with Delia hanging on his arm. She'd frequently laugh and look up at him with an adoring look. It made my stomach clench. *I* was the one who gave him adoring looks. Only *me*.

Don't let it bother you, I told myself. She's a big Philadelphia gallery owner. He needs to be on good terms with gallery owners. He needs them professionally.

"I hear her local gallery is having its grand opening Wednesday night," Mac said as he watched me watch her. "Naturally we'll cover it."

"Her local gallery?" I said.

"Sure. Intimations."

I stared at Mac in dismay. "Intimations is hers?"

"You didn't know?"

"Well, no," I said. "I mean sure. I mean I knew about Intimations. Curt's very excited about it. He's the first show and there's the gala opening and all kinds of exciting stuff. The owner has great connections in art circles."

Mac nodded. "That's true. She does."

I studied my little black bag. "I just didn't know she was Intimations." I pulled at a loose thread until I realized I would have little black beads bouncing all over the floor if I continued. I willed myself to let the thread alone. "In all honesty, though, it wouldn't have meant anything to me before tonight anyway."

Mac looked across the room where Delia and Curt were talking with Mr. Montgomery. "I never did like her much when we were kids, didn't miss her at all when her mother died and they moved away. But I've got to admit that she's done all right for herself."

"I don't think I like her much as an adult," Jolene said as Delia's laughter floated above the rumble of conversation. "Look at her, hanging onto Curt like she has a right." She reached out and patted me sympathetically.

I stared across the room at Curt and Delia. He's been so low-key about the gallery owner he'd been working closely with that I hadn't paid any attention to the fact that she was a woman. No big deal.

But now I'd seen the woman.

Chapter 6

Y ou never even told me you knew him!"

Curt and I were sitting in my living room. Or rather Curt was sitting comfortably on the sofa with Whiskers snuggled against him, shedding white fur all over his black dress pants. I was pacing, flinging my arms and ranting, the very picture of what any man would want in a woman.

The reception at City Hall had finally ended after an interminable evening during which I pasted a smile on my face and made believe I liked being left with Mac. Every time I heard Delia's musical laugh play its tune across the room, I stretched the smile wider to hide my hurt. I didn't fool anyone, not even Edie.

"It'll be okay, Merry," she whispered after one particularly charming laugh floated across the room. "It'll be okay."

When I collected my coat, resigned to the fact that Mac was going to have to take me home, Curt appeared at my side.

"Ready to go?" he asked as if we'd separated a mere five minutes ago. I gave him my most haughty expression, but he missed it because he was looking across the room. I followed his sight line, determined that if he was smiling at Delia, I was walking home. He was watching Edie.

"I must say I'm surprised at her, showing up in her condition. It's not like her." He wasn't critical or nasty, just making an observation.

I stiffened, feeling protective of Edie. "Her husband's missing. There was a dead man in her garage. Her son is driving her crazy with his rebellion. I'd say the woman has a right to be upset."

He quirked an eyebrow at me. "So you've appointed yourself her defender?"

"She's my friend."

"And no one better pick on her while you're around, right?"

"You've got it."

"Well, she's not driving herself home, is she?" He was genuinely concerned.

"No. Jo and Reilly are taking her."

"Good." He smiled down at me, and against all my will, I smiled back. As he patted me on the shoulder in a friendly way, I upbraided myself for my lack of character. I couldn't even stay mad at the man!

But as we drove home, I regained all my spleen and then some.

"You should have told me!"

"I thought you knew that the Montgomerys used to live in Amhearst." He looked surprised at the emotion of my outburst. "You always seem to know everything at that paper of yours."

"Well, I didn't know this little tidbit. You should have told me."

"If I'd known you didn't know, I would have," he said reasonably, waving his hand in the air. "It's no big deal."

"And I suppose Delia Big Deal-ia Montgomery is no big deal either?" Just thinking about her raised my internal temperature several degrees.

Suddenly it dawned on him that I was genuinely angry. And hurt. He looked at me cautiously. "Maybe."

"Maybe she's a big deal? Maybe?" I gave him as scathing a look as I could manage. It was quite a stretch for the Saccharine Queen.

"Well, of course she's important." He spoke hesitantly, ready to recant immediately if needed.

"Hah! I knew it!"

He backtracked. "Well, not important important, of course. Not like you. Just sort of important. A small big deal. She runs a well-connected gallery in Philadelphia, and she's opening Intimations out here. She's a professional friend."

I glared at him. "Intimations. Intimations. What kind of a name is that? Sounds like Imitations."

"I think the idea," he said patiently, "is as in 'intimations of greatness.'"

"Oh." Wouldn't you know there was logic behind that ridiculous name and I'd been too blind to see it.

"Merry, honey, you're overreacting here. There's no need to get all in a huff."

"You think not?" I huffed. "You know you ignored me all evening, don't you?"

"I didn't."

"Once she came into the room, you did. I had to hang around with Mac. Now there's a treat. At least Dawn had a legit reason for standing him up."

Curt was getting defensive. "I did not stand you up."

"As good as."

"If it weren't for me, my sweet, you'd still be on the front porch in your undies."

Leave it to a man to rub it in. "It would have been less embarrassing."

"What?" Suddenly he was standing, towering over me, scowling fiercely. "You're saying I'm an embarrassment?"

"Yes! No! Not you. Your absence."

"I wasn't absent! I was right there!"

"But not with me!"

"Aha!" He waved his finger under my nose. I made a lunge to bite it but missed. "So that's it. You. That's the real issue here, isn't it. It's not me or my career. It's you! Who cares that I was attending to business all evening."

"And I wasn't? That was a reception for *The News* and its employees, not you!"

"Oh, come on, Merry. You're being a bit touchy here, don't you think?"

"Yeah." I clenched my teeth against my tears. "But that's better than being a fool like you."

"A fool like me?" His voice was dangerously quiet.

"That's what Mr. Montgomery called you, remember? A fool." I conveniently neglected to mention Curt's follow-up comment about being a fool over me.

Curt stared at me for a minute. "I must be a fool," he ground out. "I'm having this idiotic conversation."

"It is not idiotic! It's important!"

"Why? What's so important? I talked with Delia. Big deal!"

"Sheesh, you're dense," I shouted. "If you can't figure out why I'm upset, then I don't want to talk about it anymore. And I don't want to talk to you anymore!"

I stalked to the front door and pulled it open. "And don't worry. I have my keys." And I stormed out.

I stomped to my car, climbed in, and drove off into the night. I did not have to put up with a man who had no sense of how he'd hurt me. I did not.

I was three blocks from home when it dawned on me that I had stormed out of my own apartment, leaving Curt behind with the warmth, light, food, and comfort, to say nothing of Whiskers. I felt the flush of my embarrassment envelop my entire body in waves. Now I was not only furious and deeply hurt; I was mortified.

I pulled up to a stop sign and sat, staring straight ahead, trying to decide what to do now. A beep from a car waiting behind me pulled me from my blue funk.

"Yeah, yeah," I muttered as I turned the corner to get away from him.

I drove around a bit more, trying to find a graceful way out of my situation. No matter how hard I thought, no matter how many angles I tried to play, if I was willing to be honest with myself, I had only two basic choices.

I could drive around all night, or I could go home.

The first was stupid; the second was humiliating.

I sighed. I pictured Curt and Whiskers, lying together on the sofa, eyes closed, gentle snores mingling harmoniously. It was such a peaceful scene.

I, on the other hand, was driving around town with no place to go and no one to go to, suddenly aware of the lateness of the hour and the dangers lurking out there, just waiting to pounce on a poor innocent like me.

Dear God, what am I doing? What's wrong with me? How could I have done something this stupid?

I heard Stephanie Bauer say, as clearly as if she were sitting next to me, "The power of choice."

What choice, Father? He left me alone all evening!

"The power of choice."

I didn't deserve that humiliation, Father.

"The power of choice."

But I have the right to feel upset.

"The power of choice."

Yeah, yeah, yeah. I know what you're trying to say. It's just that I don't want to hear it. Did I ever tell you that there are times that I hate it that you're always right?

"The power of choice."

What you're saying is that though I can't choose how Curt will act, I can choose how I act, right?

I thought of my temper and my pettiness. I had chosen to put the worst possible spin on the evening. So Curt had left me alone. It wasn't very polite, it was embarrassing, and it hurt me. But had he meant for me to feel these emotions?

In all honesty I had to admit that he had not. I had chosen to be embarrassed, to be jealous and nasty. I had chosen to be more concerned about my image and my evening than about Curt's professional opportunities.

Not that I didn't recognize that Delia was trolling for Curt, her hook cleverly hidden in the lure of a showing. But Curt had never given me any cause to doubt his affection for me. In fact he had declared it openly in front of Delia's father.

The truth, dear Father, is that I'm afraid. She's gorgeous. She comes from money. She has two galleries that can help Curt immensely professionally. Why would he want me when he can have her?

"The power of choice."

So I choose to let my fear overwhelm me and make me do crazy things like run out of my own apartment. Or I choose to trust you and him.

I pulled into the parking area beside my apartment and climbed out of the car. I knew I needed to apologize for my outburst, but I dreaded the thought. I quietly closed the car door and stood there looking at the light streaming out my front windows.

My mind came to a screeching halt every time I tried to imagine what Curt thought of my infantile behavior. I condemned myself so strongly for being nasty and stupid that I couldn't imagine him forgiving me.

A cold chill traveled down my spine. What if Curt wasn't here to apologize to? What if he'd thrown up his hands and left, maybe for good?

I squared my shoulders and walked past the lilac and up the walk to my door. I paused and peeked in the window. Curt and Whiskers were together on the sofa, but they weren't sleeping. At least Curt wasn't. He was stroking the cat who looked like he'd died and gone to heaven. Curt himself was staring into space, a frown on his brow.

I would have given a lot to know what he was thinking. Then again, maybe I was glad not to know. What if he was thinking that he couldn't wait to get rid of a ditz like me? It would break my heart if he made that decision, but I wouldn't blame him. If someone had attacked me like I attacked him, I'd think twice about continuing the romance too.

I reached for the door and pushed it open. Curt must have vaulted off the sofa the minute he heard me touch the door because he met me on the welcome mat. He grabbed me in a great hug.

"I'm sorry." I started to cry. "I'm sorry." His arms felt so good.

"No, sweetheart. It was me. You were right. I did ignore you. Please forgive me."

"But I was so nasty about it."

"But I should never have spent all that time with Delia. It was your night."

"Well, I should have been more understanding of how important she is to you and your career."

He pulled back and took my hand. "Now we're going to argue about who's the sorriest?"

I shook my head. "Just who's the wrongest—or most wrong. And it's me."

"That's what you think."

"That's what I know."

We grinned hesitantly at each other. He led me to the over-stuffed chair and sat, then pulled me into his lap. He wrapped his arms around me again, coat and all.

We sat quietly like that for a few minutes. Whiskers padded over by way of the sofa arm to the chair arm, but we both ignored him and he got the hint. He returned to the sofa.

"I was afraid," I finally whispered. "So afraid."

I felt him start. Whatever he'd expected, it wasn't this. "Afraid?"

"Of Delia."

His arms tightened. "Why?"

"She's beautiful!"

"She's attractive. You're beautiful."

"She's rich."

He shrugged. "You have a wealth of character."

I looked up at him. "You can say that after my performance tonight?"

He gave a tiny half smile. "Everybody has little aberrations now and then."

I laughed softly and tightened my arms about him. He bent and kissed the top of my head.

"She's part of your world in a way I can never be." I felt the fear flood me again. I clutched his arm. "That terrifies me."

He nodded. "She is *part* of my professional life, that's true. But you, my Merry, are my life, my heart."

"Oh, Curt." I wrapped my arms about his chest and cried into his pleated shirt.

He ran his hand over my hair. "I sat here after you left and thought about my life before and after you came along. I thought about you and your gallant heart, always out to right a wrong or write the best story or fix some problem."

"A gallant heart? You think I have a gallant heart?" What a wonderful thing to say.

"And then I thought of all you've brought to my life."

I thought of all I'd brought too. "Stress, arguments, possessiveness, pettiness. Poor Curt."

"Shh, sweetheart." He laid his finger across my lips. "I'm trying to give you some compliments here."

I nodded and rested against his shoulder. "What have I brought you?"

"Joy. You make me laugh. I hadn't laughed for several years before you came along. And excitement. There's always something happening around you. And ulcers. All the excitement, you know."

"Ulcers!" I sat up and mock-glared at him.

He grinned and pulled me back against him. "See? Humor, too. And love." His voice became tender. "Most importantly, you've given me love." He leaned down and kissed me gently.

After a few quiet minutes, I whispered. "I do love you."

"I know. And I love you." He looked at me solemnly. "You know what that means, don't you?"

His face was so serious I couldn't begin to guess what was on his mind. "What?"

He laid his hand on my cheek. "It means you're going to have to trust me, darlin' girl."

He knew how to go right to the heart of the matter. I sighed and nodded. "'Love always protects, always trusts, always hopes, always perseveres. Love never fails.'"

He nodded. "'Always trusts.'"

"But it's not you I mistrust. Truly it's not. It's her. She's got her cap set for you, Curt." Even saying it made my heart beat fast with trepidation.

He made a face. "I know. It's very awkward. But the show at Intimations is important. The invitations are out." He took my hand in his. "It'll only be four more days."

I lifted his hand to my lips and kissed each of his fingers. One for each day. "Only four."

I tamped down hard on the fear that threatened to gnaw holes in my trust.

Day One, Sunday, was a quiet day. I went to church and sat shoulder to shoulder with Curt. We were about to stand for the opening song when I felt a presence at the edge of our pew. In disbelief I looked at Mac standing there. He'd come to church three or four times since Christmas Eve and always with Dawn. Now he was alone. We slid over to make room for him.

Our church sings a combination of worship songs and traditional hymns.

"I don't know any of these songs," Mac muttered during the opening bars of the first song.

"Then listen and learn," I encouraged.

"When they look in the Bible, I can never find where they are."

"Use the table of contents in the front."

"What do I do if there's Communion? Am I allowed to take it? How do you do it here? Who cares? I'm just going to sit it out. Then I can't offend anyone. Unless sitting it out offends someone. What do you think?" If he hadn't been so serious, he would have been comical in his extreme distress.

Curt looked at him with understanding. "Dawn's still at the hospital, isn't she?"

Mac clenched his jaw. "Long labor."

I nodded. "Me too." I pointed my finger at Curt. "Him too."

Mac stared at Curt. "What?"

"Me too," Curt said.

"Well, sure, if she won't."

Curt shook his head. "Not just because of Merry. I've always held that position."

Mac was incredulous. "You've never?"

We both shook our heads.

"But why not? Is there something wrong with you? I mean, who's it hurting?"

"There's nothing wrong with me, believe me," Curt said, grinning at me in a way that curled my toes. "I take this position because it's the Bible's position."

"Amazing." Mac shook his head. "I'm hanging around with a bunch of throwbacks to the Victorian era. And I'm doing it on purpose."

"Why?" I asked.

"Why what?" he asked.

"Why are you hanging out with a bunch of throwbacks like us?"

He looked at Curt and me. Then he glanced toward the ladies' room. "You two I'm not sure about, but her?" He grinned. "I can't believe I'm saying this, but she's even worth a second virginity."

Our salads arrived, and Dawn still wasn't back.

"Let me go get her," I said. "You guys can start if you want."

Curt shook his head as Mac picked up his fork. "We'll wait."

"Right," agreed Mac as he quickly set down his fork. "It's only polite."

I found Dawn in the ladies' room standing in front of the mirror staring at herself without really seeing.

"Are you okay?" I looked at her with concern.

She shook her head without turning. "Not really. I'm scared."

I looked at her in the mirror. "About what?"

"Mac." She began to study the washbasin intently.

"He's coming on too strong?"

She shrugged. "I don't mind that. He seems willing to let me set the standards."

"Yeah. He was just telling us. Amazing."

She made a face. "He has to tell the world?"

"He's just so taken with you, he can't not speak. He's usually flippant about women. I always disliked that in him. He's not that way about you."

She smiled ruefully. "What scares me is that I don't mind that he cares so much. In fact, I like it."

I shrugged. "It's good for the ego."

"It's more than that," she said softly, her face flushing.

I clicked my tongue against my teeth. "I was afraid of that. Dawn, he's so different from you. You don't have anything in common, certainly nothing important like faith."

She nodded. "Tell me something I don't know. He comes to church once in a blue moon, and he thinks that makes him 'religious.' He's got no concept of real faith. He thinks I go overboard, but he's willing to overlook it." She spun around, her sweet face full of anguish. "I don't want someone who's noble enough to overlook my faith. I want someone who shares it with me like Curt does with you."

Of course she did. Who wouldn't? "But you care a lot for Mac anyway?"

She nodded. "Too much. When I made that crack about him being a bachelor too long, I saw his face. And it reflected my heart." Her chin began to tremble. "I'm really scared, Merry."

"I don't blame you." I gave her a hug, giving her my patented pat on the back. *I'm scared for you too,* I thought.

She pulled free and turned to the mirror, checking under her eyes to make certain her teary moment hadn't made her mascara run.

"Now listen," I said. "We've got to get back out there. Dinner'll be on the table any minute, and the guys are going to start wondering what happened to us. But before we go, I've got a piece of advice. I spent six years dating the wrong guy before I met Curt. Six years. Don't make the same mistake, Dawn. The longer you see him, the harder it will be to let go."

"What if I can't let go?" Her voice was a whisper.

The romantic in me wanted to say, "Then hang on for all you're worth. It'll all work out for the best." Instead the realist in me said, "Never underestimate the power of choice. You can let go if you must. You tell that to the girls at His House all the time. You can't do any less than you ask of them."

She nodded. "I know." Tears sat in her eyes again. "But he's so wonderful!"

I thought of Mac as I knew him and knew *wonderful* wasn't the word I'd choose. Crabby, demanding, driven, clever. But wonderful? No.

"Dawn, he'll only make you very unhappy."

She sighed. "But he's a great kisser."

I wanted to laugh at her expression but I didn't. "That's because he's had so much practice."

She looked at me, hurt that I'd say such a thing. But it was all too true, and she needed to remember that.

"Dawn, you're a woman who has spent her whole adult life in ministry. Serving God has been your priority. You can't sell out for a guy like Mac. Sheesh, you can't sell out for anyone!"

She closed her eyes and leaned back against the sink. "You're right. I can't."

We were quiet for a moment. Then she blew out a mouthful of air and straightened. "Come on. Let's go eat."

I followed Dawn to the table. I watched Mac's face light up when he saw her. I could only imagine her expression.

Dinner was almost over before Mac remembered to pass on a tidbit of information to me.

"By the way, Merry," he said between bites of crab cake. "I got a phone call about you late yesterday."

"About me?" I laughed. "Good or bad?"

"Bad."

I blinked, surprised.

"I'm to keep you reined in or *The News* will be the object of the biggest lawsuit we've ever seen."

Chapter 7

I know who that was." I shook my head in disgust.

"Good." Mac attacked his baked potato. "Then you can tell me. It was an anonymous call."

"Afraid to give his name. I'm not surprised. He's a coward."

"So who is it?" Mac looked expectantly at me as did Curt and Dawn.

"He's Tina Somebody's husband."

"Tina Somebody's husband." Mac looked at Curt and laughed. "And I have to correct her copy before it makes the paper."

"There's nothing wrong with my copy and you know it," I said. I cut the final section of my stuffed chicken breast into three neat pieces. "Tina is a woman I met at Freedom House yesterday. Well, I didn't meet her there exactly, but Stephanie put us in contact."

"Stephanie Bauer?" Dawn asked. "Isn't she great?"

"Yeah, yeah, she's great," said Mac who had never met her. "But who's Tina?"

"A battered wife. I helped her move out of her house yesterday and drove her to her parents."

"And her husband came home and found her gone and somehow knew you were the culprit?" Mac asked.

I shook my head. "He was there when she left."

"You moved her out in front of the husband?" Mac was appalled. Curt didn't look any happier.

I frowned. "Well, someone had to help her."

"Where are your brains, woman? What if he'd had a weapon?" Mac asked.

I shrugged. "Someone still needed to help her."

"Have you ever heard of the police?"

"It was for my story!"

"Oh." Mac was instantly mollified. "Okay."

"Wait a minute here," Curt said, veal cutlet halted halfway to his mouth. "It's okay for her to risk her life for a story?"

Mac raised his hand to quiet Curt. "But there wasn't any danger. She said he didn't have a weapon."

"She did?" It was Dawn. "I didn't hear her say that."

I lay my knife and fork carefully across my plate. "Listen, all of you. I will tell you what happened. But first I will tell you that I can make decisions about my safety and danger on my own. Got it?"

I looked around the table, pausing as I looked at Curt. He and I had had "discussions" in the past about what he considered the risks I took in my work.

"Got it?" I repeated as I looked at him.

He looked grim but he nodded. "Got it."

I reached over and squeezed his hand. I gave him a huge smile and said, "I think it's a matter of trust."

His eyes narrowed as I threw his own words back at him. He looked at me like he wanted to argue, and well he could. Trusting someone to remain faithful was a far cry from trusting someone not to get injured in the line of duty. A second volatile person entered into situations like mine in a way that could not be controlled. Trust was hardly the issue. Wisdom and judgment were, and I knew there were times he didn't think much of mine. In retrospect I had to agree with him. I had gotten myself into some dangerous situations, but I'd always gotten a good story.

I began talking quickly to forestall him. "Tina called Freedom House while I was there. She needed help. I went to help her. Her husband was unhappy with me. He called Mac. End of story."

"How do you know that?" Curt asked. He had on his worried look which both warmed my heart and irritated me. "He knows your name and you don't even know his. And he's got a history of being violent."

"Only toward Tina, so I'm not in danger."

Curt looked skeptical, but he managed to keep quiet.

I beamed at him. "If he calls again, we'll get worried, okay?"

The waitress appeared with the dessert tray, and I welcomed her like an old friend. "In the meantime, I want that chocolate truffle."

When we left the restaurant, we split up, Mac and Dawn each to their own cars and their own homes, Curt and I to his car.

"Let's drive up to Hibernia Park." I buckled my seat belt. "I can collect information about the mansion for the great homes article I need to write."

Curt looked at his watch. "I don't know. I've got so much to do before the opening."

"Oh, come on." I put a hand on his arm and all but batted my lashes. "It'll be fun."

"Fun's not the issue." He looked uncertain. "Time is."

"What's an hour?" I leaned over and gave him a quick kiss on the cheek.

He closed his eyes, obviously debating with himself. He straightened his shoulders, having reached a decision. He turned to me, opened his mouth, and saw my hopeful look. His shoulders sagged. "Okay," he said. "But just a quick trip."

I tried not to feel guilty as we drove through the warm Palm Sunday sunshine. He'd have plenty of time to do all he needed before Wednesday.

We drove into Hibernia Park between the white pillars with the lion heads embedded in them and up the winding narrow road past the whitewashed cottages, some occupied, one boarded shut, over Birch Run Creek and past the fishing pond. We rounded the sharp S curve, and there sat the mansion, its coppery peach stucco a soft flame in the sunshine.

"Wouldn't it be fun to live in a place like this?" I asked as we parked in the lot behind the mansion.

"If you've got lots of servants," Curt said as he climbed out of the car. "This park was a huge estate at one time."

We walked around the mansion with its slate front steps bordered by boxwood, its quarter-round turrets cuddled against the wings on either side of the main house. The white trim and red metal roof made the unusual color of the house more vibrant.

I tried the white door beside a sign that read "Mansion Entrance." It was locked, surprise, surprise.

"They give tours in the summer on Sundays," Curt said. "And near Christmas."

I looked at him. "How do you know that?"

"I've lived in this area all my life. I know all sorts of stuff." He looked mysteriously down his handsome nose at me.

I grabbed his hand. "Come on. Let's go to the ranger's office and see what information I can get."

We walked hand in hand to the beige building over the rise behind the mansion. Inside on the counter was a collection of brochures on various features of the park, including one on the mansion. I picked it up and began scanning it.

I learned there had been an ironworks on the property from the 1790s to the 1870s. At the height of the ironworks there had been two iron forges, two heating furnaces, a rolling mill, a gristmill, and at least sixteen men and boys working the facility.

I was impressed and turned to Curt to comment. I gave up the idea of sharing when I saw he was intently reading about Chambers Lake, a recent addition to the features offered in the park. I thought I saw canoeing in our future.

The door behind us slammed open. A man in jeans and a flannel shirt walked around the counter into the office area.

"Yo," he called.

A ranger walked out from his office.

"We've got a visitor," the first man said.

The ranger looked confused. "We've got lots of visitors."

"This one's staying."

"Overnight? How do you know?"

By now my ears were stretched as far as they could reach without appearing to be listening. I knew the park gates closed at dusk, so overnight stays were illegal.

"Pete found blood in the rest room early yesterday morning and again this morning. He knows he cleaned up yesterday, but there was more today."

"A visitor cut himself."

The first man shook his head. "Not that badly two days in a row. We're talking blood and bloody bandages, not Band-Aids. And Andy's lunch disappeared yesterday. And someone slept in the maintenance barn last night."

The ranger nodded. "I'll contact the police."

I grabbed the oblivious Curt and dragged him from the office.

"Do you think it's Tom?"

His head swiveled back and forth, looking. "Where?"

"The guy who's hiding here." I repeated the conversation I'd overheard.

"But why would a bleeding Tom hide in Hibernia Park? If he were hurt, he'd go to the hospital."

"But if he stole the money?"

"Same question. Why would he hide here? Why wouldn't he run?"

"He's waiting for Edie to join him?"

Curt looked at me with his bemused I-can't-believe-you-said-that look. "Are you sure you don't want to be a mystery novelist instead of a journalist?" He glanced at his watch and grimaced. "Come on. I've got to get going."

I sighed and let him drive me home. It would have been such a great story.

It was after four when I rang Edie's doorbell. While I waited for someone to answer, I studied the daffodils nodding among the yews. Their heads bobbed in the soft breeze in time to a tune only Mother Nature heard.

Yes, I thought, they're just the thing. I scurried to the closest cluster and broke off a stem close to the ground, then another and another. I broke off some of the long, slender leaves too.

I had a fistful of yellow sunshine in my hand when the front door finally opened. Randy leaned out with a frown when he saw no one.

"It's me," I said, straightening. "I'm over here." I smiled and hurried to the door.

If anything, his frown deepened when he saw me. "I take it you want something besides my mother's flowers?"

I checked a reciprocal frown. The kid was so galling! "I'm getting the flowers *for* your mother. They might cheer her up a bit."

He seemed to relish towering over me due to a combination of his own height and the added lift of the step up to the house. He looked down his handsome nose, his blue eyes cool and condescending.

I smiled at him warmly, refusing to be intimidated. If I could drive Mac nuts with my smile, maybe I could do the same thing to Randy. "How's she doing?" I sounded as sickeningly chirpy as a spring robin.

He shrugged and stepped reluctantly aside. My smile seemed to do nothing to him, good or bad. Oh, well. You can't win them all. "She's in the living room."

She was lying on the great blue couch much as she'd been the other night. Her face was a mask of misery with dark circles under her closed eyes and the lines from her nose to her chin deep and cruel. She had the same blanket I'd retrieved from the linen closet Friday pulled up over her. If I hadn't seen her last night, I'd have thought she hadn't moved since the body was discovered.

I walked quietly into the room, my heart breaking for her. As usual I wanted to fix her hurt, and this time I truly had no idea how.

"Hey, Edie." I kept my voice soft in case she was asleep.

She wasn't. She turned to me immediately, hope in her eyes. When she saw it was only me, the hope died. Irrationally, I felt guilty.

"For you." I held out the sunshine I'd picked from her yard.

She took the bouquet and stared at it as if she'd never seen a daffodil before.

"I thought you might like some cheer." I grinned in what I hoped was an encouraging manner.

She smiled faintly. "I think I had too much of that yesterday, didn't I? Did I make too big a fool of myself?"

I knew she referred to her tipsy condition of last evening. "I've seen you in better shape," I said gently. "But no harm was done."

"Only because you guys took care of me." She stretched out her hand with the daffodils in it. "Thanks."

"Thank Jolene and Reilly. They brought you home."

She nodded, and her arm collapsed like it was too great an effort to hold it upright. The flowers dangled on the floor.

"Why don't I put the daffodils in some water for you?" I took the flowers from her unresisting hand. "And while I'm in the kitchen, why don't I get you something to eat?"

"Not hungry."

"I'm sure, but that's not the issue. You must get some nourishment. What have you eaten today?"

She frowned as if searching her memory. "I don't know."

"She hasn't had anything." It was Randy. I hadn't realized he was still lurking in the doorway.

"But I haven't had anything to drink either." Edie offered this information like we would then be satisfied if she didn't eat either.

"Good for you."

She turned her head and skewered her son with a sudden, fierce gaze. "Randy threw it all away."

The boy immediately began to excuse his actions. "She was going to kill herself, driving in that condition. As if having a thief for a stepfather isn't bad enough, I'm not going to have a mom who kills herself and someone else because she's a drunk."

I realized with surprise that he was genuinely concerned about Edie beneath his façade of ridicule.

"You know, Randy," I couldn't resist saying. "It's okay to do nice things for people. You're allowed. In fact, it's encouraged."

He looked at me as if I had a second or third head, made a disgusted noise deep in his throat, and walked out.

I watched him disappear down the hall and reminded myself that he'd had some rough knocks in life. He had the right to be testy.

The power of choice.

I promptly reversed my opinion. If the legal system could do it, so could I. Randy did not have the right to be difficult. All he had was the right to choose. And he was choosing wrong. Sad. So sad.

I turned back to Edie. "Do you have any chicken broth or instant soup?"

She made a face. "I don't want anything."

"I'm sure you don't. But you're going to get it."

I went to the kitchen and began rooting through the cupboards until I found some Lipton's instant chicken noodle soup. I poured a packet into a mug that read Amhearst Bicentennial 1797–1997, added water, and after several attempts before I got the sequence of commands on the microwave correct, heated it.

While it heated, I filled a vase and arranged the daffodils. Somehow they looked like pencils stuck in a jar, all weird angles and no grace. Where was Jolene when you needed her? I took the flowers into the living room and put them on an end table where Edie could see them.

"Sit up," I told Edie when I brought her the steaming cup of soup and a plate of saltines. "And drink."

She looked at me without moving, rebellion strong in her eyes.

"Edie, sit up. It won't be good if Tom comes home and finds you sick. Now come on. Eat like a good little girl."

She pulled herself upright and grabbed the cup. "I never knew you were such a pushy person."

I laughed. "Ask Curt about that sometime."

Edie blew at the edge of the cup and took a small sip. She frowned as it burned her tongue, but she kept sipping.

"I guess I was hungry after all." She inhaled a couple of saltines. Eventually the cup was empty and most of the saltines gone. I like to think it was because she knew it was right and necessary to eat, not because I loomed over her like Randy hovering over a weaker kid.

I took the empty cup from her and went back to the kitchen. I rinsed it and put it in the dishwasher, a generic machine that comes in many new houses.

"Did she eat anything?" Randy asked from behind me.

I spun around, my hand over my heart. "I didn't hear you. You scared me to death."

He smirked. "Maybe that's what happened to Tom-boy."

"What?"

"I scared him to death."

"Right." I studied him, wondering what made him tick. Because of my strong desire to please people and fix everything, I had trouble comprehending someone like Randy, who purposely chose to hurt.

"What's the matter with you?" His tone was ice, his eyes cold.

"Nothing." I shook my head and looked away. "And yes, she ate. She had a cup of soup."

"Um." He turned to leave. "She wouldn't eat for me."

I walked back into the living room, trying to imagine a conversation in which Randy demanded Edie eat and she refused. The mind boggled.

"I'm assuming you've heard nothing from William." I sat in my cushy chair across the room from Edie, my legs tucked beneath me in an attempt to keep from sliding on the creamy leather.

She shook her head. "Not a word. I sit here and wonder, do I want to hear from him or not?"

"Don't you want to know what's happened?" I asked, amazed at her comment. "I've always thought not knowing was terrible, worse than knowing, even when the information's bad."

"That's strictly a theoretical position on your part. If the possible information was that your husband was dead, you'd never want to hear."

"Do you really think he's dead, Edie?"

She slid back down on the sofa, and though her color was still bad, she looked more alert. The soup had been good for her.

"I've been lying here all day, thinking about just that question. One minute I think, of course he's not dead. I'd know if he were dead. I'd feel it. If I had my heart torn out, I'd know. Then I think that that's just metaphysical nonsense. How would I know? I'm not clairvoyant. I'm just a wife who loves her husband." She raised a shaky hand to her forehead and rubbed.

"Headache?" I asked.

"You wouldn't believe."

"Can I get you some Tylenol or aspirin?"

"Would you? Now that I've eaten the soup, I think I can handle it without my stomach acting up."

"Where will I find them?"

"Upstairs in the bathroom off our bedroom. On the second shelf in the medicine closet."

I climbed the stairs and walked down the hall, carpeted in nondescript, inexpensive beige, past two bedrooms and a bath. It wasn't hard to identify which room was Randy's.

The door was open and I could see every electronic device known to man or teen: TV, CD system with speakers that would overwhelm a small stadium, computer, laser printer, cordless phone, portable CD player, videos, and a collection of CDs that would make any disc jockey at any radio station in the country drool. I even thought I saw a fax machine on his desk, though I couldn't imagine why a kid needed a fax machine.

Edie and Tom's room was at the end of the hall. I followed the beige carpeting from the hall across their bedroom to the bath. The cabinet hung above a small pedestal sink, and I easily found the Tylenol on the second shelf, just like Edie had said.

When I walked back into the bedroom, I flinched and ducked as I saw someone rushing at me. Even after I realized I was looking at myself reflected in the mirrored doors of the closet, it took a while for my heart to stop pounding. I shook my head at my jumpiness and hurried downstairs to Edie. I gave her the medicine, then went to the kitchen to get a glass of water. I recognized her glasses as just like mine, a blue-light special from Kmart.

Excess in the living room and dining room. Low budget in the rest of the house, Randy's room excepted. I frowned. Somehow Edie didn't strike me as the type to try and impress with the fancy rooms people saw when they visited. Tom either.

"I scared myself in your mirrored closet," I said as I returned to the living room and handed her the water. "I thought someone was coming after me."

"Those mirrors were a mistake." She swallowed three Tylenol. "The decorator magazine said the mirrors would expand the size of the room." She snorted. "It's still just as small, I still bump my thigh on the corner of the footboard more times than not, and I scare myself every time I get up during the night."

She closed her eyes. "Tom likes the mirrors though." She smiled to herself. "He says he likes seeing multiples of me, if you can imagine that."

"I think that's sweet," I said.

"Yeah, it is." She turned her head and looked at me. "You know, Tom has never even told me if he has any brothers or sisters."

"Oh." I didn't know what else to say. I couldn't very well tell her how strange I thought that was.

"Once when he was almost asleep and very relaxed, I asked him where he went to high school. Without thinking, he said he graduated from Audubon High School, hooray for the green and the gold. But every other time he was willing to talk about the past, he said he was from Camden. He even denied he'd ever mentioned Audubon. I looked up Audubon and Camden on a map. Audubon is a town in New Jersey not too far from Camden, but you'd never live in one place and go to school in the other."

She looked at me, her eyes filled with fear and distress. "What's going on?"

"I don't know, Edie," I said gently. "I don't know."

She closed her eyes and a tear ran down her cheek. "Me neither."

Soon she was asleep. I stayed curled in my chair, reading and thinking. I stood by my original sentiment that Tom loved Edie deeply. So why wasn't he contacting her? I sighed heavily. I could think of no good reason that Tom wasn't calling home, and I could think of several bad ones.

Lord, where is he? If he's still alive, take care of him, okay? And let him come home safely. Please.

I heard Randy rummaging around in the kitchen and assumed he was making himself something to eat. Good for him. Maybe I had been misjudging him, and he would turn into a decent human being after all.

"There's nothing in this house to eat," he bellowed.

Nope, I hadn't been wrong about him after all. I jumped from my chair and ran to the kitchen.

"Quiet!" I hissed. "Your mother's sleeping."

"Like I care." He stalked down the front hall and out the door. I followed and watched out a window as he disappeared down the street on his bike.

Did he often take off like that without saying where he was going? If my brother Sam or I had ever left without saying where we were going and when we planned to return, my father would have called us on the carpet but good.

"Families talk," he'd lecture. "We tell each other things. It's not to limit anyone's freedom. It's to give peace of mind. Your mother and I tell you where we are going. You tell us where you are going. I don't care how old you are. Families talk."

Randy had not been gone long when the phone rang. I ran to grab it before Edie awoke. "Hello?"

A man's voice growled in my ear, "If you say anything to the cops, I'll get you too."

"What?" I could barely push the word out of my throat.

"You heard me. I'll blow you away too. Just like your old man."

The dial tone had been buzzing in my ear for a while before I could breathe again. I missed the cradle the first time I tried to seat the receiver. The second time I succeeded. I leaned against the wall, trying to rid myself of the tainted feeling the menacing voice had somehow conveyed. I shuddered.

"Who was that?"

Edie stood in the doorway, her face filled with the warring emotions of hope and fear.

"I don't know." I shuddered again. "It wasn't Tom. I'm sure of that. But whoever it was made his voice sound creepy."

"It was a threat?" Edie looked shocked.

I nodded. "Big time. We need to call William."

I dialed William's number. "Come at once. I'm at Edie's."

I could feel him snap to attention. "What happened? Tom?"

"No. A threatening phone call. Can you trace it?"

"Do they have Caller ID?"

I asked Edie and she said, "Randy does on his line, but Tom and I don't."

"We probably can't do much," William said. "But we'll be right there. Tomorrow call the phone company and get a special Call Trace account set up. If he calls again, we'll at least get his number."

I made a note to call the phone company and get Edie set up with the service that traced calls of an obscene or threatening nature, recording the number at the phone company where the police could obtain it. Edie herself would not be given the number.

"Let's go wait in the living room," I said to Edie, attempting to walk around her, attempting to put off telling her the content of the call. No, I wasn't anxious to tell her that information at all.

She moved directly in front of me and looked me in the eye. "What did he say?"

"He threatened me," I admitted, "though of course he wasn't threatening me. He thought he was talking to you."

"And he said?"

I took a deep breath and knew I had to tell her. "'If you say anything to the cops, I'll get you too.'"

Edie lost what little color she had, and she grabbed at the wall as her knees buckled. "Too? He said too?"

I nodded.

"Was that all?"

I shook my head. How I did not want to repeat the rest of the message! "I said, 'What?' and he said, 'You heard me. I'll blow you away too. Just like your old man.'"

"Just like—" Edie gave a low groan and started to sway. I caught her just before she collapsed.

I laid her on the floor and ran to the sink. I grabbed a towel that lay on the drainboard, wet it, and hurried back to her. I placed it on her forehead, grabbed her hand, and began to rub.

Her eyes fluttered. "What hap—?" Then memory hit.

"He's dead." Her voice was a whisper. "Tom's dead." Tears filled her eyes.

"We don't know that," I protested.

"But you said—"

"I know what I said, but I don't know that he knew what he was talking about. Maybe he just wants to upset you. Maybe he's just trying to scare you."

She pulled the cloth off her forehead with a shaking hand and sat up. "Well, he's succeeded." She used the cloth to wipe her face. "I don't think I've ever been so terrified, not even with Randolph."

With Randolph? How did he get into the conversation?

She looked at me with sad eyes. "Tom's never going to come home."

"Edie! Don't say that."

"Don't ask me how I know, but I do. Tom Whatley's never going to come home."

Chapter 8

I knew something was up as soon as I walked into the newsroom on Monday. The air pulsed with awed wonder.

"What's going on?" I asked Larry, the sport's guy. He was standing by his desk staring in mute fascination, an unusual thing for him. He was a doer, a fidgeter, not a starer.

"Just take a look over yonder." He jerked his thumb in the direction of the big picture window.

I saw nothing unusual. "Window cleaners are coming?" That hardly seemed reason enough for the air of disbelief and surprise so palpable you could almost touch it. "The pigeons are having an open house and have invited us out to their sill? The African violets are being resettled?"

"Look again."

I studied the window and the windowsills and still saw nothing. My eyes drifted casually to the right.

"Oh, my!"

Larry looked at me with a raised eyebrow. "That's a mild expletive for the radical nature of the situation."

"I can't think of anything else to say. As a nonswearer, I rarely get rawer than that."

"Remind me not to take you into the locker room after the home team has lost," Larry said. He flopped into his chair, still staring. "Something big is up." His voice was full of doom. "The question is what."

I continued to study Mac's desk. It was neat for the first time since he'd become acting editor. "Does it mean he's been fired? Or does it mean he's trying to make a good impression? Or does it mean he's lost what little sanity he had?"

"You tell me," Larry said. "He'll never find anything now. We're all doomed to fits of temper unlike any the human race has ever seen."

"You looking at something?" Mac's voice said softly from directly behind us.

I spun around, my face red as I recalled my crack about his sanity. I refused to even recall Larry's comment. I decided attack was my best defense. "It's bad enough when Randy sneaks up on me. You don't have to do it too!"

He studied me for a minute as I glared at him. "I think I like you better all grumpy than smiley."

Larry laughed. "Either way, she sounds like one of Snow White's dwarfs."

"Just what I always wanted to be." I opened my bottom desk drawer and dropped my leather shoulder bag inside. I looked at Mac. "How did you accomplish the cleanup between Saturday, when I last saw the indescribable mess, and this morning?" I asked. "And more importantly, why?"

He grinned. "I had help."

I frowned at him. That grin could mean only one thing. "You asked Dawn to neaten up your desk? I thought you liked her."

"When she heard Mr. Montgomery was coming in today, she volunteered to help me. We spent yesterday afternoon working. Together."

I couldn't decide which concerned me more, Mr. Montgomery's impending visit or Mac's continuing infatuation with Dawn and its effect on her.

"Montgomery's coming to the newsroom?" Larry sat up straight, all nerves and rattled energy. It was obvious what was his major concern. "When? Maybe I've got time to organize my desk too."

We all looked at Larry's working space with its dog-eared books of statistics and well-read sports magazines, wire-service printouts, handwritten notes, professional team mugs with dried coffee crusts, and a new box of doughnuts that he might or might not choose to share. Then we looked at each other and shook our heads. Not a chance he could order the inches-high clutter before next weekend.

"But it's okay," I assured Larry. "Your job's not hanging by a thread."

"As is that of someone else we all know and love," announced Jolene as she plopped her handbag down on her desk and opened the Waterloo Gardens paper bag she had been holding carefully by the handles. She lifted out a basket of small flowering plants: primroses, tiny mums, tête-à-tête daffodils, grape hyacinths, and cyclamen.

"Oh, Jolene." I stared at the basket, as bright as the spring it heralded, and promptly forgot all about Mr. Montgomery. "How beautiful. Did you arrange it?" I glanced at her face and knew by the satisfied look she wore that she had indeed clustered the flowers together and draped the graceful, airy Spanish moss around the edges to hide any holes or pots careless enough to show.

She nodded with a remarkable amount of modesty as she plucked a leaf that looked good to me and tossed it away.

Mac studied the basket. "Not bad."

"Not bad?" Gone was Jolene's humble manner as she glared at Mac. "What do you mean, not bad?"

"Great as a matter of fact," Mac said, recalling belatedly that Jolene was only as efficient as his compliments were frequent.

Jolene nodded. "Right answer. Now put it on the corner of your desk and maybe Mr. Montgomery won't notice the mess." She stopped cold. "Where's the mess?"

Mac reached for the basket. "Can't I have it if there's no mess? And how did you know Mr. Montgomery was coming today?"

"I didn't. I just knew that if I were deciding whether to keep you or fire you, I'd come see you in action. So here." She handed him the basket. "Now we'd better get to work, so that when he comes in, it looks like we actually do things around here."

Mac stood there with the basket dangling awkwardly from his fist. "Does this mean you want me to keep being your boss, Jolene? You actually like me? You recognize that I'm the best boss you've ever had? You can't live without me?"

With each question Mac stepped closer to Jolene. I would have been retreating at the same pace as his advance, fearing a return of his Mac the Lecher persona. Jo stood her ground until he was almost touching her.

She looked him calmly in the eye and said, "One step closer and I'll scream sexual harassment. Or better yet, I'll tell Dawn."

Mac stepped back with a sour look on his face. "You are the most irritating woman I know. Can't you take a joke?" He turned toward his desk, then turned back. "Thank you for the flowers."

"Me irritating? I'm not the one stalking me. I'm the one being nice! And you're welcome."

The door at the back of the newsroom opened and we all spun, expecting to see Mr. Montgomery come to catch us at our leisure. We all breathed a huge sigh of relief when it was only Edie.

She looked terrible. Her face was pale, her eyes were puffy, and her skirt actually fit, a sign that she wasn't eating. I was willing to bet she hadn't had anything since the cup of soup I made her eat yesterday.

I hurried over to her, Jo right behind me.

"No word from Tom yet?" I asked. Foolish question considering how she looked.

She closed her eyes as if in pain.

"Edie." It was Mac. He held out the basket of flowers. "Take these and go home. Put your feet up and relax. You don't need to be here today. We'll manage just fine."

"No, please." Her face was desperate. "Let me stay. I need to be out of the house."

Mac blinked. "Sure you can stay. Whatever's best for you."

I was proud of him for his kindness. Sometimes I actually liked Mac a lot.

He still held out the flowers, ignoring Jolene's accusing look. "These can cheer up your desk."

She looked at them, then turned her head from the basket. "They look too much like something you might get if someone died," she whispered.

I didn't think they looked like that at all, but I understood what she was saying. She was terrified Tom was dead. I could hear her saying to me yesterday with desperate conviction, "Tom's never going to come home."

Poor Edie.

Wisely Mac took the basket and went to his desk, where he set it on the corner. Between the African violets on the sill and the basket on the desk, he looked like he was lost in a flowering jungle. It looked great.

I watched Mac sit down and stare in bewilderment at his neat desk. He looked like he didn't know what to do in such an ordered setting, and he probably didn't.

Edie went to her seat and began moving papers around. Jolene and I watched her out of the corners of our eyes, but she seemed all right. Gradually we relaxed and went about our own business. We did have a 9:30 deadline.

First I called the police station for the latest on the body in Randy's car. William wasn't in and wouldn't be until the afternoon. I spoke with Jeb Lammey, a cop who served as their press liaison and PR specialist.

"Nothing yet, Merry," he said. "We've sent fingerprints to AFIS, but who knows how long it will take to hear. It depends on how busy they are. And that's assuming the FBI has the guy's prints on file to begin with."

I turned my back to Edie and said as softly as I could, "What about Tom Whatley? Any word there?"

"Nothing there either. We're making inquiries."

Ah, those all-encompassing, ever-convenient inquiries.

"Any idea why the man was in the Whatleys' garage?"

"None whatsoever."

"Jeb, you're not making this very easy for me, you know."

He laughed. "If it's hard for you, imagine what it's like for us! We have to find the answers. You only have to write about them."

We hung up and I wrote a story that depended heavily on Jeb's quotes about the Automated Fingerprint Identification System.

The business of comparing the arches, loops, and/or whorls from the fingers of John Doe to the millions found in the FBI computer is amazingly quick, but requests for possible identification have to be taken as they come. On a busy weekend, a request may be one of many and must take its place in line. When several similar prints are finally found by the computers at AFIS, the possibilities are examined by a fingerprint expert. The final identification is made by human eye.

I even ended up writing about Randy's birthday car, a gift from his father now damaged before it was even driven. I think I kept my personal feelings about a gift of this magnitude out of the article. I certainly meant to.

I reread my copy, pushed the right buttons, and sent my story to Mac in his flowering jungle for approval and editing.

It was shortly after nine when I found time to call Tina at her parents' home.

"I'm just checking to see how you're doing."

"We're doing all right." Her voice was hesitant.

I leaned back in my chair, frowning. "Tina, what's wrong?"

"He came last night."

My hands grew clammy on the phone. "Your husband? To your parents' house?"

"Yeah. He wanted to make me and the kids come home."

"Obviously he didn't." *Thank you, Lord.*

"But my father's in the hospital."

"Oh, Tina! What happened?"

She gave a little sob. "When he grabbed me, my father tried to stop him. Bill pushed him." She started to cry, something she seemed to do often. I didn't blame her. I think I'd cry in her situation too.

"What happened? Did he fall? Hurt himself that way?"

"No. He had a heart attack."

I closed my eyes, wishing I could make all of Tina's pain go away. "Will he be all right?"

"We don't know." She took a huge sobbing breath. "Mom's at the hospital now, but I had to come home because of the kids. Oh, Merry, he's such a good man!" I assumed she meant her father, not her husband. "It's all my fault! I should have just stayed at home. I should have. Then Dad'd be all right and Mom wouldn't be crying and everything would be fine."

"Except it wouldn't be fine, Tina. You know that. You'd still be getting knocked around."

"But at least I'd deserve it!" And she began to sob again.

I let her cry for a bit until the racking sobs became soft weeping. Then I said, "Tina, it'll be okay." I hoped it would be someday. "Now listen to me. You need to remember that you *never* deserve treatment like he's given you. Never."

"But neither does my father."

"You're right. He doesn't. It's just another sign that your husband is out of control. You can't go back to him."

She said nothing, and I read a lot of bad things into that silence. I sighed. "Will he bother you again if he knows you're alone?" Who do I know in Phoenixville? I kept asking myself. Who do I know who could come stay with her? Who do I know who could protect her? The answer was always the same: no one.

"He won't bother us today. My mom called the police when he showed up. They arrested him." She cried harder. "They were putting him in the police car and he's yelling, 'I love you, Tina. All I want is for you to come home. I'll never touch you again in anger. I swear. I love you!' It was horrible!"

"Are you going to get a restraining order to protect you and the kids from him?"

"I don't know. I get so confused!"

"Tina, you're not going to go back to him! Tell me you're not!" Her only answer was more tears.

"Tina, will you let me interview you for the paper? I won't use your name or anything. I'll protect you and the kids."

"You want to talk to me? Why me?"

"I'm doing an article for *The News* on domestic abuse. That's why I was talking to Stephanie when you called on Saturday. I'd like to have your perspective on what it's like to be in your situation."

Tina's tears lessened as she thought about the interview.

"Think of how you could help other women caught in situations like yours. Maybe something you say would help one of them be as brave as you and leave."

"I'm coming to Freedom House tomorrow," she said. "I could see you then. Is that too late?"

"No. That's just right."

"I have a black eye," she said suddenly. "He clipped me last night when I tried to protect my father."

I thought of Curt holding me in his lap, comforting me even though I had been the foolish one.

Dear God, I don't even know how to articulate my thanks.

M ac, I'd like to go to Audubon, New Jersey, and see what I can find out about Tom Whatley." It was early in the day yet, only about 9:30. Audubon was a small town just across the Delaware River, and there should be plenty of time to get there and back before Sherrie showed up at 4:00.

"Why Audubon? I thought Camden was the town of choice."

"That's the official line, but Edie told me that Tom once let slip that he had graduated from Audubon High School. He later denied he'd said any such thing. I looked in the Camden County phone book, and there are three Whatleys listed, all with the Audubon exchange. I called the numbers. Two claim they don't know anything about any Tom Whatley, but they were awfully belligerent for not knowing him. The third was an answering machine. Maybe in person they would talk to me."

Mac didn't even need to think about it. He just got a cat-who-ate-the-canary grin. "You've got good instincts, Kramer."

I hugged the rare compliment to myself.

Mac nodded. "Why don't you try the high school while you're there. Check the old yearbooks. Talk to some teachers. After all, Tom's not that old."

I could feel the excitement thrumming. "Sure. There have got to be some teachers there who remember him. Maybe I can find out something that will give us an idea about why he's hiding."

"It'll take you an hour fifteen, an hour and a half to get there," Mac said. "Go down Route 82 south to Route 1 east to Route 322 south to I-95." I wrote the directions as he talked. "Be careful when you get on 95 north. You enter the road in the far left lane and have to cross four lanes of traffic in less than a mile to make the Commodore Barry Bridge."

"Four lanes?" The thought of trying that move with Philadelphia traffic made me cringe. "Isn't there another way?"

"Yeah, there is. My mom always does it the way I'm going to tell you when she goes to visit her brother Tony down the shore in Ventnor." His tone of voice made it clear that he thought it was the coward's way. "When you come to the Y just before I-95, take the right fork instead of the left to 95. Then take three lefts and you'll get on 95 from the slow lane instead of the fast. You'll also be in the lane to get off for the bridge."

Feeling much relieved, I took off for Audubon. When I saw the volume of traffic on 95, I was very thankful for the coward's way to get to the bridge. I went north on 295 in New Jersey and got off at the Lawnside exit and drove down the White Horse Pike to Audubon. I turned left at the light at Pine Street and found the high school, a solid-looking tan brick building.

I climbed the front steps, went to the office, and signed in. I had to show both my press card and my driver's license. I felt like I was trying for a boarding pass at the airport. The secretary directed me to the library.

"You want Mrs. Russo. She's been here forever, she never forgets a student, and she'd love to help you. Just look for the lady with the curly hair."

When I walked into the library, several students were sitting at tables reading. I looked around and found Mrs. Russo immediately, a short, thin lady of indeterminate years. Hennaed curls stood out all over her head. Her red dress fought with her hair, but her personality beat both into submission. She was lecturing a linebacker-sized student, her finger wagging under his nose. He stood, patiently enduring, eyes on the floor.

I approached her, arriving just in time to hear her say, "You're a good boy, Jay. A bright boy. Don't you go doing something stupid like trying to get by on Cliff Notes again. Read the whole thing, young man. Never settle for the easy way out."

"Yes, ma'am," Jay mumbled.

"Now get out your copy of *Moby Dick*. Read it. Sit right over there where I can see you."

"But I paid money for those notes," Jay protested in what he must have known was a vain effort. I knew it and I'd only seen Mrs. Russo in action for two minutes.

She nodded. "Yes, you did. I'm sorry that you are losing money on a poor investment like this." For the first time I noticed the yellow and black Cliff Notes in her hand. "That will teach you to consider the consequences carefully next time. No easy way out!"

Jay turned and walked to the table she had indicated, a sheepish grin on his face as the other kids smirked at him. He reached in his bookbag and pulled out a copy of *Moby Dick* and began to read.

"Senior honors class," Mrs. Russo said to me, her sharp eyes watching the class to see if anyone dared challenge her lecture to Jay or tease him about receiving it. "They come in here each week for some sustained reading. Can't have them taking the easy way out. No, sir, we can't. They're too smart for that."

They don't make them like her anymore, I thought as I studied Mrs. Russo. And these kids don't know how lucky they are to sit under someone like her. Her eyes sparkled with a zest for books, for kids, for life in general. She was definitely old enough to have known Tom. In fact, she looked old enough to have been his mother, and what a mother she would have been. I wondered if she had kids of her own and what they had grown to be.

"I'm trying to trace a man I think went to school here about twenty-three years ago," I explained after I introduced myself and showed my press card.

Her eyes lit up at the idea of tracing someone. I could tell I was looking at a woman who thrived on research. "What was the man's name? I've taught here for almost thirty years, so I might well remember him."

Somehow I knew her comment was mere modesty. I bet she remembered just about everyone who had gone through this relatively small school since the day she arrived.

"Do you remember a student named Tom Whatley?"

Immediately she smiled and began shaking her head in the reminiscent way some people have. "Who doesn't remember Tom Whatley?"

I grabbed my tape recorder out of my purse. "Can you tell me about him?"

"Come on into my office where we can talk," she said, indicating a small closet of a room off to one side. She faced her readers and announced, "I'm stepping into my office with this young lady. I expect to hear no noise whatsoever while I am absent."

She walked ahead of me into the office, confident that the students would obey her. I glanced over my shoulder and thought that they probably would. Nobody wanted a dressing down like Jay had gotten.

"Everybody knew Tom," Mrs. Russo said from her seat behind her desk. "He was one of those kids who was into everything. Football, basketball, track, National Honor Society, yearbook, class plays, choir. You name it and Tom seemed to be involved."

Football? Basketball? Tom Whatley? Not only was he short. He was slight even as an adult. As a teenager he would have been as substantial as dandelion fluff.

"All the girls had crushes on him, you know. So handsome. If I'd been a few years younger, he would have turned my head too."

I stared at Mrs. Russo. Maybe she wasn't as sharp as she seemed.

"Do you have old yearbooks that I could look at?" I asked. "I'd like to see what he looked like back then." I'd like to show her she wasn't talking about the right person.

She got up from her seat. "Wait until you see how handsome he was." She shook her head. "I haven't thought about Tom in years, though come to think about it, it's been ten years, hasn't it? You doing one of those recap pieces?"

I mumbled something noncommittal as she led me to a shelf where years of books sat, the pictorial history of the school. A recap piece? Ten years? What was she talking about?

She went unerringly to a yearbook, flipped to the senior pictures, and thrust the volume into my hands.

"There he is." She pointed to the picture of a young, handsome, very large kid down in the lower righthand corner of the right page. I blinked and looked again.

The name read Thomas John Whatley, but he definitely wasn't Edie's Tom.

Chapter 9

Comments like *Class Everything*, *Ladies Man*, *Prom King*, and *Three-Letter Man* were inscribed next to the picture of an incredibly good-looking hunk. There was no other word that came to mind when I looked at the picture of Tom Whatley except *hunk*. He had lots of dark, wavy hair hanging to his shoulders and a killer smile. He even looked comfortable in the suit and tie he'd obviously been forced to wear for the photo.

I stared at this stranger in fascination. "Tell me about him. Anything and everything you can remember."

"Well, he was definitely a star in our little firmament." Mrs. Russo reached out and ran a finger across the picture. "And he was a nice kid too. I think he was as popular with the faculty as he was with the kids."

"What did he do after he left high school?"

"He went to Annapolis and played football for them."

"Mr. All American." I smiled as I said it so she wouldn't think I was being snide.

"Not in the sense of making a specific team," Mrs. Russo said, "but in the sense of being well-rounded, yes. You can see from the picture how big he was. What doesn't show is how smart he was. A very gifted student. He'd never have tried to get by with Cliff Notes." Poor Jay. He was forever marked in Mrs. Russo's mind. Mine too, come to think of it.

"Well, he'd have to be an excellent student to go to the Naval Academy."

"True enough. He did well his first two years, too, and then the trouble began." For the first time since we began talking about Tom Whatley, the real Tom Whatley, she wasn't smiling.

"What trouble?"

She looked out the window, squinting against the bright light or against the memories, I wasn't sure which. "From what I heard and read in the paper, he got caught up in drugs somehow. He lost his place at the Academy in a scandal about drugs on campus. After that, he bounced around for several years, taking jobs but never sticking with anything for very long. It was quite sad."

"Did you ever see him during this time?"

She nodded. "Just once. I bumped into him down the shore one summer walking on the boardwalk. He was as charming as ever, but I realized for the first time that he was only charm, no substance. I remember wondering whether he'd always been that way and we'd all been blind to it, or whether he'd become that way as life got away from him. I still remember how sad I felt that night. The only time I felt sadder was the night I heard he'd died."

"He's dead?" My heart paused midbeat at the unexpectedness of the comment. Though why it should surprise me, I don't know. No one usurps the name of a living individual. The living individual tends to complain. "How did he die?" I asked.

"Again I don't know all the details, but it had something to do with a drug deal gone bad. If you access the files of the Philadelphia *Inquirer* and the Camden *Courier-Post*, you can probably get the details. I just remember that his best buddy was somehow involved."

"His best buddy?"

"Yeah. Tom Willis. They were like brothers all through school. The kids used to call them the TomTom Twins." She shook her head and her hennaed curls seemed to come alive. I half expected them to reach out and grab me. "Most unlikely pair of friends you ever saw."

I pulled my fascinated gaze from her head and asked, "Why?"

"Well, there was Tom Whatley, king of the school, and there was Tom Willis, nice little guy but not even a princeling, let alone a king." She reached across the yearbook and flipped the page. "There. That's Tom Willis."

Again my heart gave an irregular little beat. Smiling up at me was Edie's Tom, younger, slighter, full of innocence, but definitely Edie's Tom.

The comments beside Tom Willis's picture ran to the generic phrases reserved for the nonroyalty of high school, things like *Nice Guy, Pleasant Personality, a Twin, Good Student.*

I stared at Tom Willis and wondered how he got from being Tom Whatley's best friend to being Tom Whatley. What had possessed him to drop his own name? What had happened that night of the bad drug bust? Did any of this history have anything to do with Tom's present disappearance? And what would Edie say when she learned all this convoluted information?

"Tom Willis surprised me," Mrs. Russo said as she stared at his picture. "I admit that I was so blinded by Tom Whatley's glory that I didn't see what, or I should say who, Tom Willis was. And he turned out to be quality. He didn't win any scholarships or appointments to prestigious schools, but he went to Rowan College back when it was still Glassboro State. I think he studied psychology. After he graduated with honors while working two jobs to pay living expenses and help support his widowed mother, he went to the police academy and became

stayed home these days waiting for phone calls from the press, specifically me. I dialed the Willis number, and a lady answered. I hung up without speaking and immediately drove to the address I'd gotten from Mrs. Russo. As I might have expected, her directions were perfect.

I stared at the Willis house. It was a typical Audubon bungalow, gray with white trim, the front porch closed in to make a sun room. The sparse grass in the front yard was in need of a good lawn service, and the globe yews hadn't been trimmed in forever. The only bright note in the yard was a fat azalea, planted for some reason in the middle of the lawn. It was full of plump buds just waiting for their time to burst in spring's warm sun.

I walked to the front door and rang the bell. As I waited, I peered through the little glass panes into the house. The sun porch was furnished with some moth-eaten white rattan furniture that had undoubtedly been cheery and inviting once upon a time. Now it looked ready for trash pickup. I couldn't see into the rest of the house through the wooden door that separated the porch from what was probably a living room.

When the inside door opened, a little bird of a woman peered out at me. She must have decided I looked safe because she came across the sun porch to the outer door, her little feet barely touching the floor. She opened the door a mere crack.

"Can I help you?" she asked with a tremulous smile.

I gave her my best smile, the one that Curt loved and Mac hated. "Hello, Mrs. Willis. I'm Merrileigh Kramer and I think I know your son, Tom. And your daughter-in-law Edie."

Instantly the smile disappeared. "I'm not interested," she said in a desperate voice and began to close the door.

"Mrs. Willis," I said quickly, putting my hand on the door. "I mean it when I say I'm a friend. I work with Edie. Please talk to me. I'm very confused."

The whole time I talked, Mrs. Willis shook her gray head. "Go away, please. Just go away."

"But Mrs. Willis, we need to find Tom. Edie's beside herself with worry. Do you know where he is?"

"Go away," she pleaded yet again. She glanced back into the safety of her house, obviously regretting answering the door. "I don't know anything."

I looked at the small woman, and I saw genuine fear in her face. I recognized once again that I didn't have the killer instinct necessary to make it in the news business big time. I sighed and took my hand from the door. "Please."

Mrs. Willis shook her head. "No." The door shut in my face with all the finality of the gates of hell snapping shut behind an unrepentant sinner. The only difference was that I was on the outside while the sinner would be on the inside.

When I arrived at the newsroom shortly before four, I draped my blazer over my chair, dropped my purse in my drawer, and started for Mac's desk. I stopped when I realized he was in deep discussion with Larry, the sport's guy.

"Arrgh!" I muttered in frustration. Here I was sitting on the story of my life and Mac was busy!

I went back to my desk and found myself unable to sit still. My left leg bounced up and down faster than a crying kid's chin. I booted up my computer and went to the Web. I typed in the URL for the Philadelphia *Inquirer* and went to the archives, seeking any available information on Tom Whatley. While I waited for the information I requested to be called up, I turned to Jolene.

"How did Mr. Montgomery's visit go?"

"He never came, and if he doesn't hurry, Mac's desk is going to revert to its natural chaotic condition." She wrinkled her nose, showing her beautiful capped teeth. "We're all just waiting around practicing our smiles and our paeans of praise about Mac."

I raised my eyebrow and cocked my head toward Edie, asking how she was without saying anything aloud. Jolene shrugged her eyebrows back: who knows?

"I'm fine," Edie said tartly. "And I'm not an idiot. I know what this means." She jerked her head a couple of times.

"Sorry," I said. "I didn't want to bother you. You looked busy."

"I am. I'm a reporter and I'm working on a story. And I'm fine."

"No, she's not," Jolene said, leaning back in her chair. "She wouldn't go to lunch with me. I even offered to pay."

Jolene might be a millionaire, but an offer to pay was a rare occurrence and a sign of the depth of her concern.

"I asked you to bring me a cup of noodle soup," Edie defended.

"Which you carried to the rest room and threw away when you thought I wasn't looking." Jolene's lethal nail pointed straight at Edie's nose.

"You are one nosy woman," Edie griped.

"I am," said Jolene proudly.

Larry left Mac, and I stood to grab his attention while it was free. I picked up my notes just as William Poole entered the newsroom and distracted me. It was the focused look on his shar-pei face as he approached Edie's desk that caught my attention. He was a man normally given to taking things as they came. The melancholy cast of his face was due more to gravity's action on the deep furrowing than actual sorrow.

Now his face was so intense that I sat back down again. I did not want to miss whatever was coming.

"Edie, may I talk with you in private?" William asked.

Edie, who had watched his approach with trepidation, seemed to shrink into herself. "Is this about Tom?"

William nodded.

"Do I need a lawyer?"

William blinked. "I don't think so. This isn't an official interrogation or anything. We just need to talk."

She looked at Jolene and me in a panic. Obviously she felt his intensity too.

"It's okay, Edie." I came and stood by her, putting my hand on her shoulder. "You can trust William." I shot him a look that said he'd better be trustworthy. "He's a friend."

But Edie wasn't having any of it. "Stay with me, Merry. You too, Jo."

"Like you could get us to leave." Jolene joined me beside Edie. Her expression dared William to tell her to go.

William looked exasperated. "Edie, I need to talk about some very private things with you. I don't think you want an audience."

"I have no secrets. I want them with me."

"There's a conference table over there," I said, pointing to the scarred collapsible table about the size of two card tables that sat along the far wall. It was so unstable that if Mac got angry during a meeting and pounded his fist, everyone's beverages jumped and spilled. "Why don't we sit around it?"

William looked unhappy but resigned. After all, he'd said it wasn't an official interrogation.

We paraded across the newsroom and clustered about the table, William at the head, Jolene and Edie on one side, me across from Edie. When Mac saw the parade to the table, he came to see what was going on. I'm sure Larry would have come too, but he'd just left to interview some high school athlete.

"What's all this?" Mac asked.

"I need to talk with Edie," William explained again. He was looking beleaguered and undoubtedly wished he'd sent Jeb or someone else to bring Edie to the station.

"Oh, okay." Mac pulled out a chair and sat next to me.

William sighed deeply and cleared his throat. We all looked at him expectantly, me especially. I wondered if he was going to mention Tom Willis or if I had beaten him to the punch. I schooled my face to be impassive, something that does not come naturally to me.

"Edie," William began, "do you remember when I questioned you about Tom's background?"

She nodded. "And I knew very little."

"Well, we've learned a bit more. By tracing Tom's social security number, his birth date, and birthplace, we've learned a fascinating piece of information."

We all waited while he paused for dramatic effect.

"Tom Whatley doesn't exist."

"Oh, no!" Edie put her hands to her face and began to cry.

Jolene scowled at William like it was his fault Tom didn't exist. "Are you sure?"

Mac frowned and reached across the table to pat Edie on the shoulder. You would have thought he had taken patting lessons from me. But he was alert enough to pick up on William's choice of words. "What do you mean, doesn't exist?"

I sat still and said nothing because I knew how right William was. A terrible thought struck me and knocked my complacency for a loop. Was he referring to the real Tom Whatley or Edie's Tom Whatley? "Is 'doesn't exist' a euphemism for Tom's dead?" I blurted.

William nodded. "Tom Whatley is dead all right." He talked right over Edie's wail. "As a matter of fact, he's been dead for ten years."

As a conversation stopper, William's comment was one of the best I'd ever heard. I looked around the circle and tried not to smile at everyone's dropped jaws. I looked at William, who was looking at Edie.

She turned her earnest, tear-streaked face to William. "Then you haven't found my Tom's body or anything?"

William shook his head, surprised. "Your husband's body? No."

Edie laughed and looked at the ceiling. "Thank you, God."

"But Tom Whatley's body?" William glared at all of us. "Yes."

Mac was having a hard time assimilating William's information. He was probably still hung up on *doesn't exist*. "Tom's not dead but you've found his body?"

"Edie's husband isn't dead, to the best of our knowledge," William agreed. "But Tom Whatley definitely is. We have found his death certificate at the Camden County Courthouse dated almost exactly ten years ago."

Mac narrowed his eyes. "If Tom Whatley's dead, then who's Edie's husband?"

William nodded. "The question of the hour. We don't know yet. I've sent Jeb out to Edie's house to get something with Tom's fingerprints on it. We'll begin a trace immediately through AFIS."

"Don't bother, William," I said. "I can save you the trouble."

Everyone looked at me like I was crazy, and I have to admit that I kind of liked the power of knowing what no one else knew. Childish, of course, but fun.

"Edie's husband is named Tom Willis."

Everyone looked at me in surprise, including William, who wasn't happy about being beaten to the punch. Edie dropped her head onto her chest, but was that relief I saw in her eyes before they closed?

"Tom Willis is from Audubon, New Jersey, and he's an ex-cop." I acknowledged William with a nod of my head as I passed on that bit of information. "He was somehow involved in the death of his best friend, Tom Whatley, in a drug bust. His mother, that is, Tom Willis's mother, still lives in Audubon, but she wouldn't talk to me."

"Edie," cried Jolene. "If Tom Whatley isn't Tom's real name, are you really married? If he signed the marriage certificate Tom Whatley, are you legal?"

We all turned to Jolene in disbelief. Talk about the least important issue at the moment.

"Well, is she married?" Jolene asked all of us, refusing to back down.

Edie's married state or lack thereof didn't interest William. "What I need to know, Edie, is why your husband is calling himself Tom Whatley."

"I don't know."

"But you've been married for how long?"

"Five years."

"And you expect me to believe you don't know about the false identity?"

"I do not know why he calls himself Tom Whatley."

"Where would he go if he ran away after committing a crime?"

"I don't know, and he didn't commit any crime!"

"Did you know he was using a false identity?"

"I—"

The back door of the newsroom burst open and Randy flew in, startling all of us.

"Mom!" His eyes went to her empty desk.

"Over here, Randy." Edie waved her hand.

Randy came charging over, his face full of anger. "The cops were at the house again. You'll never guess what they were after."

He skidded to a halt beside our table and for the first time noticed William. "Oh."

"Hello, Randy," said William, standing and indicating the chair at the far end of the table. "Would you like to join us? We're talking about your stepfather."

"Here," said Jolene. "Sit next to your mom." She got up and moved to the seat at the far end, the mother to William's father for the family around the table.

"I don't want to sit." Randy moved to the vacated chair, but true to his word, he didn't take the seat. Standing with his back to the room, he didn't see Sherrie enter to keep her appointment with me. I did though, turned as I was to look at Randy. I held up a finger to Sherrie to show I'd be a minute here. Suddenly her insights into domestic abuse didn't look nearly as compelling as they had seemed when she suggested the idea. There was too much exciting stuff going on right here at the table.

Sherrie nodded and sat in an empty chair along the far wall, patiently waiting until I was free. I rose and began moving toward her, my ear trained to the table. Maybe she could come back tomorrow.

Randy, full sneer, made one of his patented statements: "That man is not my stepfather. Just because he's married to my mother doesn't mean I have any relationship whatsoever with him. In fact, he makes me sick." The last four words were separate and emphatic.

"Randy!" Edie was embarrassed and distressed. She reached for his hand. He pulled it away and sank angrily into the chair beside her, crossing his arms over his chest so she couldn't grab at him again.

I smiled at Sherrie as I approached her, noting that her usually bright eyes were clouded with concern.

"Hi," she said to me absently, her attention riveted on Randy just as mine was. "What's wrong?"

"The police are talking to Randy's mother about the disappearance of his stepfather."

"His stepfather has disappeared?"

"He's been missing since Thursday night."

Sherrie looked confused. "He said today that he had just gotten rid of a huge problem and was feeling light as a feather in relief." She turned to me. "You don't think he was referring to Mr. Whatley, do you?"

I thought the chances were about one hundred percent that he was referring to Tom, but I didn't want to upset Sherrie. "Who knows what he meant. Maybe he had just finished a huge term paper or something."

Sherrie hitched her backpack higher on her shoulder. "Nice try, but I doubt it."

Just then Randy went wild again. He stood up abruptly and his chair, a rickety folding thing about as sturdy as the table, went flying. He stood glaring at his mother.

"How can you defend him, Mom? How can you be so stupid?"

Edie said something we couldn't hear, her face pleading.

"He's a thief! And I bet he's a murderer too." Randy struck the table with the flat of his hand, the sound reverberating through the room like thunder. "I bet he killed that guy in my car just to make my life miserable."

I glanced at William who was listening to the outburst with grave concentration. He was not going to interfere.

Edie's voice had become a little louder in response to Randy's harangue. "I doubt that anyone would kill someone just to make your life miserable, Randy. Especially not Tom. That was a very self-centered comment."

"Self-centered? Me?" He leaned into Edie, his nose mere inches from hers. "You leave my father and marry that man and you call me self-centered? You've ruined my life!"

"Ruined your life? Ruined your life?" Edie stood, glaring at her son. "You're doing that all by yourself."

"You married a thief and a murderer!"

"I did not! I married a wonderful man!"

"Then why do the cops want his fingerprints, huh?"

"Stop it, Randy. You don't know what you're talking about." She turned to sit down.

But Randy wasn't finished yelling yet. He grabbed Edie and spun her around so fast she lost her balance. She reached out for Randy's arm to steady herself.

"Get your hands off me!" Randy pushed at her. With her previous loss of balance compounded by the push, she started to fall. She grabbed for Randy more desperately than ever. His face contorted with rage. "I said get your hands off me!"

Randy shoved his mother as hard as he could. Her chair flew behind her, striking Larry the sports guy's desk with a great crash. She completely lost her balance and fell, striking her head on the edge of the table as she went down. The table flipped, falling on her and pinning her to the floor where she lay absolutely still.

The incident happened so fast that none of us could intervene. Mac leaped from his seat and rushed to subdue Randy. William lurched to his feet and around the table with the same goal. Jolene screamed and I grabbed the phone on my desk to dial 911 and ask for an ambulance.

But the fastest responder was Sherrie. She went running across the room yelling, "Nooo!" She threw herself at Randy, beating William and Mac by a good five strides. She wrapped herself around him, pinning his arms to his sides. She was panting and crying and screaming, "How could you do that? I thought you were nice! You're just like my father! You're just like my father!"

Randy stared at his mother, appalled at what he had just done. His face was white and his eyes wide with horror. "Mom!" He tried to move, but Sherrie, tears streaming down her face, hung on.

"Don't you dare touch her again!" the girl screamed. "Don't you dare! I can't believe it. You're just like my father!"

Randy looked at Sherrie's tear-streaked face and shuddered. "No, I'm not," he whispered. "I'm just like *my* father."

Into this chaos walked Jonathan Delaney Montgomery.

Chapter 10

Mr. Montgomery, the epitome of professionalism in his navy blazer, gray slacks, light blue shirt, and red and blue rep tie, brown leather briefcase clutched in his hand, took one look at the emotional tornado streaking through our newsroom and closed his eyes as if to deny what he was seeing. Then he turned very deliberately on his well-shod heel and left.

Just like that.

No "What's going on?" No "Can I help?" Not even "Do you need help?" The least he could have done, I thought critically, what with Edie lying there on the floor unconscious, was to ask, "Is she all right?" But nothing. Not one word.

It was abdication pure and simple. At least the Duke of Windsor had run because of the "woman I love." Mr. Montgomery just ran.

And, I thought ruefully, *it is my great joy to work for this man.*

I looked at Mac who was watching Mr. Montgomery's exit with resignation and sorrow on his face. Obviously he felt his goose had just been cooked, and I was afraid he might be right. It seemed apparent that upheavals were not tolerated in Mr. Montgomery's newsrooms. The unfair thing was that Mac was innocent of any responsibility for the chaos.

I caught his eye and smiled with sympathy.

He sighed, shrugged, and took a deep breath. He turned to Edie and hunkered down beside her.

"Hey, Edie," he said softly. He took her hand in his and began rubbing it. "Can you hear me?"

When she groaned and started to move, he said, "Shhh. You stay nice and quiet here. Help's on its way. Merry called the ambulance for you." He sat beside her tailor fashion, talking quietly and soothing her, until the ambulance arrived.

In the meantime I hustled the hysterical Sherrie back to my desk and pushed her gently down into my chair.

"How could he? How could he?" she kept saying over and over again. She looked bereft, thoroughly shocked, her eyes wide and tear-filled.

I went down on my knees and threw my arms around her, holding her, patting her back. I didn't know what to say, so I said nothing. I wasn't certain she would hear me anyway.

Eventually the tempest eased somewhat though she was still hyperventilating when I called Stephanie.

"She's had a bad time." I heard Stephanie gasp and hastened to reassure her. "She's all right, truly, but she needs you." I was pretty sure Stephanie could hear her daughter crying, no doubt striking fear into her heart regardless of what I said.

"I'll be there in less than five minutes," and she was gone.

After I hung up, I knelt before Sherrie again and pushed her hair back off her forehead. Her face was flushed and her hands shook.

"It'll be all right," I said, trying to comfort her. "Mrs. Whatley will be fine. You'll see."

She shuddered violently at my words. "No, it won't be all right even if Mrs. Whatley is fine." Her eyes overflowed with a new sea of tears, and I suspected that a lot of her own past, a past she probably thought she had licked, was flashing before her eyes. Her sorrow broke my heart. I patted her hands helplessly.

"Tomorrow we'll try again to talk, okay?" I said for want of anything better to say. "It's even more important now, don't you think?"

Sherrie mumbled something that sounded like an affirmative. Then after a mighty sniff, she said clearly, "Is he still here?"

I nodded as I glanced at a distraught Randy. "He's very upset."

"Good!" She kept her eyes fixed on the floor so she wouldn't accidentally see him. "He should be."

Randy looked terrible, all white and wide-eyed, as he stared first at his mother, then at Sherrie.

"What have I done? What have I done?" he mumbled over and over. I wasn't certain which bothered him the most: his mother's injury at his hand or the blighting of his romance with Sherrie, again by his own hand.

"I'm sorry, Sherrie," he whispered a few minutes later in an anguished voice as, head down and taking care not to look his way, she left with her mother. "I'm so sorry."

"You ought to be, boy," said William Poole as he walked to Randy and took his arm. His voice was devoid of sympathy and his eyes drilled a hole right through Randy. "And now you need to come with me." He reached toward his belt like he was going for his cuffs.

"No!" Randy looked frantic. "I don't have to! Mom? Do I?"

Edie lay on the floor, the emergency techs strapping her to a backboard. Her neck was already in a cervical collar. "Oh, Randy," she sighed and a tear tumbled out of her eye and rolled back into her hairline.

Randy sank to the floor beside her. "I didn't mean to hurt you! It was an accident!"

"Was it?" asked William coldly.

"Mom! Tell him! It was just that something came over me. I couldn't help it!" He grabbed for her hand, but one of the techs reached out and restrained him. Randy looked distractedly at the tech, then back to his mother. He balled his large fists awkwardly on his knees.

"The something that came over you, boy, is your own lack of self-control." William was giving him no quarter. "And the sooner you admit that you're the one to blame, the better off you and your mother will be."

"No," Randy cried. "I didn't mean—"

"Sure you did." William glared at him. "I've seen your kind for years, and you make me sick."

Edie made a protesting sound at the harsh words, and William looked at her, his gaze gentling. "Edie, don't be easy on him, or there's a lifetime of this treatment awaiting you and some woman foolish enough to marry him someday."

Edie smiled at him sadly and nodded. "I know," she whispered. "But he's my son."

"Don't let that get in the way of what needs to be done."

Edie looked at Randy again. Then she shut her eyes in pain. "Do whatever you need to, William."

"No, Mom! I love you. I do! I'm so sorry." Randy's eyes were red, his nose was running, and he looked more like five than fifteen.

"That's just what your father used to say, Randy." Edie looked hopelessly at the ceiling. "You're becoming just like him, and it breaks my heart."

"No! No, I'm not!" He grabbed for Edie's hand again, and this time he connected. "Don't say that! Please! I promise, I'm not!"

Edie smiled wanly at him and said nothing.

"Randy." Mac lowered himself to Randy's eye level. "We all care for your mother a lot, from Sergeant Poole to all *The News* staff. That you would dare touch her in anger upsets all of us. Not only were your actions morally reprehensible, but assault and battery is against the law."

"Assault and battery!" Randy couldn't believe his ears.

"What else would you call it if not that?" Mac asked quietly.

"Get up, son. We're leaving." William put a hand beneath Randy's arm and lifted.

It seemed impossible, but Randy's face turned paler, and he clung to Edie's hand.

I didn't know whether William could or would actually do something official to Randy or if he was just trying a scare-him-straight type thing. Either way, I thought Randy was a thoroughly broken young man, and I was pleased to see it.

Ah, God, use this to make something of him. May he turn to you for help.

"William, may I see you for a minute? Alone?" I motioned him to my desk.

He released Randy. "Don't you move."

Randy nodded, compliant. He was taller, younger, and undoubtedly fleeter of foot than William, but all fight was gone. Besides, where would he have fled?

William walked across the room. "Yes?"

"He's underage and has no other family in town." We both knew I meant Randy. "If you need somewhere for him to stay tonight, you know, if they keep Edie at the hospital, he can come to my place. The sofa will be fine for one night."

"You're not afraid he'll hit you?"

I looked across the room at the boy in question. I don't think I'd ever seen anyone so contrite, so forlorn. "Should I be?"

William gave a sad smile. "I don't think so. I just hope this is the kid's wake-up call. His mom'll forgive him even if the girl won't. He can still recoup things nicely if he's got a mind to." He looked at me. "But I'm not going to make it easy for him. I'm going to make him squirm."

I nodded. "Sort of like Mrs. Russo and Jay, only more so."

"What?"

I shook my head. "Just call me if you need me."

Finally only Jolene, Mac, and I remained, and Jolene didn't stay long. She was itching to get home.

"Wait until Reilly hears! He thinks my job's dumb." She cracked her gum in delight. "This'll show him!"

I looked at Jo. The woman never ceased to amaze me at the way she saw things, always slightly skewed. Here I was, emotionally drained, and she was as perky as a high school cheerleader. All that was missing were the somersaults and splits.

"I don't think he thinks your job is dumb." Mac looked more weary than I'd ever seen him. "He thinks that you *having* a job is dumb."

"You mean because of the lottery money?" Jo asked.

Mac nodded. "Twenty-five thousand dollars a month for twenty years makes the idea of working as a general assistant at *The News* sort of redundant, doesn't it? It's not like you need the money."

"Well, I've got to do something with my life," Jolene said. "I can't just sit around all day getting my nails done. I mean I could, but come on. How boring is that!"

"Oh, I don't know," Mac said with a wry grin. "I bet I could learn to become so bored."

I smiled. "You'd look especially good in a bright pink polish, I think. A nice contrast with your dark hair and eyes."

159

Mac grimaced. "I'd been thinking more mauve, whatever that is."

"You couldn't stand being bored," Jolene said. "You've never sat still a day in your life."

At least she saw that fact correctly.

"What do you do with it all?" Mac asked, blatant curiosity compelling the question.

"You mean the money?" Jolene just looked at him. "That's a very personal question."

"And you won't answer it?"

She nodded and shot him with her forefinger. "You got it." She grabbed her purse and headed out the back door. "See you tomorrow."

I listened to their exchange as a brilliant, absolutely wondrous idea blossomed at the back of my head, sort of a beautiful Easter lily of an idea, fragrant with possibilities. I didn't know why I hadn't thought of it before. I just had to figure out how to pull it off without Jolene realizing she was being manipulated.

I left the hospital parking lot at 9 P.M. Edie was resting comfortably, and I hoped I soon would be too. I was driving on empty, both literally and figuratively.

The first problem was easy to fix, and I stopped at the gas station at Eighth and Main. The latter was also fixable, I realized, and I headed for Intimations. I called Curt's home as I drove, just to be certain he wasn't there. He wasn't. I hung up rather than leave a message on the answering machine.

I knew that all I had to do was share my Audubon story with Curt, and I'd immediately feel better. He'd congratulate me and give me a great hug and kiss, and I could forget Edie's pain and Sherrie's tears and Randy's white face and bask in the glow of my love's approval. Already I felt brighter, refreshed.

By the time I reached Intimations, I was dancing inside, the prima ballerina in a mental ballet, doing great and graceful arabesques and pirouettes while the corps de ballet (Mac, Jolene, and Edie) spun behind me in tight spirals of grateful appreciation. Then I leaped with abandon in one elegant grande jeté into the arms of my pas de deux partner, a leotard-clad Curt in a red velvet tunic trimmed in gold and ermine. He was so impressed with me that he carried me off into the wings to show me how wonderful I was.

I was grinning as I pulled up in front of the gallery and parked right behind Curt's car. I looked at the quietly elegant sign over the door, unlit since the grand opening had not yet occurred, then at the picture tastefully displayed in the window—Curt's latest from which prints had been made. The picture was softly lit, its deep red barn and silo glowing in a setting sun that streaked the evening sky with soft pearl pinks and mauves.

I had to admit, albeit unwillingly, that Delia knew what she was doing. Intimations looked great. Presentation and image were so important, and she clearly understood this truth. Give them style if you don't have substance, but when you had both like she did with the understated elegance of the gallery front and with Curt's work radiant in the window, you had power to be reckoned with.

I sighed. I'd have liked it better if I could be mad at her for pulling Curt and his work down to some tacky level that diminished his abilities and threatened his reputation. The truth of the matter was just the opposite. She was going to be a professional godsend.

I climbed out of my car and walked to the front door. As I expected, it was locked. I knocked loudly, but got no answer. I peered through the door into the gallery, dark and falling away into black shadows except where dim light seeped in from a street lamp. Way in the back of the room I saw a sliver of light peeking out from the bottom of a door. The workroom, I guessed.

I knocked again as loudly as I could. I didn't stop in spite of sore knuckles until the closed door at the rear of the gallery opened and a woman dressed all in black emerged. As soon as she pulled the door closed behind her, all that showed was a glimmer of blond hair gliding across the gallery toward me.

She opened the gallery door a scant two inches, her elegant face set in a winsome, friendly cast.

"I'm sorry. We're closed." Her voice was gracious, her smile sorrowful. She regretted turning away a potential customer. "Please come back Wednesday night for our grand opening."

"Thanks." I smiled with equal grace and charm. "I'm looking for Curt Carlyle."

Her eyes narrowed for the briefest of moments. It was as if she suddenly recognized me.

"I'm sorry. Curt's not here."

I blinked. "Sure he is," I said. "That's his car."

She followed my pointing finger with her eyes. Her lips compressed ever so slightly.

"It's not that he's not here." She backpedaled with an agility that came from long practice and made me wonder how seriously afflicted she was in the truth-versus-misleading-statements department. "It's more that he's not available." Again the smile, but all the charm was now gone. It was her predator's smile. "He's working."

I nodded. "I'm sure he is."

"And he can't be disturbed." It was like she dared me to contradict her.

I accepted the dare. "Please tell him that Merry'd like to see him for a minute."

I knew she wanted to tell me to get lost. I knew she wanted to shut the door in my face. I watched as her agile mind looked for a way she could manage to do just that without Curt ever learning. I could practically see the wheels turning. She was saved from such gauche behavior when the rear door opened and Curt, bathed in a swathe of light, stepped into the gallery.

"Hey, Delia, I've got an idea for the—"

"Curt!" I called before Delia gave into her base desire and slammed the door in my face.

"Merry?" His voice held both surprise and pleasure. It was all I could do not to look at Delia and smirk. He hurried across the room. "Hey, darlin' girl, how are you?"

Delia had no choice but to step back and let me in.

Curt covered the distance between us quickly and came to a stop well inside my private space. I was delighted to have it invaded, especially with Delia watching.

"I'll be in the back, Curt." Her voice was cool and impersonal for the most part, but in the end she couldn't quite keep her claws sheathed as she continued, "Don't be long. We have a lot to do. We don't want to waste too much time."

I think it was the slight emphasis on *waste* that made me look at her and smile sweetly enough to give cotton candy a run for its money. Mac would have ground his molars if he'd seen.

"We won't be long," Curt said as he took my hand. He found it full of my car and house keys. Without a second thought he took them from me and slid them into his pocket. Then he took my hand again and pulled me in for a quick hug.

Since he stood with his back to the rear door, he didn't see Delia pause in the doorway and turn. Of course if he had been facing her, the glare she leveled at me would have been a soft smile, I'm sure.

"You'll never guess what I learned today," I said, dismissing Delia Big Deal-ia as unworthy of my thoughts at the moment.

"You mean you didn't come just to see me?" Curt asked.

"Well, yes." I wrapped my arms around his waist and rested against his chest. "But I've got big news too."

"Me too. You should see how things are coming together for the opening," he said into my hair. "Delia really knows her business. And tomorrow—"

I pulled back enough to see his shadowed face. "Tom Whatley isn't really Tom Whatley," I said dramatically.

"Tomorrow," he continued as if I hadn't said a word, "Delia's taking me to some big lunch down in Philadelphia where I'll meet not only people from the art community in Center City but several down from New York."

"Nice," I said. "But listen. Tom Whatley is dead and our Tom Whatley is really Tom Willis. Edie's been married to an imposter!"

"I thought it would take me years to meet some of these people, if ever. Amhearst isn't exactly the center of the art world, you know, and these people aren't readily accessible to any old person. Imagine if I got some of my work hung in some New York galleries!" His eyes gleamed in the dim light at the wonder of it all.

I nodded, staring thoughtfully at his chest, about a foot from my nose. He wasn't listening to a word I said. "I beat the cops to the story."

"Mr. Whitsun from the Broughley Gallery is even thinking of coming back down from New York for the opening!"

The door in the back of the room opened, and Delia appeared in her black turtleneck, black tight jeans, and black half boots. "Curt, dear heart, I need you."

He dropped his arms from about me and turned. "In a minute. I'm almost done here."

"Dear heart?" I looked at him with one eyebrow raised.

He flapped a hand negligently. "Sort of I-call-everybody-darling, only it's dear heart."

"Somehow that doesn't make me feel much better. Now did you hear me tell you that Tom Whatley is really Tom Willis?"

Curt squinted into the dark room, obviously trying to recast the conversation. He smiled brightly, his teeth white in the dusky gloom. "Yep. I remember. And this is supposed to mean something?"

I blinked. "Sure. Tom Willis was masquerading as Tom—"

Curt nodded. "I got that. But why?"

I shrugged. "It has something to do with the way Tom Whatley died in a drug bust, but we don't know exactly what yet." I grinned. "And I'm the one who discovered all this!"

He patted my shoulder. "That's great, Merry."

But it was more like patting your collie after he had fetched for you about a hundred times in one afternoon. You're polite but abstracted, wishing he'd just give up and leave you alone. Curt wasn't really paying attention to me but looking at something behind me with an intensity I wanted for myself.

I turned and looked but saw nothing except the window display. "What's wrong?"

"Not much. Don't worry. It'll be okay." He walked over to the picture in the window. He leaned into the display and shifted the easel upon which the picture sat about a quarter inch to the left.

"There. That's better." He stood back, satisfied.

If he had bothered to look at me, Curt would have seen my mouth hanging open. I had prepared a scenario for this conversation, and this wasn't it. I'd expected congratulations, applause, acclamation, adulation. If he were truly my pas de duex partner, I'd be splatted all over the stage, because he'd missed the catch completely.

Instead of appreciating my cleverness, he was fixated on the stupid angle of his picture.

The back room door crashed open. "Curt, are you coming?" Delia demanded.

"Be right there," Curt called.

"Right." Delia's sarcasm would have curdled the blood of a lesser individual.

"Right," Curt repeated, unfazed.

"Well, hurry up, lover," she said, emphasizing the *lover*. "There's still much to do back here." Somehow she made those words very suggestive.

"Lover?" I repeated, jaw clenched. "Is that like dear heart?" What I wanted to do was scream in the direction of the back room, "Don't you dare call him that!" That would be after I screamed at him, "Will you listen to me?"

Curt, unaware of my anger, shrugged. "What can I say? It's my charm."

"Charm, schmarm." I grabbed the door handle and gave him one last hostile glare. "You haven't heard a word I've said, have you?"

Curt looked bewildered. "Sure I have. Tom Whatley is— something. Missing."

"Try dead."

Curt looked surprised. "Tom Whatley's dead? Poor Edie."

"For ten years."

"What?"

"Curt!" The tattoo of Delia's boot striking the floor in frustration or anger cut across the gallery.

"See?" I scowled at him. "I knew you weren't listening!"

He looked down at me, his face thrown into sharp planes of dark and light from the open door to the back room. "And have you heard anything I've said?" His voice was hard.

"Yeah. You're going to lunch with her highness tomorrow." I was appalled at how nasty I sounded, but I was too hurt to take it back. I pulled the door open. "Have fun." I slammed the door as loudly as I could. With luck, the glass pane would shatter under the tension.

Fat chance. Safety glass had been invented for protection against tempermental idiots like me.

I was in the car reaching for the ignition before I realized I'd left my keys behind. In Curt's pocket. I let my head fall back against the headrest. Not again! I thought of the humiliation of going back to Intimations and banging on the door and felt the heat rise. All my anger dissipated like mist before a strong breeze.

I closed my eyes, trying to work up the courage to go back, when a knock on my window startled me. I swallowed a scream at the huge shape shadowing me and reached out automatically to slam the lock down. I wasn't fast enough.

The door flew open and my keys dropped in my lap.

"I think you'll need these."

It could have been worse. It could have been Delia come to gloat.

"Thanks, Curt." I sighed. "Twice an idiot."

"Thrice," he corrected, ever the gentleman. "Move over."

I slid across to the passenger side and he climbed into the driver's seat.

"What happened back there?" he asked. He sounded genuinely perplexed.

"We had a fight?"

"Um. But about what? Delia?"

"I don't think so, though I don't like her calling you dear heart and lover."

"It means nothing," he said, reaching for my hand. He began rubbing his thumb back and forth over my wrist. "At least it means nothing to me."

I felt better already. "I know."

"Then what? I wasn't excited enough about your story?"

"To the head of the class with you." I reached out and straightened his collar. Then I brushed back the curl that always fell over his eye.

"But you didn't pay any attention at all to my good news either."

I looked at him, stung at his accusation. "Of course I did."

"You call your crack about lunch with her highness noticing?"

Now it was my turn to recast our conversation. Try as I might, I couldn't recall one nice comment about what was a great career opportunity for him. My shoulders sagged. "You're right. I'm sorry."

He smiled slightly. "I didn't mean to diminish your big news either. You did a nice piece of investigative reporting to discover something like that."

"Thanks." My eyes filled with tears. "And I'm delighted for your opportunity. Truly I am. I know how much it must mean to you."

I don't know who moved first, but as makeup kisses after an argument go, this one had to be among the best ever.

We sat silent for a couple of minutes, arms about each other.

"Are we too different?" I whispered. "Or is this type of misunderstanding typical of all couples?"

"If I had to hazard a guess, I'd say typical, but I don't know. I've never paid all that much attention to the dynamics of being a couple." He smiled and kissed my cheek. "I never had to before."

All the lights in Intimations erupted into the night, golden, brilliant, and demanding. Delia.

"I've got to go," Curt said, pulling back. "Really."

I nodded. "Have a wonderful lunch tomorrow."

"How about dinner tomorrow night?" He squeezed my hand. "I promise to listen very carefully to your Tom story."

"And I to your luncheon report. Can Delia spare you for the evening?" I slapped my hand over my mouth. "I didn't say that last sentence. I didn't. Or at least I didn't mean it to be nasty."

"Give me a kiss, darlin' girl." He leaned in and I complied.

As I drove home, I told myself over and over that we'd get this communication thing figured out. We would.

Oh, Lord, we will, right? What we've got developing here is too special to lose.

I thought of my mother and father and some of their communication struggles.

"If ever you need money, you take it," Dad told Mom more than once. "After all, it's a joint account."

Knowing him to be a man of his word, Mom took money from their account whenever she felt she needed something. The trouble came in the definition of *need*. For Mom, need meant it was spring and a new spring dress was called for. One of the old ones was worn, out of style, and/or in need of replacement. She wasn't spendthrift in the least. She just needed another something for work or church or a special event.

For Dad, need meant you'd go naked if you didn't buy that. After all, he bought a new sports coat once every ten years whether he needed it or not. If it weren't for holidays, he wouldn't have a dress shirt or tie to his name. And shoes? A good pair would last forever with an occasional resoling or reheeling. And holes in underwear meant nothing. No one but Mom saw them anyway.

"What's this item on the charge card bill?" Dad would demand.

"I needed it, dear," Mom would counter. "You said that if I needed—"

"You've got a closet full of clothes! How could you need something more? Why, if you'd take as much care of your things as I do of mine—"

"I'd look like a frump." Mom'd stand in front of him, hands on hips. "Do you want to be married to a frump, Alan? Do you?"

My brother Sam and I always made a fast escape to our rooms. Mom and Dad rarely if ever argued except over *need*, and listening made us both very nervous.

It took Mom and Dad a while, but they solved the need problem by having separate checking accounts. They decided together how their money would be allocated, Mom made certain she had her portion in her account plus some grace funds, and Dad never asked her how she spent it. As long as he ate, groceries falling under her area of responsibilities, he didn't care if she bounced checks or spent thousands on clothes. It was all up to her.

If they could find a way to handle things, so could Curt and I. Yes, we were different. We liked different things. We had different careers. But we were learning to love each other, and we both loved the Lord.

We could do this, I told my rapidly beating heart.

We would do this.

Right, Lord?

Chapter 11

I'd been home barely fifteen minutes when the phone rang. I was sitting on the sofa watching an old John Wayne movie on AMC while I ate a chicken cheese steak with onions and tried to convince Whiskers that he would like what was in his plate on the kitchen floor better than what was on mine. I wasn't making much headway, but since I'd dished up his dinner and had smelled it, I couldn't blame him for trying for mine. When I went to the phone, I carefully took my plate with me.

"Merry, you said to call." It was William Poole.

"Randy?"

"I am not willing to release him on his own recognizance, regardless of what he wants."

"I should think not." The idea of Randy out on his own gave me the chills for several reasons. First, he was so distraught, I didn't know what he might do. I didn't think he'd hurt himself, but kids sometimes do the strangest things. Or he might show up on Sherrie's doorstep trying to make things right, something neither Sherrie nor Stephanie would appreciate. Or he might try to get to his father, which could be disastrous for several reasons—like rejection or acceptance.

"Look," William continued, "if you take him tonight, can you keep him for a couple of days longer?"

I clamped my lips shut to keep from sputtering. A couple of days longer? When I'd said he could come for tonight, I'd never given a thought to any longer. I was so busy as it was. Where would I find time for Randy? There was my job. There was Curt. There was Tina and Sherrie and Stephanie and Tom and Edie and—

There was Randy.

I pushed nobility and need away in favor of practicality. Did I want a volatile teen around? I mean, what would I say to him? What would I do with him? I had visions of the furniture in kindling and the house ransacked. Then I remembered the quality of my furniture and the dearth of ransackable goods and acknowledged those thoughts for the excuses they were.

"Will Edie be in the hospital that long?" I asked for something to fill the stretching silence.

"I don't know. But even if she comes home tomorrow, which she probably will, she'll be in no shape to keep an eye on the kid."

I wondered about the unhappy Randy and his reaction to being in my care. "What does he say about this?"

"He doesn't get a choice. It's you or I'm taking him to juvenile detention down in Lima."

Me or the juvenile facility. No pressure here, Merry. *Lord, this is scary! It's one thing to help out sort of peripherally, like taking Tina to her parents or making Edie soup, but getting involved like this?*

I knew I should say yes because I knew that as a Christian I had no other choice. WWJD. Even if my furniture were valuable and my goods worth stealing, I should put the boy before the things, no matter how risky. Still, my heart beat against my ribs and my stomach churned like a malted in a blender.

"I've got to go to work," I cautioned.

"Take him with you."

"What about school?"

"There's only a day or two before Easter break. He can miss the time or you can take him and pick him up. I really don't care."

"Are you at the police station?"

"Yes."

I took a deep breath and jumped. "I'll be right there." *And Jesus, you'd better come right with me!*

Randy was not the finest of companions as we drove to his house for clothes and necessities, which I was interested to notice included both a portable CD player, several CDs, and a laptop computer. He was sullen and embarrassed and angry, to say nothing of less than monosyllabic.

"Do you have school tomorrow?"

Grunt.

"Do you have homework and stuff?"

Swing his backpack before my nose.

"Do you want to go to school or to work with me?"

Grunt.

"Is your car okay?"

Grunt.

And just because I couldn't resist, "Don't forget clean underwear."

That didn't even rate a grunt.

Looked at from his fifteen-year-old vantage point, I understood. After all, I'd seen him slug his mother, fall to pieces, and get dragged off by the police. Our common experiences were hardly the stuff of meaningful conversation and deep friendship.

"Have you had dinner?" I asked as we neared my place.

He shook his head.

"McDonald's okay?"

He nodded.

I pulled up to the drive-through order mike. "What'll it be?"

He stared straight ahead without speaking for a few seconds, tumultuous emotions pouring from him in waves. It was almost as if he were so consumed by the internal conflicts he felt that he couldn't articulate a coherent thought. Apparently reason finally moved him enough to remind him that starvation would solve nothing.

"Two Big Macs, two large fries, two large Sprites, and two boxes of McDonaldland cookies."

"Thanks, but I already ate," I said, trying to lighten the atmosphere.

He looked at me blankly.

I smiled sadly. "Forget it." The boy of ten who took my money was definitely more fun than Randy. He might struggle to reach the cash register, but at least he knew how to smile.

Randy wolfed down the food the last couple of miles to the apartment and left the paper sack stuffed with trash on the floor of the front seat when he climbed out at the carriage house. He stared at the place in disbelief long enough for me to collect his trash. He barely blinked when I shoved it in his hand.

"Trash basket's in the kitchen."

"What is this building?" he asked. "It looks weird. And it's not on the street. It's on the alley." I could definitely hear his lip curl in disdain on the last comment. I guess if I were getting a classy sports car for my sixteenth birthday, living on the alley would definitely look déclassé.

"It's an old carriage house that's been converted into four apartments. The mansion that it serviced has been torn down and those houses built where it used to be." I gestured toward the residences fortunate enough to be on the street. "My apartment's on the first floor. I hope you don't mind the couch, because that's what you've got."

He barely restrained a grimace.

"One thing you need to be aware of is that the bathroom has two doors, one in the living room—yours—and one in the bedroom—mine."

"So?" he said, ever charming.

"Neither door has a lock."

He looked at me like I had lost my mind.

I chatted like an idiot as I got out extra sheets and blankets and a pillow. From the linen closet I pulled a set of new, fluffy pink towels that I'd bought myself just last week at Kmart. If he thought them unmanly, that was his tough luck. It was pink or use paper towels.

The whole time I made up his bed, I kept up a one-way conversation, answering myself when he refused to respond.

"Yeah, Whiskers is a great cat. I got him at the pound, but he has decided that he won't tell anyone of his lowly background. After all, he's already come a long way, living on the alley. He suspects that it's just a matter of time before he moves up to the street. Right, baby?"

Whiskers responded by butting against my shins. I reached over and fondled his head, and he purred in delight.

Randy leaned down and spoke. "Here, cat." The command had all the grace of a drill sergeant telling his men to stand at attention, but for some reason, wonderful Whiskers responded. He wrapped himself around Randy's ankles, and the boy actually managed a smile.

I tried to think back to when I was fifteen. Had I been so sullen and withdrawn? Of course, my parents hadn't divorced, my father hadn't forgotten the date of my birthday, my stepfather hadn't disappeared, and I'd never flown into a rage and struck my mother, so it was difficult to make a comparison. I looked at the boy as he awkwardly petted Whiskers, and my heart broke for him all over again.

Oh, Lord, he needs you so badly!

When I had him all arranged, at least to my satisfaction, I said, "You can watch TV if you want. Just keep the sound down so I can sleep, okay?"

He stared at me blankly in answer.

"Right." I gave my fist a shake, a little homeboy sign to make him feel comfortable. "Now I know you can easily walk out of here during the night." He started as I said that, making me wonder if he'd already been planning to leave. "However, let me tell you that I don't think it would be a good idea. Enough people are upset with you as it is." I smiled with what I hoped was sweet encouragement. "I'm trusting that you're wise enough to know what's the best thing to do here even if it's not the most fun or the most exciting."

He looked over my left shoulder and out the window into the night and made no response.

I bit back a sigh. "Tomorrow morning after breakfast we'll call the hospital and see if your mom's coming home. If she is, we'll arrange a time to go get her. Until she's released, you can come to work with me if you don't feel up to school."

At that pronouncement, he actually looked at me, and his pained expression showed clearly what he thought of this plan. Still, I got the definite impression that it was better than school. After all, he'd have to face Sherrie at school.

"Coming to work with me was Sergeant Poole's suggestion," I said. I didn't tell him that I wasn't wild about the idea either. What would happen when Sherrie came by? I didn't even want to think about that scenario.

"I'll use the bathroom first and get out of your way." I spoke to the top of his head because he had dropped onto the sofa and was contemplating the floor. Whiskers was winding around his ankles, and he raised a limp hand to rub the animal's head. The cat purred in ecstasy. "I'll let you know when I'm finished."

I turned and noticed for the first time the little blinking red light on my answering machine. Someone had called while I was getting Randy. Maybe Curt? With a smile I pushed the play button.

"Stay out of it! It's none of your business! Or you'll get hurt!"

I stared at the phone in fascinated horror.

"Who's that?" Randy demanded.

I blinked. "I don't know." I hit the save button just before I lost the message, then hit replay. I grabbed a pencil and wrote down the number displayed in the Caller ID box as the nasty male voice taunted me again.

"What did you do?" Randy was so curious that he forgot to be self-conscious.

"I don't know." I played the threat again. Was it the same voice I'd heard at Edie's?

"What kind of pervert is stupid enough to leave messages?" Randy asked, voicing my thoughts exactly. "Hasn't he ever heard of voice prints?"

I quickly called the police and reported the threat. It was only a matter of minutes before William called back.

"Can you identify the caller? Is it the same person who called Edie?"

"No, I can't identify him. And I don't know if he's the same guy. Maybe. I want it to be. How many weird callers does Amhearst need? But I don't know."

William sighed. "It'll be a phone booth. I'll bet you anything."

"No takers here. I agree."

"What do you agree with?" Randy asked as I hung up.

"Phone booth."

He nodded and looked at me with interest. Then he walked back to the sofa and collapsed, his long legs turning to spaghetti as I watched. Gathering Whiskers to him, he buried his head in the cat's ruff and suddenly made believe I was no longer there.

I shrugged my mental shoulders and went into the bathroom. Working as fast as I could, I washed and dried my face on the old green towels I'd brought with me when I moved to Amhearst eight months ago. I made sure I left no toothpaste spit in the sink or dirty foam on the soap. I knocked cautiously on the bathroom door that opened into the living room, then cracked it a couple of inches. I was surprised to see the living room in darkness. I expected Randy to be glued to the TV.

"I'm finished, Randy. It's all yours."

I heard a deep breath that sounded an awful lot like a sob. "Thanks." It came out as a croak, and he quickly cleared his voice and tried again. "Thanks."

"You're welcome." Maybe there was hope for him after all. "I'm glad you're here."

I could hear Whiskers purring all the way across the room, and I figured he was curled up on the sofa next to Randy. That was good. The boy needed uncomplicated affection. I stepped back and started to close the bathroom door.

"Merry?"

I stuck my head back in the room. "Yes?"

"Will that guy hurt you?"

I tried to keep the surprise out of my voice. "The one on the answering machine? I don't think so. Sergeant Poole will take care of it. There's something sort of cowardly about a phone threat, don't you think?"

"Yeah," he said, contempt for the caller making his voice fuller, surer. "Yeah."

"Good night, Randy."

"Merry?"

"Yes?" I smiled, thinking of all the nights when I was small and had lain in bed and said, "Mom?" and come up with some foolish question, anything to keep from actually having to go to sleep. But Randy wasn't a little child and his questions weren't foolish.

There was a long pause, like he was trying to work up courage. Then: "She'll be all right, won't she?"

"Your mom?"

"Yeah."

"I think so. I don't know why not."

He grunted, a sound that somehow conveyed relief. There was a small silence. I was moving to close the door again when he said, his voice thick with apprehension, "Will she ever forgive me?"

"Sure. Moms always forgive, especially nice moms like yours."

"Not Mom. Sherrie. I know Mom'll forgive me. She's like that. But I don't know about Sherrie."

I heard the distress in his voice and knew that young love was such a painful thing in the best of circumstances. I remembered how I had pined over Bob Frantz all through high school, an unrequited passion if ever there was one.

"I don't know about Sherrie either, Randy. You behaved very badly in front of her and you brought up some very unsettling memories for her."

He sighed in pain. "Sometimes it's not good to have things in common."

Not when one of them was an abusive father. "She's only fifteen. You've handed her a situation that many adults couldn't deal with."

"I know." He seemed freed to speak by the darkness. "I wouldn't blame her if she never talked to me again."

I flicked out the bathroom light and slipped into the living room. All I could see of him was a darker shadow against the dark shadow of the sofa. "But Sherrie's also a girl of uncommon grace and faith. Maybe in time she'll be okay."

"You think so?"

There was such hope in his voice that I felt tears spring to my eyes. "I hope so, for both your sakes."

He seemed satisfied with that, as if recognizing that that was the best he could hope for right now. We fell silent for a minute. Then he took a deep breath.

"Tom's not a terrible man." The words rushed out of him like water from a ruptured dam. "He's been nice to me always. I'm the one who's been terrible."

"I know."

"Yeah." He made a choking sound. "I haven't been very subtle about it, have I?"

"Mm."

"I don't want him to be in trouble." There was an urgency in his words that underscored the truth of his statement.

"I know."

"My mom loves him. He's so nice to her. He takes care of her." There was wonder in his voice.

"Do you think that's unusual?"

I heard him shift on the sofa, the sheets murmuring in the darkness. "I used to think it meant he was weak. A real man made a woman fear him, not love him. That way he was always in control."

"And now?"

"I—I think I've changed my mind."

"Why?"

"I've seen how upset Mom is over Tom."

I took a minute to try and digest his answer, to understand his logic, careful all the while to remain close to the door, far enough away to be nonthreatening. "Explain that to me, Randy."

He shifted on the sofa again. "I think that if my dad had ever disappeared, Mom's strongest response would have been relief. I wouldn't want Sherrie to be relieved if I disappeared. I'd want her to care." His voice caught on a muted sob that he tried to swallow. "Not that she's ever likely to care about me."

The conversation had come full circle.

"Randy, how do you think God fits in all this?"

"God?" He sounded surprised.

"You know how important God is to Sherrie, don't you?"

"Sure. I mean, her mom's got a mission."

"Do you realize that if Sherrie forgives you, it will be because God gives her the strength to do it?"

I could almost feel him thinking. "Does that mean she talks to God about me?"

"It does."

"That makes me feel—weird. Or special. I don't know which."

"Maybe both?"

He gave a half laugh. "Maybe both. I don't think anyone else talks to God about me."

"I do."

His surprise bounced off the walls.

"I have to admit that I used to pray mostly for your mom, that she'd survive you." *Oh, Lord, don't let that offend him so much he stops listening!*

He grunted.

"But from now on I will pray that you become the man that's inside you, the man that God would like you to become. And I'll pray that you realize that God's the only one who can help you become that."

I held my breath and awaited his reaction. Eventually I heard a muffled, "Thank you."

"Good night, Randy. Like I said, I'm glad you're here."

The next morning, Randy was back to less than monosyllabic.

"Cereal or toast?"

Point to the Captain Crunch my mother would never buy for me and which I enjoyed each morning in sweet rebellion. Point to the bread.

"Both?"

Nod.

"Whole wheat or oat?"

Point to the oat.

"Orange juice?"

Nod.

We listened to each other crunch while I tried to imagine several days like this.

WWJD. I poured him some more Captain Crunch.

When we got to work, I settled Randy at his mother's empty desk. He pulled out his laptop and started typing away, ignoring me and everyone else in the newsroom. Considering the startled expressions on everyone's faces, I couldn't blame him. It was obvious that the last thing they expected to see was Randy trailing after me.

I shot everyone a warning glance, especially Jolene, and got to work, calling the police station first thing.

"Anything exciting overnight?" I asked.

"Nah," said Jeb. "Dead night."

"I can never tell if you're pleased or upset when things are quiet," I said.

"Neither can I," he admitted.

"No identification yet on the body in Randy's car?" I could see Randy's hands stop still on his keys as I asked the question. "Hasn't AFIS come through?"

"You know, I think they have." I could hear Jeb shifting papers around. "I think something came through after I left yesterday. I saw it mentioned in somebody's report. Yes. Here it is."

I waited impatiently while he read the report to himself, apparently to determine if it would jeopardize police confidentiality to read it to me.

"The deceased was a petty criminal named Barney Slocum," Jeb finally said. "He has a list of priors going back twenty years, and all for small-time stuff like selling pot to an undercover agent or being bag man for a bookie or acting courier for a drug shipment."

"What does any of that have to do with Tom Whatley or Tom Willis?"

"We don't know yet. But my money's on drugs. Willis was involved somehow when Whatley died in that drug bust. I bet he's involved again."

At least he was no longer accusing Tom of taking the money. "Is that a hunch or do you know something you haven't told me yet?"

"Strictly a hunch. Oh, and there is one more thing. There's a car missing from the Hamblin lot."

I waited for more but none came. "I don't get it, Jeb."

"Every month they do an inventory of the lot to track and verify all the cars so none just sort of disappear."

"And they did this inventory and one's missing? Any idea what happened to it?"

"This is a special inventory done at our request, a between-times tabulation, if you will. Apparently a car could be borrowed off the lot between inventories, and no one would be the wiser. It just needs to be returned before the next count is taken."

"So what do you think it means that this car is missing?" I asked.

"Missing car, missing man, drug courier killed. Three guesses."

"You think Tom is involved?"

"More than involved, if you want my opinion."

I didn't, if that was his opinion. I couldn't imagine the hurt such involvement would bring Edie and Randy.

"And then," he continued, "there's the fact that Tom was the last to sign the car out."

"Sign the car out?"

"You know. When they let you drive a car or when they take a car home themselves to try it out."

"They have to sign it out?"

"And in."

"And Tom took the missing car? He signed it out?"

"But not in."

"And you actually think he'd steal a car he signed out? He'd put his name there confirming that he stole it? Come on. That doesn't even make sense."

"He took the money."

We were back to that. "Jeb! You don't know that. You don't know any of this."

"I can't take it to court, but I'll bet it's an accurate scenario."

I stared at my blank computer screen and wondered if he could possibly be right. "What do you think any of this has to do with Tom Whatley's death?" I asked.

"The Audubon PD faxed us a bunch of stuff late yesterday, but I'm not free to pass it on without authorization. I can tell you though that something was funny the night Whatley died, and Willis was right in the middle of the funny stuff. That's all I can say right now."

I knew I wouldn't get any more out of Jeb if he was in authorization mindset. I disconnected and wrote steadily to get my Whatley/Willis article finished before deadline. I took one break to call Bill Bond, Tom's boss at Hamblin Motors, to see if I could get a statement from him about the inventory and missing car.

I had to call him at home because of the hour. Dealerships open later than newsrooms. When I looked in the phone book, there were four William Bonds. The first was an elderly gentleman so anxious for conversation that I had trouble getting away.

The second was a woman who said Bill had moved out six months ago and good riddance, but if I found him, please let her know; he owed scads of child support. "And you won't find him at his office either, the louse." And she reeled off the next number in the book.

I called it anyway and she was right. It was a disconnected number.

On the last number, all I got was an empty ring, not even an answering machine. Either this guy was online or he was behind the times. I went back to writing.

When I sent the finished work off to Mac, I turned to Randy, who had been madly inputting who-knew-what the whole time I was at work. I bet he was a hacker to be reckoned with.

"I need to see a couple of people." I got to my feet and slipped on my navy blazer. "Bring the laptop and let's go."

Our first stop was Hamblin Motors. The showroom was finally open for the day, and I hoped Bill Bond would be around for me to interview.

Randy came to life as we walked into the showroom. His eyes roved lovingly over the models on floor display. Next thing I knew, he was sitting in a low-slung blue number, hands on the wheel, mind on the free and open roads.

I, on the other hand, was drawn to a display case filled with old-fashioned toy cars, the heavy metal ones from the 1920s and 30s. I know nothing about cars and have no desire to learn one from another, but I was fascinated by the cumbersome toys, mostly because they had been fortunate enough to escape the great scrap metal drives of World War II. There was no doubt that I was looking at a collection of some value.

"Wonderful, aren't they?"

I turned to find a salesman standing behind me, all smiles and good will. His name tag read *Howard*.

"That's a Reo." Howard pointed. "And that's an early Cadillac. And that, of course, is a Model T."

"Of course," I mumbled.

He continued to name every car in the case and the case against the facing wall.

"Mr. Hamblin himself collects these toy cars. He has more than a hundred, though he only displays the finest."

I nodded as we walked to the center of the showroom and the real cars. Howard's brown oxfords squeaked on the shiny tile floor with every step, and he should never be allowed out of the house in the deep green twill shirt he was wearing. It made him look sick. Still, since it said Hamblin Motors over the heart, he probably didn't have a choice. But he had nice eyes and an earnest spirit.

"Are you interested in a nice car for your son?" he asked, nodding toward Randy.

My son? I didn't know whether to hit him or kick him in the shins. I settled for looking at him sourly. He might have nice eyes and an earnest spirit, but he had the brains of a nit.

He realized his mistake immediately, not a great intellectual feat given my facial expression. "Your brother?" he offered hesitantly. "Boyfriend?"

"I'm baby-sitting for him." The chill in my voice should have had everyone running for tire chains due to icing conditions. "He's a high school freshman."

The poor man wilted completely and asked without hope, "Can I help you?"

"Yes," I said, and was fascinated to watch him perk up, sort of like a wilted plant that finally gets a drink. "I'd like to see Bill Bond, please. Tell him Merry Kramer from *The News* would like to talk to him if he has a minute."

He nodded cooperatively. "I'll get him for you." He all but ran through a frosted glass door in the middle of the room. In his haste to please he neglected to shut the door firmly.

"What did you do to him to make him run like that?" Randy stood just behind me.

I glanced over my shoulder at the tall blond, then caught a glimpse of my short, dark self in the window. "He thought you were my son." It still rankled.

Randy blinked in surprise, then started to laugh.

"It's not funny," I protested. "I'm only eleven years older than you!"

"Yes, it is funny," he managed between sputters of laughter. "It's hilarious. Especially your face!" He grinned at me. "Does that make Curt my father?" Fresh gales of laughter erupted from his throat and he wandered off to find another car to mind-drive, happier than he'd been in days. I suppose I should count it an honor to be able to so lift his spirits.

I felt my own lip begin to quirk up at the corner. I had to admit, at least to myself, it was kind of funny in a warped way.

A voice that was anything but fun-filled cut through the showroom silence. It came from the frosted glass door Howard had entered.

"Who did you say?" It was a low roar.

I couldn't make out the answer. I assumed poor Howard was giving my name again.

"I'm not here." The statement was abrupt and emphatic. "I will not talk with her."

There was a low rumble from the salesman again, then a resounding, "I said no! Just tell her I'm not here. If she gives you any trouble, go get Joey."

I walked toward the frosted glass door. If Bill Bond was so anxious not to talk with me for some reason I couldn't begin to imagine, I was suddenly dying to speak with him. I was reaching for the knob when the door swung open and Howard emerged, effectively blocking any approach I might make.

"I'm sorry," he said, looking acutely uncomfortable. He pulled the door firmly shut behind him. "Mr. Bond isn't available."

"Sure he is," I said. "I heard him talking with you."

Howard blanched. "Oh, no. You must be mistaken. Mr. Bond isn't here."

I looked at him, disappointed that he lied so willingly. "Oh, Howard."

He flushed and looked away. "Mr. Bond isn't here," he repeated.

"Sure he is." I pointed to the car lot. Howard looked, just as I'd hoped he would. I stepped around him quickly, taking him by surprise, and threw open the frosted door.

"You can't go in there!" Howard cried in a panic.

"Sure I can." I walked into what was essentially a hallway with two small offices opening off it on each side. The first door had a sign that read *Bill Bond, sales manager.* The room was empty but the desk looked very neat.

I glanced in the other three offices as I walked quickly toward the door at the far end of the hall. A woman sat in one, her eyes fixed on rows of figures on her computer screen. Another woman sat equally mesmerized in the other, her screen showing order blanks that she was busy dealing with. The fourth office with a sign on the desk reading *Mike Hamblin* was empty.

I pushed through the far doorway and found myself in a great, cavernous space filled with cars of varying ages and descriptions, all with men and an occasional woman working on them in some fashion. Bill Bond was nowhere in sight. At least I assumed he wasn't. I saw no one with a shirt like Howard's.

A couple of the mechanics looked at me curiously, but none spoke. Between the blare of music and the whir of power tools, a conversation would be difficult. But worth a try, I decided.

I walked to a young woman who rested against the front fender of a car, her head bowed, her arms lost in the bowels of its motor.

I tapped her on the shoulder and she jumped like I'd bitten her. I smiled placatingly.

"Have you seen Bill Bond?" I yelled over the pneumatic roar from the mechanic at the next car freeing lug nuts on a tire. "I think he came through here."

She shook her head and turned back to her motor, which was obviously more interesting to her than I was.

I walked along the wall, peering between cars and searching on my own. A person in a dark green twill shirt was nowhere to be seen.

I turned to go back to the showroom, disappointed that I wouldn't discover why Bill Bond wouldn't see me, when I saw a once-white door with a permanent black, greasy stain just above the chrome push plate that was supposed to prevent just such a stain. *Men*, the door read.

"See if he's in there," I ordered the fretting Howard who watched me like a nervous mouse watching a hungry cat. I don't know what he expected me to do, but eating him would be too offensive to the palate.

He looked shocked at my request. "I can't do that."

"Why not?" Randy'd do it, I thought. Where was the kid when you needed him?

"I just can't." He'd cast our little drama as an us-against-them scenario, and he wasn't going to do anything to help me. I sighed. "Then I guess I'll have to."

He looked shocked and I expected him to step forward to prevent me from opening the men's room door. He didn't. He probably didn't believe I'd breech that male bastion. I was forced to go ahead and do just that or look like an idiot. I refused to consider what I looked like as I pushed the door open.

Squeezing my eyes shut against I didn't know what, I burst into the room. "Mr. Bond! I need to speak with you. You can't hide from me using this old ploy."

"Well, well," said a voice appreciatively. "What have we here?"

"Pretty little thing, isn't she? Obviously lost."

My eyes snapped open and I stared at two mechanics who stared back, goofy smiles on their faces. Unfortunately Mr. Bond wasn't anywhere in the room. I know because the door to the single stall was hanging drunkenly open, and every other facility was right out in the open. I backed out quickly, my face scarlet, immensely grateful that the two were merely washing their hands.

I turned to flee back to the showroom and ran into the solid chest of Joey. I know it was Joey because the name was written on his blue Dickies workshirt.

"Can I help you?"

I looked up at him and wondered how he could say something so innocuous and sound so threatening.

"I'm looking for Bill Bond." I was pleased to hear myself sounding firm and rational in spite of my behavior and pounding heart. Joey made me nervous.

"Who?" Joey growled.

"Bill Bond. The sales manager."

"Don't know him," Joey said. "Never heard of him."

Right.

"Is there another Joey here?" I asked, hearing Bill Bond's *if she gives you trouble, go get Joey.*

"Not hardly." He puffed out his already impressive chest. "One Joey's all this place can handle."

I could tell he expected me to be impressed, but I didn't play along. His face darkened.

"You need to leave, lady." He pointed to the door to the hallway. "It's dangerous out here. Lots of possibilities for accidents."

Again what should have been just a statement of the obvious sounded like a threat. I turned and left, aware of Joey's smirk and resenting it mightily. I refused to look at Howard as we made our way back to the showroom. He had finally found something to smile about in our brief but tumultuous relationship. When we were back in the showroom, I spun to face him.

"Tell me about Tom Whatley," I said, hoping my abrupt change of subject would take him off guard. It worked.

"Nice guy," Howard said. "I couldn't believe it when they said he stole all that money."

"Why do you think he stole the money?"

"I don't know. Maybe his wife's sick or something. He loves his wife. Always talks about her."

"No," I said, pleased that Howard verified my feelings about Tom and Edie, "I don't mean why, for what purpose. I mean why do you think he's the guilty one? Especially since you said he was so nice."

Howard looked at me like anyone could figure that out. "The money's missing and so's he and so's a car he signed out."

"Howard, if you were going to ruin your life, would you actually sign out the car you were stealing?"

"No, but if he didn't do it, then where is he? And where's the car?"

I stuck out my hand and shook his like I was congratulating him. "You're a genius, Howard. If we answer those questions, we solve the mystery, don't we? Will you call me if you think of anything that might help Tom? Or hurt him for that matter." I handed him my card.

He stared at it a minute, stuck it in his shirt pocket, and nodded. "I liked Tom."

"You should still like him," I said. "He's a nice man. Even his stepson says so."

Howard snorted. "Not hardly."

"Hey, Randy," I called.

He looked up reluctantly from his inspection of the motor in a black car.

"Do you like Tom?"

He nodded. "Nice guy." He abandoned the motor and climbed in the black car.

"That's Randy, the monster stepson?" Howard stared in amazement.

"He's recently had a change of heart. Come on, Randy, we're leaving." I waved my hand in his direction. He climbed reluctantly out of the black car which had so many bells and whistles that its name was in gold letters.

While he schlepped across the floor to me, I turned to Howard. "One last question. What's Joey's last name?"

"Alberghetti. Joey Alberghetti." He looked at me thoughtfully. "Be careful." He walked away as Randy reached me.

"Come on, son. Time to leave."

He grinned. "Right, Mom."

We went out to the car and climbed in. To maneuver out of the congested lot, I had to back up across the entrance to the service bays. I looked over my shoulder just before I drove off and there against the far back wall was Joey Alberghetti talking to a man in a green twill shirt. The man's back was to me, but I was willing to bet it was Bill Bond. He was sticking his finger in Joey's chest and gesticulating wildly with his other hand.

Bill Bond, if that's who it was, was upset with Joey Alberghetti.

Better him than me.

Chapter 12

By the time we arrived at the hospital to pick up Edie, Randy was in a terrible state. He had cracked his knuckles enough to guarantee arthritis for the rest of his life, and the twitch beneath his right eye was driving me crazy. I could only imagine how it was making him feel.

As he climbed out of the car, he looked young and scared in spite of his height and the breadth of his shoulders. He gave a toss of the head that was supposed to appear casual but was more like a nervous jerk. As we walked down the halls, I noticed he couldn't look at people. If they saw his face, he seemed to feel, they'd see his guilt.

One part of me wanted to comfort him because he was still young. It was easy to forget how young because of his size and mature good looks. Another part of me thought that the nervousness, guilt, and regret might be a good thing. Sweating out the consequences of his actions had to be a strengthening experience. Certainly anything that painful must produce character.

When we arrived at Edie's room, she was dressed and waiting, resting on her bed with a book she wasn't reading. She was alone, her roommate off somewhere, doubtless being tested for some catastrophic something. To look at Edie, you wouldn't know there had been any physical injury, but her eyes were so full of pain that the emotional turmoil was more than evident. I walked to her and hugged her, willing my chin not to wobble.

"Hey. Ready to go?" Another of those dumb questions. What would I expect her to say? "No, I like it here. I want to stay."

Randy hung back at the door and sort of peeked in. I don't know what he expected, but all he saw was his mom looking much like she did every day, just a bit more worn.

"Hi, Mom." He walked awkwardly to the bed. "How are you?"

He heard himself and apparently decided he sounded too much like an uninvolved stranger. "I mean, are you feeling okay? Does your head hurt?" Then his eyes filled with tears. He stared at the floor, trying to control himself. He cleared his throat once, twice, and again.

I watched Edie watch him. Her face was a study in love and trepidation. She wanted so much for him and feared so much for him. She understood, even if he didn't, that he was teetering on the edge of good and evil. He would fall one way or the other, setting a pattern that would govern his life for years. Since neither of them thought much in terms of the place of Christ in their lives, I wondered where she got her hope. Maybe just from her mother's heart that couldn't believe her kid would go bad.

When Randy finally lifted his head, his face was full of anguish. "I'm sorry, Mom. I'm so sorry." He barely managed to whisper the words. "I can't believe I—" He couldn't continue.

Edie slid to the edge of the bed and stood. She reached for him and wrapped her arms about his waist. He threw his arms around her and his shoulders began to shake.

"I don't want to be like Dad."

"You won't be, Randy," she promised. "You won't be."

I left the room and waited in the hall, sniffing a fair amount myself.

It was ten more minutes before a nurse arrived with a wheelchair. She went blithely into the room, unaware of the emotional breakthrough inside, and emerged in a couple of minutes with Edie in the chair and Randy, red eyed but obviously lighter in spirit, walking beside her, carrying her tote bag.

When we were on our way home, Edie gave a great sigh. "I hated being in the hospital."

"Most people hate the hospital," I said. "I'd worry about you if you didn't."

Edie nodded. "But I hated it more because Tom didn't know I was there. What if he tried to call me?"

She amazed me with her unfailing optimism about Randy and her faith in Tom.

But Tom hadn't called. At least if he had, he'd left no message. I watched her shoulders sag and the hope in her eyes dim.

"He'll show up, Mom. He loves you too much not to."

Edie and I looked in surprise at Randy. Talk about a turnaround. Apparently he meant some of the things he'd said last night in the darkness.

"Thanks, honey," Edie said in a voice made wobbly by emotion. "You're going to make it too, you know."

Randy gave a quick, self-conscious nod and became busy settling Edie in. Together he and I set her up on the blue leather couch with everything we could think of that she might need. Finally she held up her hands.

"Enough, you two! I'm not dying here. I can get anything I need all by myself. Or Randy can get it for me."

Randy and I looked at each other.

"What?" Edie said, an edge to her voice.

"I have to stay with Merry." Randy looked apologetic. "Sergeant Poole gave me the choice of staying with her or going to juvenile hall."

"And he chose me." I tried to sound bright and positive.

Edie glanced from me to her son. "Well, at least you made the better choice. I don't mind telling people my son is staying with a friend."

"A *female* friend," Randy said, wagging his eyebrows.

"Hey, now," I groused. "It's bad enough that Howard thought you were my son."

"Your son?" Edie laughed out loud. "Howard, whoever he is, needs glasses."

I nodded, still feigning disgust. "Don't set me up as a cradle robber, too. Besides," I grinned at Randy, "Curt's bigger than you."

"Not by much," the boy said, straightening to his full height. He liked it that I had to look up so far to him.

"How soon they forget," I said to Edie. "Yesterday he was pining over this young beauty, and now he's—"

Wrong thing to say. I saw the unhappiness fall over his face like a curtain.

"I'm sorry." I reached out and touched his hand.

He gave a half shrug. "Fact of life."

We were all quiet for a moment, thinking about Sherrie. I shot up a quick prayer for her and her peace of mind.

"Enough of that," Randy said. He became very businesslike. "I've got stuff to tell you two before Merry and I leave."

Edie and I glanced at each other. I had no idea what he had up his sleeve and neither did she.

He pulled out his laptop, turned it on, and as soon as it was ready, scrolled down his screen for a bit. He had settled in the big chair I'd sat in the other night, his laptop on his knees. I noticed the chair fit him a lot better than it fit me.

"I've been online most of the morning looking for information about Tom."

Edie gasped. "Randy!"

"Look, Mom, I figured we needed to find out all we could about what happened ten years ago so we could better defend Tom today."

"Better defend him?" Edie stared at her son.

"Yeah," he said, head buried in his laptop. "Somebody's got to speak for him since he isn't here to speak for himself."

"I thought you didn't like Tom."

"I didn't." His fingers flew over the keyboard. "Not at first. Then I couldn't admit I'd been wrong." He glanced at his mom. "It's a teen thing, you know?"

Edie nodded weakly.

"But I've learned a lot these past couple of days, most of it about me and how dumb I've been." He fell silent as he continued to work over his computer.

Edie sat, poleaxed. I had to smile at her expression. Of course she didn't have the benefit of hearing last night's musings as I had.

"Edie, I've got a couple of questions for you while we wait for Randy." I hoped I wouldn't come to regret what I was going to ask.

"Ask away."

"Was Randolph an abuser? Is that what Randy's referring to when he says he's afraid he'll be like his father?"

Edie nodded, brushing the wrinkles from her slacks. "You'd think I'd have known better, being raised by an abusive father, but I stepped right into my marriage without seeing it coming."

"That's why you didn't want to write the article on abuse? It was too painful?"

"But that's proven not to be true." She still looked surprised at this discovery. "I've found writing about abuse has been cathartic."

"The other night," I said. "You referred to thinking your days in the paper were over. What did you mean?"

"We ended up in the police report in the paper a couple of times when I had to call for help." She shuddered. "What an embarrassment! I hated it."

"Thanks. That answers those questions."

"Then let's not talk about Randolph again, okay? He gives me the chills even now."

I cleared my throat. "Edie, I've got one more question. It's presumptuous, but I've got to ask it as a reporter and as someone who wants to find the truth."

Edie swallowed. "Go ahead."

"Your furniture in here." I waved my hand at the living room, dining room, and entry hall. "It's gorgeous."

"And expensive, right?" Edie looked relieved. Obviously this was a question she could answer.

"It's from my father," Randy said without looking up from whatever he was doing. "When Mom left, Dad sold the house and got an apartment. He wanted all new furniture because he was starting over again. He was going to give all the stuff we had to the Salvation Army."

"He was going to give away all this beautiful stuff?"

Randy nodded. "He has money coming out his ears."

I thought of Randy's silver sports car, wherever it was at the moment. I guess Randolph did at that.

"I talked him into letting me have whatever I wanted. I took the stuff you noticed and my bedroom stuff." He glanced at his mother, embarrassed, a kid about to make a confession. "I was mad at Mom then because I blamed her for the divorce, so I refused to get her anything."

"Oh, Randy, don't worry about that. I didn't want anything, believe me. The last thing I needed was the bedroom suite I shared with him." She fluttered her hands rapidly like she was trying to shake something sticky and unpleasant off. "Some days even the living room is a bit much."

Randy looked at the beautiful furnishings. "You can get rid of all this stuff if you want. I don't care. I don't need it anymore." He spoke like it was a revelation to him, this fact of not needing the furniture. "Just keep the pictures." He looked at the watercolors hanging on the walls. "I really like them."

"Me too," Edie said. "And I don't think we'll get rid of anything else either. It's a cinch Tom and I will never be able to afford anything this nice." She ran her hand over the soft arm of the sofa. Then she looked up, her impudent grin in evidence for the first time in days. "Who needs great furniture when you've got Tom?"

I grinned back. "Recast that sentence to say when you've got Curt, and you're more on target."

"It's all in the eye of the beholder." She leaned back, resting her head against the massive pillow that passed for the back of the sofa. She sighed. I watched as slowly Edie's grin faded and the worry returned.

"I'm glad you asked about the furniture, Merry. All this talk about missing money. Our furnishings are definitely beyond our income level, at least in this part of the house."

I thought of the plain beige carpet upstairs and the Kmart glasses in the kitchen. There was no question but that the rest of the house was ordinary. Nice enough but ordinary. I thought of Jeb's comments about a drug connection and Tom, talk I didn't think Edie had heard yet. Lots of money in drugs. I was relieved to my toes to know the prosaic origin of the furniture, though I couldn't help but wonder what William Poole had thought of the opulence found here when he visited twice on Friday.

"Okay," Randy said, "here we go." He cleared his throat. "Tom worked for the Audubon PD for ten years. He was a sergeant at the time of the drug bust. The Audubon PD cooperated with the Camden PD and the Drug Enforcement Agency to break up a ring that was using the mall on Black Horse Pike in Audubon and the park down the street from the high school like they owned them. Of course they were also working Camden like crazy. They had a DEA guy and woman go undercover, he with the gang, she in the high school. They set up the bust at a drop in an old warehouse in Camden."

He hit some more keys and Edie watched him in total fascination.

"The cops surrounded the building and did their usual 'Freeze; it's the police' thing. But one of the drug guys panicked and started shooting. Gunfire was exchanged and when the dust settled, Tom Whatley was fatally wounded and one other guy named Felix Estevez was dead."

He looked at us. "That's all available in the newspapers and is general knowledge. I got it from the Philadelphia *Inquirer* and *Daily News* sites. Now comes the interesting part." He went back to his screen. "Tom—our Tom—"

Edie turned to me and mouthed, "Our Tom?" and patted her heart like she couldn't believe what she was hearing.

Oblivious, Randy continued. "Our Tom rushed in with the rest of the force, and when he saw Tom Whatley, he went sort of crazy." He looked up apologetically at his mother, hoping he hadn't upset her. "He fell on his knees beside the wounded Tom and kept saying, 'You aren't supposed to be here! You aren't supposed to be here!' His superiors thought that was an incriminating comment given the TomTom Twins history, so they had Tom's involvement with Tom Whatley and the drug bust investigated. But before they could come to any conclusions, Tom resigned from the force and disappeared." Randy snapped his fingers. "Just like that."

"Nobody had any idea where he was?" I asked.

Randy shook his head. "He was just gone."

"Even his mother didn't know where," Edie said. "I don't think he realized how hard something like that would be on a mother. I know he never meant to hurt her. He's too kindhearted."

Randy went back to his story. "The Audubon PD found no evidence to indicate Tom had anything to do with trying to taint the bust. He was cleared in absentia. But the kicker is that the lab tests showed that the bullet that killed Tom Whatley came from our Tom's gun. It was one of many shots fired, but it was the one that struck. The police kept that bit of information quiet for several months before it was leaked to an *Inquirer* reporter. No one ever admitted letting the report get out, and the reporter refused to talk, protecting his source. But there's no question. Our Tom accidentally killed the other Tom."

Randy looked at Edie and blinked. Whatever he had expected her emotional reaction to be to this news, he hadn't expected a smile. Neither had I. But her face was alight with joy.

It only took me a minute to jump to the obvious conclusion. "You've known this all along, haven't you?" I accused. "You've always known that Tom Whatley was Tom Willis."

She turned her smile on me. "Do you really think that Tom would deceive me?"

Given what I and everyone else said about the depth of their affection, the answer had to be no, he wouldn't deceive her. But he had deceived the rest of us, including Randy. And so had Edie.

"How long have you known?" I couldn't decide if I was mad or just frustrated.

Randy stared at his mother, confusion all over his face. "You knew all this? I did all this work for nothing? I even hacked my way into the Audubon PD system!"

Ignore that you've been lied to for five years. Forget the ethical issues involved in living a lie. Be hot and bothered by the unnecessary work you've done, by feeling used, taken advantage of. Here was Randy's great gift offered in love—for the first time in who knew how many years—and it wasn't wanted or needed, and he was ticked.

Oh, Lord, don't let this revelation undo all the good of the past day or so!

"Honey, you have done me one of the biggest favors of my life." Edie walked over to him and kissed him noisily on the cheek. "I thank you, I thank you. You have helped me more than you'll ever know."

Though still confused, Randy seemed somewhat mollified by her appreciation. *Thank you, Lord.*

"So when did you find out?" I asked, pleased I didn't sound too peeved.

"Tom told me all about Tom and the shootout before we were married, but he swore me to secrecy. It didn't really matter until Thursday when he didn't come home. I didn't know what to do. Maybe the truth would sort things out, though I couldn't imagine how. I decided I'd just keep quiet until I had to tell what I knew. But it was killing me inside. Now, thanks to this wonderful kid who uncovered all our secrets"—and she glowed at Randy—"I can talk about everything with a clear conscience."

"Would you have kept quiet indefinitely?" I asked, still peeved that she hadn't shared what she knew. And maybe, I confess, peeved because she forgot to give me at least some credit for opening this particular Pandora's box with my trip to Audubon.

"I don't know. It would have depended on what happened. But it's a moot point now." She smiled at Randy. "I'm free."

He didn't smile back. "Why did you go along with it at all?" Much of his pique was passed, but there was still a touch of starch in his question.

Edie leaned back on the sofa and clutched a pillow in her lap. "Tom was already known here in Amhearst as Tom Whatley when I met him. How do you tell people that you've been using a false name without them wanting to know why? And then all that pain would be raked up all over again. I mean, who wants to live through that twice?"

"How did he come to be known as Tom Whatley in the first place?" I asked.

"Ah. Now there's a weird story. I bet you didn't find that in your magic little machine, did you, Randy?"

"You know I didn't," he said. "Come on. Talk. Tell me why I shouldn't be mad at you all over again."

"I love you."

He rolled his eyes and slouched down on his neck. All his body language yelled, "Prove to me that you're okay!"

She paused and ordered her thoughts. "You already know that Tom and Tom were best friends and had been for years. The TomTom Twins. My Tom"—she looked at Randy—"*our* Tom had done well, graduating from college and the police academy with honors earned through hard work. He was doing well on his job. Tom Whatley, the golden boy of Audubon High, had done poorly, dropping out of college, drifting from job to job, unable to cope when no longer the golden boy."

"The moral here," Randy said, "is that I should be glad I'm only second string JV and not one of the popular jocks in the starting lineup?"

His mother smiled at him. "You're popular with me, kid."

His expression said clearly that while he might be having a change of heart about many things, being popular with his mother still didn't cut it. The new Randy managed to keep his comments about this to himself, but he looked constipated with the effort.

Edie and I looked at each other and laughed at his expression.

"It was a joke," Edie said.

Randy looked immensely relieved.

"I take that back. No, it wasn't." She shook her head. "You are popular with me, guy."

Randy's smile was sickly. "Just don't tell my friends, okay?"

Edie nodded solemnly. "Deal."

I'd had enough mother-son bonding. "So Tom Whatley was a failure. I found that out in Audubon."

Edie looked sad. "He fell into drugs big time. My Tom was never sure how it began. He asked and asked, but the other Tom was always frustratingly vague. But as the years passed, Tom Whatley became more and more heavily drug dependent. Tom put him in detox programs more than once, but the other Tom would always leave, sometimes before even one day had passed.

"Tom knew that the other Tom was going to die soon if something wasn't done. The problem was that the other Tom didn't seem to care. Then came the word that Tom Whatley was involved with the ring about to be busted."

"How did Tom hear that?" I asked. "A source on the street?"

"A comment from his chief, if you can believe that. 'A hero's going to fall in this one,' he said the afternoon before the bust. Tom asked what he meant. The chief was an older guy who had a son named Bobby who had graduated with the Toms. Bobby played football, and he always lost out to Tom Whatley for everything from starting position to team captain. There may have been a bit of satisfaction in the chief's comment when he said, 'Such promise wasted, not like you and Bobby.'

Right away Tom knew what the chief meant. It was his worst nightmare."

I could imagine. Talk about an ethical dilemma. You can't tell Tom what's going to happen because he might tell his associates. Then they would either disappear and set up shop elsewhere, or they would arrange an ambush. But how can you let your best friend get caught up in a situation that could lead to him getting arrested or shot?

"Tom went to the other Tom's apartment, by this time little more than a mattress on the floor in a horrible part of inner-city Camden. 'Don't go out tonight, Tom,' was what Tom ended up telling him. 'Promise me you won't go out.' The other Tom didn't even ask why. He just promised to make Tom happy, then did what he wanted. As Tom has said many times since, he should have realized that druggies will agree to anything, then do what they need to."

"So Whatley went to the drug drop." I found the story fascinating. "I take it he was financing his own habit by selling?"

Edie nodded. "He went out and got shot, and Tom still holds himself accountable."

"But it wasn't Tom's fault," Randy protested. "He told the other Tom to stay home. Besides the other Tom was killing himself anyway."

Edie nodded. "Tom knows that, but the other Tom is still dead and he was unable to save the friend he loved better than a brother."

Randy looked thoughtfully at the rug. "Maybe I don't understand because I don't have a friend like that," he said. "But if something happened to Sherrie and I couldn't save her ..." His face said it all.

I thought of Tom Willis, quiet, unimpressive, kind, living with all this hurtful history while he helped Edie overcome hers. And I looked at Edie, living with all these secrets, protecting the man she loved, helping him learn to cope. How much easier it would have been if they had known that God sent Christ to bear just such pain for them.

Dear God, help me help them.

Edie wasn't finished. "I'll say one thing for Tom Whatley. While our Tom was weeping beside him, knowing his wound was fatal but not knowing the bullet came from his own gun, Tom Whatley looked at him, smiled, and managed to say, 'Thanks. You tried.'"

I thought about that for several minutes. "You tried." How would I react if someone I loved said that, trying with his last breath to free me from guilt?

"What?" Edie asked me. "You're shaking your head."

"'You tried.' I was wondering if that would free me. I don't think it would any more than it did Tom. I think that's one that only God can set you free from."

Edie looked at me with something like respect in her eyes. "Tom still has nightmares about that night."

"But it wasn't his fault," Randy said again. "It's not fair."

"It's not," his mother agreed. "But then life's not fair."

That's sure true, I thought. "By the way . . ." I smiled at Edie. "I met your mother-in-law."

She stared at me. "Mom Willis?"

I nodded. "When I went to Audubon. She wouldn't talk to me. I think I scared her to death."

"I'll bet. Tom has impressed on her not to talk about him, especially to strangers. They might be newspaper reporters, looking to revive the Tom Whatley story for one reason or another." She smiled at the irony of her own occupation and mine.

"And I showed up at the tenth anniversary of Tom Whatley's death without even knowing it. Just what Tom warned her against, though she didn't know I was a reporter. But she was sure suspicious, let me tell you."

Edie stood and began to pace. "I don't think Mom understands all that happened to Tom. She just knows he's living here in Amhearst and using a different name. He visits her often, usually at night so there won't be questions from the neighbors, and he sends her money every month. Without it, she wouldn't be able to keep her home. I think she talks about him to her friends. I know she brags on Randy a lot."

Randy looked at his mother, surprise writ large on his face. "Tom's mom brags about me?"

Edie smiled. "I heard her once on the phone talking about her handsome grandson."

He blinked. "But I've never even met her."

"That doesn't stop Tom and me from talking about you."

"If she thinks I'm nice," Randy looked uncomfortable as he spoke, "then you haven't been telling her the truth."

"Let's just say we're selective," Edie said. "You do well in school, you play a mean game of football, and you are a computer whiz. We tell her things like that."

He blinked rapidly a few times. "Thanks. Can I meet her?"

"When Tom comes home."

"She's a little, tiny lady, Randy," I said. "You could carry her around in your palm."

"Sort of like Tom." But he smiled and there was no mockery in his voice.

"Yes," his mother said as she made her way back to the sofa. "Sort of like Tom."

Randy had shut down his laptop and closed its lid. He leaned an elbow on it. "I still have two questions. Why or how did Tom Willis become Tom Whatley?"

Edie took a sip from the now lukewarm cup of tea I'd made for her. "It's one of those dumb things," she said. "Tom had gone to ground after the shootings, staying at a friend's cabin in the Poconos."

"Did the friend know he was there?" Randy asked.

"I don't think so," Edie said. "He'd stayed there before. In fact, he and Tom had stayed there a couple of times in failed attempts to clean Tom up. This time my Tom went to be alone and grieve. He stayed there for a couple of months in the winter, reeling with the pain, only venturing out to go to the store for the bare essentials. But come spring, he knew he couldn't live the rest of his life like a hermit, eaten with regret and what ifs.

"He got in his car and began to drive. Somehow he ended up in Amhearst just as his car died. He coasted into Hamblin Motors prepared to buy a car. Mike Hamblin himself was the salesman he talked with, and Mike was impressed with Tom's knowledge of cars. 'I need a salesman,' he said. 'I need a job,' Tom said. 'What did you say your name was?' Mike asked. Before Tom could answer, Mike was called away for a minute.

"While he waited for Mike to return, Tom saw a newspaper on the corner of Mike's desk. The headline read COP IN DRUG BUST KILLED BEST FRIEND. A picture of him in his uniform stared out at him. He wasn't worried about being recognized as the man in the picture. He looked much different than the rookie cop with the earnest face staring out at him from under the bill of his hat. Regret and sorrow had aged him. But it was the first time he knew he had been the one to kill Tom."

My stomach clenched. What a terrible way to learn something of that magnitude!

"When Mike came back, Tom's mind was still reeling. 'What's your name?' Mike asked again. And because his mind was full of his friend, my Tom said, 'Tom Whatley.'"

"'Well, Tom, what do you say? Willing to give us a try?'

"Tom opened his mouth to correct the mistake in the name when he caught the first two words in the article: Thomas Willis. What if Mike Hamblin made the connection? Besides, he only planned to be there for a very short time. All he wanted was a little ready cash and he'd be on his way. Who cared if they called him by the wrong name?"

"But what about Social Security and his paycheck and all?" I asked. "How could he get paid in the wrong name?"

"When Tom Whatley died, none of his family came to the hospital. They had all washed their hands of him long before. So the hospital gave my Tom all the other Tom's effects. He kept all the things with him all those months, actually carrying the papers in his own wallet. If Mike Hamblin thought it strange that he had to pull his Social Security card and read his number, he didn't mention it. And of course"—she spread her hands—"Tom found out he liked Hamblin's and selling cars and Amhearst."

"And you," I said. "And he was trapped."

"Well, there's nothing very sinister in that," Randy said, relief evident in his voice.

Edie nodded as she collapsed against the arm of the couch, exhausted now that the story was told. "Nothing sinister. Just sort of stupid. One of those things."

I stood, worried at how weary she suddenly looked. "You need to rest. This has been hard on you."

"Yeah," Randy added. "You just need to get better so you're fine when Tom comes home."

Edie looked at her son. "You almost sound like you want him to come home."

"Well, yeah. Because it's what you want." He turned bright red but forced himself to continue. "So it's what I want."

Edie was still reeling from the shock of Randy's comment when we left.

"I still have one question," Randy said as we pulled out of the driveway. "What does all that long-ago stuff have to do with now?"

What indeed.

Chapter 13

Randy and I arrived at Freedom House at two o'clock. I was looking forward to my interview with Tina, and he was cringing with embarrassment. What if he saw Sherrie? Or her mother, who had undoubtedly heard about the events of yesterday from Sherrie.

"It's called facing the music," I said as we climbed the steps.

"Yeah, I know. But the tune is so ugly." He tucked his laptop under one arm and looked around the porch. "So's this building. Why don't they fix it up?"

"Money." I thought of the quality furniture in his family's living room and the multitude of gadgets in his room and all the money those things represented. "Or lack of it."

He grunted as a young woman I'd never seen before opened the door. Not having enough money was a concept that was hard for him to grasp.

"Hi, I'm Karen." She stepped back to let us in. She was pretty in an overblown sort of way with lots of long curly blond hair and way too much makeup. Still, I could see the bruise on her right cheek.

She smiled like she hadn't a care in the world. "We're having Bible study now, but Stephanie's almost finished. She asked me to take you to her office."

I noticed that the collection of equipment and offerings for Like New had grown and was threatening to overtake the entryway. Randy stared with distaste at the clutter, not understanding its eventual use.

"Isn't it great?" Karen grinned as we stepped over two super-sized plastic bags of clothes, their cinches pulled tight and tied in red bows. "Some lady Stephanie doesn't even know dropped these bags off just a few minutes ago. Word's getting around."

"Word about what?" Randy muttered in my ear. "That the place is the town's new dump site?"

"God is so good," Karen said, beaming at us as she stopped in Stephanie's office door. She touched the dark shadow on her cheek. "I'm going to be the first trainee at the store. I don't have any place to live yet and I don't have any money, but I know I'll be okay. I have hope." And she left us.

Randy stared after her, frowning. "Why's she so cheery? That bruise on her cheek looked pretty bad to me."

"She's got hope," I said.

"Yeah, I heard. But why? She hasn't got a place to live. She hasn't got money. She's got a husband who beats her."

"But she's got a way out."

He shook his head, confused.

"That stuff out there ..."

"That junk?" Distaste curled his lip.

"That's her way out."

"She's the town's new trash man?"

I looked at Randy. He'd come a long way in a short time, but he still obviously had a long way to go.

"Do you think Sherrie's smart?" I asked.

He blinked at the change in topic but came with me readily enough. "I should do so well in school."

"Do you think she's got class?"

"Down to her fingertips."

"How about her mother and brother?"

"Very neat people. Fun. I like them."

"Then why do you assume that they're collecting trash? Why do you assume that the property is shabby on purpose? Think a bit, Randy. Ask yourself *why* instead of jumping to what appear to be obvious conclusions."

He didn't look very happy at the not too subtle reprimand. Too bad. If I had to cart him everywhere I went, I was going to tell him a thing or two as I thought best. I wasn't just a baby-sitter, for Pete's sake.

"Okay." His voice was clipped and cool. "Why the mess?"

"Many women don't leave their abusive husbands because of money. They have no way to feed and house themselves and their kids. Stephanie wants to help them learn a marketable skill. She's opening a secondhand store and training women in sales skills there."

"Oh." He looked slightly chagrined, but he rallied quickly. "But why the mess in the hall? Why don't they put the stuff away somewhere?"

"Priorities."

"What?"

"What's more important? A temporary place for Karen to sleep or a neat hallway?"

He looked at me in silence for a minute. "You're good, you know." He walked into Stephanie's office and collapsed on one end of the sofa from the mission in Allentown. "All of a sudden you've got me thinking that mess is a wonderful thing."

"That's nice, but what I really want is for you to take time to think first, guy. Don't jump to conclusions about things. Or people."

He slid so far down on the sofa he was almost sitting on his neck. "Me? Jump to conclusions about people?" His laugh was bitter and full of self-loathing. "Not me."

He ran his fingers over a particularly dark stain on the sofa seat, then slapped at it. Dust motes flew. "Why would anybody want furniture like—" He stopped and looked at me. "They don't necessarily want it, do they? They have no choice. There's no money."

I smiled and nodded. Inside I felt like a proud mom cheering and screaming for her kid when he's hit a home run, but I said very calmly, "You got it."

He nodded and stared at the stain a minute. Then he plugged in his computer and got down to business. From that moment on he was basically lost to his surroundings and all conversation. The game he was playing had his entire concentration.

I knew when the Bible study finally ended because I could hear the women's voices, all talking at the same time, laughing, lingering. Stephanie came into the office while women still talked.

"They don't like to leave," she explained. "It's safe here."

She saw Randy, who looked up apprehensively when somehow through his game fog he heard her enter. She smiled a welcome. "Well, hi, Randy. Nice to see you."

He relaxed visibly at her accepting attitude, his fingers easing on the computer keys. He blurted, "I have to stay with Merry."

Stephanie looked a question.

He flushed but said, "It was her or juvenile hall."

"Ah. And you chose her." Stephanie collapsed in the stuffed chair. "Wise choice."

"Is Sherrie okay?" Randy asked, flushing an even more painful red.

Stephanie nodded. "Not happy, but okay. She went to school."

Randy seemed pleased. "Good. I need to apologize to her for yesterday."

Stephanie eyed him thoughtfully. "Maybe not quite yet."

He nodded sadly. "She needs time, doesn't she? I understand."

Stephanie smiled at him. "I like you, Randy. With God's help, you're going to be okay, you know that?"

Randy was bowled over by this show of confidence. He went back to his computer to hide his self-consciousness.

Stephanie turned to me. Her smile fell away. "She isn't here."

My heart dropped. "Do you know where she is?"

Stephanie shook her head. "I'm afraid to guess."

"Because you're afraid you'll be right?"

She sighed. "Yeah. I've been down this road with so many women, including myself in the old days. I was just going to call her parents to see what they can tell me."

She walked to her desk and sat down. As she reached for the phone, it rang.

"Freedom House. Stephanie Bauer speaking."

She glanced at me with a raised eyebrow and mouthed, "Tina." I nodded. I could hear a happy voice splashing through the mouthpiece like verbal sunshine, though I couldn't hear specific words. Maybe things actually were all right.

Stephanie listened a minute, leaned back in her desk chair, and closed her eyes in dismay. So much for all right.

"Oh, Tina." There were more words pouring out of the phone, but none of them eased Stephanie's fears. Then she said, "You had an appointment with Merry Kramer for an interview. Did you forget?"

Next thing I knew I had Tina in my ear. Stephanie could pass off a phone with all the flourish and skill of a relay runner passing off the baton.

"Hi, Merry. I thought you'd be there." Canaries never sounded so chirpy. "I wanted you to know I didn't forget, but I can't meet with you after all."

Rats, I thought. There goes some of the best content of my story. "Can we talk now, Tina? I can interview you over the phone."

"Can't do it," she said happily. "Bill asked me not to."

"Since when do you care about what he says?" I was more abrupt than I meant to be, but I didn't apologize.

"Merry." Tina's voice was a gentle rebuke. "Bill's my husband. I always care what he says."

"Where are you, Tina?"

"I'm at home." As my heart sank, she bubbled, "Isn't it wonderful? Bill came for me and the kids this morning before work. He was so kind and loving."

My stomach roiled. "Tina, it's an act to get you back under his control."

"No, it's not." There was anger and panic in her voice. "He loves us. I know he does. He said he did."

"Oh, Tina." She wasn't a stupid woman, so why was she being so dumb?

"He drove all the way to Phoenixville for us," she gushed. I drove all the way to Phoenixville for her, too, I thought darkly. And that proved exactly what? "He was so good with the kids, hugging them and kissing them. I could tell he really missed us and regretted what happened."

"Don't waste your time," Stephanie whispered across her desk. "She can't hear you at the moment."

I nodded. I knew she was right, but I hated it. "Look, Tina, you still have my card, don't you? If you ever have time to talk to me or if you ever need me, you just call. I don't care what time it is, day or night."

After I hung up, Stephanie and I stared at each other. Finally she shook her head and said, "One of the hardest things I've had to learn is that you can't help them if they don't want to be helped."

"But he'll do it all over again."

She nodded. "He'll do it all over again. We need to pray that he doesn't kill her in the process."

"It took my mother years before she'd leave my father," Randy suddenly said, looking from me to Stephanie. "And I know we went back several times. He could be very persuasive." And he went back to his game.

I stood. "Come on, guy. We need to go."

"In a minute. I just want to finish this one part or I'll have to start all over again."

"Obviously a fate worse than death," I muttered and left the office. Stephanie followed. We were almost to the front door when I heard a key in the lock. The door flew open and in backed Rob and Sherrie, busy waving at a car driving off.

"You're home early," Stephanie said.

Rob nodded. "Don brought us home. He's got a car for the rest of the week because his dad's in the hospital. His mom told him he could drive his dad's car to school if he promised to go visit his dad every night."

"Sounds like a deal." Stephanie grinned.

Rob grinned back. "I think Don likes Sherrie."

Sherrie looked appalled. "Oh, no."

"Oh, yes."

"But he's too old!"

"He's my age. That's only three years."

"I don't mean in years."

I looked at Sherrie with respect for her insight.

"Ah," said her brother. "Experience. Yep, Don's had a lot of that. But he's still a nice guy. All the girls love him."

Sherrie frowned. "And that's supposed to be a selling point?"

"Oh, yeah," Rob said. "I forgot. You like them tall and blond and shy."

Suddenly Sherrie's frown became real. "Shut up, Rob."

"Rob," his mother cautioned.

Speaking of tall, blond, and shy, where was he? I looked back to the office and watched as he came sailing out, laptop in hand, unaware of the ambush awaiting him.

"Hey, wait for—" He slammed to a halt as he saw Sherrie. I don't think he even noticed Rob. Or Stephanie and me.

Sherrie went absolutely still too.

Randy moved first. He glanced around at their audience, then back at her. He swallowed a couple of times. "Can I talk to you for a minute?"

"Oh. I don't—" She looked at her mother for help, then back at Randy. "You weren't at school today." She said it in a rush.

He brightened because she'd noticed. "We brought my mother home."

Sherrie nodded. "How is she?"

"Fine. She's at home now, resting."

Sherrie nodded again and fell silent. As the silence lengthened, she grew embarrassed. She lowered her head, her black hair falling forward to guard her face.

"Can we talk?" Randy asked again. "Just for a minute?"

There was no sign she heard him except for perhaps a more rapid rhythm to her breathing.

He accepted her silence as a no. "That's okay." He held out a hand, trying manfully not to let his hurt show. "I understand. I wouldn't want to talk to me either. I was pretty awful."

Her head came up, her eyes uncertain. "It's not ... I don't ... You're not ..." She looked at Stephanie again.

Stephanie stepped into the breach. "Sherrie, I know you're supposed to talk with Merry this afternoon. Why don't you two take the office? Randy, why don't you come upstairs with Rob and me and I'll get you guys something to eat while you wait for Merry."

"You're here with Merry?" Sherrie asked, her head once again lowered.

Randy nodded jerkily, then realized she couldn't see him. "Yes."

"I thought you came to see me." Her voice was a whisper, and I couldn't tell if she was relieved or disappointed that Randy had come with me.

"I'd always come to see you if I thought you'd see me." It was a declaration straight from the heart.

Stephanie and I looked at each other and smiled. It was so sad and so sweet. This time Rob saved further awkwardness.

"Come on, Randy. Mom and Sherrie baked snickerdoodles last night. It was their mother/daughter ritual to help Sherrie cope." He started toward the stairs. "You might as well benefit from their activities." He stopped and grinned impishly over his shoulder. "After all, if it hadn't been for you, there'd be no cookies."

Sherrie gasped and put her hand over her mouth, but she didn't look up. Randy flushed and manfully smiled at the gentle, precise jibe.

"Rob," Stephanie cautioned as she stood at the foot of the stairs and waited for Randy to precede her. With a lovelorn look in Sherrie's direction, Randy resigned himself to cookies instead of his love and followed Rob.

Taking a deep breath and letting it out slowly, Sherrie led the way to her mother's office. I took the sofa again and she the easy chair. I got out my tape recorder and my note tablet.

She sat and stared at her clasped hands for a minute, and I let the silence continue. She needed time.

"I still like him." She said it like she was admitting she liked Internet porn.

I grinned to myself. "So do I. He's a nice person with lots of possibilities."

She looked at me then, clearly confused with herself. "But you saw what he did."

I nodded. "And he scared himself very badly."

She thought about that for a while. "Badly enough to change?"

"I think there's a good chance."

"Can he do that without Jesus?"

"Maybe." I rubbed at the stain Randy had noted earlier. "Some people do."

She nodded. "But lots don't."

"You know what that means, don't you?"

She thought about that for about two seconds, then grinned. "We've got to pray he finds Jesus," she said.

I smiled at her. "I'd already been thinking about inviting him and his mom to church on Easter to hear you sing. Now I know I will. You pray that they come, okay?"

She nodded, excited. "I will. Oh, I will."

"Good girl. I knew I could count on you. Now let's get to work."

We talked for almost a half hour, and she did have some very good ideas for my story.

"Kids in an abusive home have one of two experiences," she said as she tucked her legs under her. "Either they end up getting hit too, or they observe it happening. Mom calls it 'pointed behavior' when the abuse is leveled at the child and 'modeled behavior' when the child observes the abuse. Each has its own special terror. But either way, they think this is normal. They don't have any other gauge for family life, especially when they see it from a little kid on up."

"So you thought your dad's temper and beatings were normal?" I couldn't quite keep the surprise out of my voice.

"Sure. It scared me, but I thought that was just the way life was. I'd wake up to Mom screaming and begging and him roaring and cursing. I'd hear the bangs and the crashes and the crying. I'd cry in fear because I didn't understand what was happening or know what to do. I hid under the bed more than once, terrified I'd be next."

"Did your father ever hit you?"

She shook her head. "He never hit either Rob or me. And he hit Mom most when he'd been drinking or had a real bad day at work. Then he'd apologize and fall all over himself saying how he'd never do it again. What a lie."

"What would you like to tell parents in abusive homes?"

She didn't have to think for even a moment. "I'd tell the moms to get out before the kids are scarred any worse. Every day you remain makes it harder for the kids to be normal adults. I'd tell the fathers to think what they're doing to their kids. They're making them scared and full of fear and teaching them that violence is an okay way to live. Go get help for the kids' sakes."

I smiled at her appreciatively. She was a good interview, her ideas organized and clear. "Why do you think moms stay?"

"They keep hoping it'll be different. They're ashamed. They don't have anywhere to go. They don't have any money. They don't have any job skills. They think God wants them to stay. Their pastor tells them they should stay." She shrugged. "All or any of those, and there are probably more reasons I haven't thought of. Take Mom. She's an optimist. She wanted to believe my father every time he said things would be different. She's a fixer-upper. She wanted to fix him. So she stayed."

"Do you remember the day she left?"

Sherrie looked out the window and into the past. "Rob asked me to get him some cookies. He was watching TV and didn't feel like getting up. I was playing with my Barbies and didn't want to get up either. I made believe I didn't hear him at first. He started to get mad at me, just like Dad would get mad at Mom. 'You got to do what I ask,' he yelled. 'I don't,' I said. 'You do,' he yelled. 'I'm the man and you're the girl.' I kept combing Barbie's hair. I wasn't expecting anything bad to happen. Rob had never done anything before to hurt me except regular brother stuff like pushing me out of his way and all."

"Why do you think this time was different?"

"I don't know." She grew thoughtful. "Maybe because he was getting older? Anyway, he grabbed me and pulled me to my feet. He put his face in my face and yelled again that I should get the cookies. I was scared now because he was hurting my arm. 'You got to do what I say! Girls have to do what boys say.'"

She looked at me and said very seriously, "I didn't like that idea then and I still don't today."

I nodded in agreement. "Wise woman. I don't either."

"But see," she said earnestly, "that's what he'd learned from my father and mother. Kids learn by example. Boys have the right to make girls do whatever they want. They're bigger and meaner. They have the power. And they make you cry if you don't cooperate."

"So he slapped you, just like he'd learned."

She nodded. "And even though I didn't think I'd been all that bad, I took the blame for his action. I was learning by example too."

"What would you want to tell girls your age to help prevent them from marrying someone like your father?"

"I'd tell them to be wary of anyone who has a temper. I'd tell them not to think they can change someone just by loving him. So many of the women my mom works with had a savior complex. They were going to love this man so much he'd become healthy emotionally. They would fix all his hurts. Love would make everything fine."

I looked at her earnest young face. "But that sounds good."

"The trouble is that he doesn't know what love really is. He only knows what control is. Love yields. Love cares. Love desires that the other person be happy or comfortable or pleased."

"But some guys are frauds, able to play the game until after the marriage." I wanted to hear her answer to that familiar problem.

She readily agreed. "Some guys are frauds. And the younger you are, the more liable you are to be taken in by a fraud. But in the long run there are no guarantees about anyone."

"How'd you get to be so smart?" I asked.

"Around here," she said, "all you have to do is listen."

"If there are no guarantees, what hope can you give a young woman?"

"Make certain the guy's a Christian. That's not a guarantee either, but it's the best I can offer. Make certain the guy loves God because God's love will change his heart, just like it'll change yours. Make sure he's dealt with any problems in his background. Make sure he's kind to his mother. I kid you not. The way he talks to his mom and grandmom is probably the way he'll talk to you. And he should be nice to animals and to old people too."

She fell silent, looking at me expectantly.

"Anything else?" I asked.

"Nope." She uncurled from the chair. "I think I said everything I wanted to."

I stood and collected my equipment. "Shall we go upstairs and get a snickerdoodle? I hate to think of those guys getting them all."

Sherrie immediately became hesitant and shrank into herself.

I smiled gently. "Life's a lot harder than theory, isn't it? My suggestion is that you be pleasant but distant. Sort of like he's your pesky though handsome brother. He likes you a lot, which shows he has good taste." She blushed. "But right now he needs to take care of his own problems, not focus on you. Maybe in a year or two?"

"Or three or four?"

"Or three or four," I agreed.

Slowly she relaxed. "A brother. Three or four. I can handle that." She nodded. "Let's go get some cookies, quick."

Chapter 14

I started when the doorbell finally rang. I glanced at my watch. Ten P.M. Curt was only three-and-a-half hours late.

Randy looked up from the TV he and I had been pretending to watch. "I'll get it."

I nodded, torn between relief that the man was finally here in one piece—they didn't call the Schuylkill Expressway the SureKill for no reason—and anger that he was so late and hadn't called. But it was the fact that he'd been with Delia when he hadn't called that made my blood chill.

Okay, girl, I said to myself for the thousandth time. *You can be a shrew, a harridan, a nag, a carper, a termagant, or you can be kind. Like you told Randy this afternoon, ask why, but do it nicely. Politely. Gently. Considerately. And if you're collecting synonyms at this rate, you'd better go very carefully. You are an emotional time bomb.*

Randy had just reached the door when the phone rang. I picked it up as Curt crossed the sill. He smiled slightly in Randy's direction, but his eyes immediately sought me out. They were filled with the unlikely combination of excitement and apprehension. I didn't know why the excitement, but I sure knew why the apprehension. I hadn't been exactly understanding recently. But then he'd been too friendly recently.

I smiled slightly at him as I said, "Hello," into the phone.

Choice.

I broadened my smile. After all, there might have been a giant pileup on the Schuylkill Expressway and he'd been held up while they cleared the roadway of the myriad bodies or the oil slick or scores of little pigs freed by the collision.

Or he'd been with Delia.

My smile soured somewhat.

"Merry?" The word in my ear was so soft I almost didn't hear. It was also slurred, indistinct.

"Who is this?" I asked. The last thing I felt like dealing with was another threatening phone call, mine or Edie's.

"Merry, it's me, Tina."

I could barely make out the words. "Tina? Are you all right?"

Her answer was a ghastly, gurgling sob.

"Tina!" Curt and Randy were both at my side, reacting to the horror in my voice. "He's hurt you, hasn't he?"

"Help me. Please." Then more sobs.

"Are you at your house? Tina, answer me. Are you at your house?"

"Yes."

"Is your husband there?"

"He went out to get some booze. Help. Before he comes back. Please."

"I'll be right there. Are the kids okay?"

"Scared. Crying."

I'll just bet, poor little souls. I'd be scared and crying too. "I'll be right there," I repeated.

I disconnected and reached for my purse even as I dialed 911. Curt's tardiness for our special dinner had become the unimportant item it was.

"You're not going alone," he said clearly and with authority. "We'll take my car. It's parked behind yours."

For once I didn't argue. I wanted his size and protection.

We raced out the front door, and it wasn't until we were pulling out of the parking lot that I realized Randy was with us too.

"She sounded so bad," I said as I buckled my seat belt. I was shaking so hard with apprehension for her and anger at her husband that I had trouble getting the clip in its slot. Finally I heard the click. "We told her not to go home. We told her." My voice caught and I had to swallow.

Curt reached over and took my hand. "She'll be okay. We'll get her out."

I nodded, comforted somewhat just because he realized my distress. I tried to smile my appreciation, but I couldn't quite pull it off. I felt overwhelmed with responsibility. If I'd argued more effectively, if I'd somehow been able to convince her of her danger, this beating wouldn't have happened.

"It's not your fault, Merry." Randy leaned over the seat and looked at me, concern for me evident in his voice, in his expression.

I stared at him. Randy? Mr. Mouth? Compassionate? I could hardly believe it. His mother would be so proud.

"I heard you and Mrs. Bauer talking to her," he continued. "You told her all the right stuff, both of you. She just didn't listen."

I sighed. I knew he was right. It didn't make my churning stomach calm, but it did relieve some of my self-inflicted guilt. "Thanks, Randy." I patted his hand resting on the seat by my shoulder.

I gave Curt directions, and we sped through the darkness. Amhearst basically pulled in the sidewalks by ten on a Tuesday night. There were a few taverns and an all-night convenience store that were open across town, but in the residential neighborhood where Tina and her family lived, all was quiet.

The flickering light of TVs flared from living rooms, and lights shone through curtains and around the edges of shades in bedrooms. An occasional dog barked, and a white cat flashed across the road in front of us. Otherwise, nothing.

"There!" I pointed to Tina's house, and Curt pulled into the drive. I sighed with relief when I saw there was no sign of another car. Her husband must still be out.

The front door opened even before Curt turned the motor off, spilling yellow light onto the little front porch. In the doorway stood Jess, looking small and vulnerable in his pajamas. He threw open the storm door as I ran up the sidewalk.

"Merry!" he called, relief all too evident. He launched himself down the steps and ran toward me. The cavalry had arrived. He could take his finger out of the dike. He could lift the world from his frail shoulders.

Stop with the mixed metaphors! I yelled to myself as I reached for him. Everything was going to be all right.

He froze midstride as he became aware of Curt and Randy coming up behind me. I thought how two tall men must appear to a little boy who was already afraid.

I knelt on the sidewalk. "It's all right, Jess. This is Randy. And this is Mr. Carlyle. They're my friends and they've come to help me help your mom."

"Hi, Jess," said Curt, going down on his knees beside me. "Are you all right?" He lay a gentle hand on Jess's head.

The boy flinched as he saw the hand coming in his direction, glanced at me doubtfully, but stood his ground. When he felt the gentleness of Curt's touch, something in him gave way. He started to cry.

"It's my mom," he sobbed, his great, dark eyes looking at me. My heart broke and I gathered him to me. He wrapped his arms around me and buried his face in my neck.

"Where is she?" I asked, standing with him still held close. He wrapped his little legs about my waist.

He mumbled something into my neck, now wet with his tears and, I was afraid, the phlegm from his runny nose.

"What?" I said.

"I'll show you." He wiggled to get down.

I set him on the ground, and he led us into the house, across the living room with its toppled lamps and upended coffee table, and upstairs to a bedroom. That room was a shambles too, with shattered fragrance bottles and wall mirrors, a bed with the linens ripped off and thrown helter-skelter, a closet with clothes ripped from hangers and stomped onto the floor. Shards of what had once been a porcelain figurine lay at the base of one wall beside a library book with its spine broken.

But the most terrible sight was Tina, lying on the bed with her eyes closed, a wide-eyed, apprehensive Lacey curled beside her holding her hand.

One eye was swollen shut and bruised. The other was ringed with black from the shiner she'd gotten in the skirmish between her husband and her father Sunday evening. Her nose was bleeding slowly, and she sniffed periodically, gagging as she swallowed the fluid. Her lip was split and swollen, and she couldn't shut her mouth. Saliva kept sliding out, and she was too despairing to care. It ran down her cheek and pooled by her ear next to the raw spot where hair had literally been pulled out by the roots.

The kids had drawn a comforter over her, covering her other injuries, but I knew there must be more.

"Tina," I called softly as I knelt beside the bed. I swallowed bile as I looked at her and fought against losing the cheese and crackers I'd been nibbling all evening as I waited for Curt. "Tina, it's me, Merry."

When she didn't respond, I was filled with momentary panic until I saw the steady rise and fall of her chest.

"I got her that ice pack out of the freezer," Jess said, coming to stand beside me. He pointed to the chemical ice packet Lacey was holding to Tina's eye.

"That was very wise," I said. "You did well."

Jess straightened his frail shoulders. "I called 911 too."

"Very well done," Curt said, standing behind us. He made certain to keep his voice soft and friendly.

Jess still eyed him with distrust but nodded, accepting the compliment.

Just then we heard a vehicle pull into the drive behind Curt's car. Jess turned white and Lacey began to whimper.

"It's okay," I said, sitting on the bed beside Lacey. I leaned in and gave her cheek a kiss. "Even if it's your father, it's okay. He can't hurt you or your mom with all of us here. We're going to see your mom gets to the hospital and you get someplace safe."

The kids looked at each other and some message flew through the air between them. Jess nodded and Lacey calmed a little. She went back to stroking Tina's hand.

Randy, silent up until now, undoubtedly seeing reflections of his own early life, turned from looking out the front window. "It's the ambulance. And the police. I'll go let them in."

Jess climbed onto the bed beside his mother and sister. He knelt, leaning over Tina. "It's okay now, Mom," he said softly. "Merry's here. And so is the ambulance. And the police. It's okay now."

Tina, who hadn't moved or seemed aware previously, relaxed at his words. I could see it in the movement of her shoulders and hear it in the deep sigh she gave. One corner of her injured mouth curved in a slight smile. A hand snaked out from under the quilt and touched Jess lightly, then Lacey, before falling heavily to the pillow. "Good," she managed in a raspy, weak voice. "Good."

Curt, Randy, Jess, Lacey, and I sat on the living room couch and waited as Tina was prepared for her trip to the hospital. Lacey's little body shook as she leaned against me, and I ran my hand soothingly over her head. Jess sat alert, listening for anything that might go wrong. I thought with sadness that things going wrong was a regular part of his life.

The most amazing and unsettling thing to me was that every one of the emergency responders, police and medical personnel alike, knew Jess and Lacey. One of the EMTs stopped at the couch and knelt in front of the children. "I'm sorry we took so long to get here, you guys. We were out on another call and came as soon as we could. Are you okay?"

Jess nodded for both of them.

"You're a good man, Jess," the EMT said as he stood. "And you're a sweetie, Lacey." He chucked her gently under the chin and she smiled shyly.

With a quick nod at Curt and me, he disappeared upstairs. How many times, I wondered, had these people been here in the past to be on such friendly terms with the kids?

And why had Tina stayed with the villain who was her husband?

As the EMTs wheeled Tina across the living room, she made a feeble motion for them to stop. She looked at me, fighting to stay alert.

"The kids," she said in a barely audible voice.

I laid my hand lightly on her shoulder. "I'll take care of them. Don't worry."

"Jess, Lacey." I stepped back as she reached out a weak hand to them. "I love you. Go with Merry. Tomorrow she'll call Grandmom." She looked at me again. "Tomorrow."

I nodded. "Is your father still in the hospital?"

"Home. Very sick." It was all she could manage. Her eyes lost focus and slid shut.

"I love you, Mommy," Lacey whispered, her voice desperate.

But Tina didn't hear. She was unaware of anything for the moment.

I picked Lacey up and held her tightly as Tina was taken from the house. "She loves you too, kitten." I kissed the little girl's cheek. "She loves you a lot."

I looked at Jess, the little boy who was forced to react like a man. "And you too, Jess. She's so proud of you for all your help."

He looked at me hopefully, his big eyes uncertain. Curt laid an encouraging hand on his shoulder. This time the boy barely flinched.

When everyone was gone but us, I said briskly, "All right, guys. Let's get your clothes and some toys. Come on, Lacey. Show me your room. Jess, will you show Mr. Carlyle yours?"

Lacey's room was absolutely enchanting, a little girl's dream with its white canopied bed, gigantic collection of stuffed animals, and more Barbies than I knew existed. Did her father think that a beautiful room would compensate for the ugly atmosphere she breathed daily? If so, he was more foolish than I thought.

Or maybe it was Tina, trying to create visual loveliness in the middle of emotional deformity.

Lacey pulled a little suitcase with wheels out from under the bed. "It's my visit-Grandmom suitcase," she said. "I'm allowed to put anything I want in it."

"Then you make your choices. Just make sure you have some clothes and not all Barbies."

I was trying to tease her, but she looked at me with such a serious little face that I knew she thought I was telling her what to do. I smiled sadly. "Take whatever you want, Lacey. If you want to take all Barbies and no clothes, go ahead. We'll go buy new outfits tomorrow."

For some reason she thought this was funny and gave me a shy giggle.

Jess wheeled a little visit-Grandmom suitcase from his room, and we loaded the suitcases and the kids in the backseat with Randy. Lacey clung to a battered, fuzzy, once-pink blanket, holding it to her face and rubbing it back and forth between her fingers. Jess had a teddy bear with a missing ear and a dangling eye tucked firmly under his right arm. They leaned into each other, and I almost cried when I saw Jess pat his little sister on the shoulder.

Just before I climbed into my seat, Curt looked at me over the roof of the car. "You want to go to the hospital to see how Tina's doing, don't you?"

I nodded.

"What about our little friends?" He glanced down at the car.

"I don't know. We certainly can't leave them. They need us as much or more than Tina."

Randy leaned out the window. "Mom and I can take care of them. Take us to our house. We've got a guest room they can stay in."

I looked at Randy, uncertain.

With a sad smile, he said, "I know you don't trust me, and I can't say I blame you, but call Mom. She'll tell you to bring them." His lips curled sardonically. "You do trust her, don't you?"

I went back inside to call Edie so we could talk out of earshot of the children. She needed to be able to say no if having the kids was too much for her right now. I just didn't want Jess and Lacey to overhear and think no one wanted them.

"Oh, my goodness, bring them," Edie said without hesitation. "And bring their mother if they don't keep her at the hospital."

"You're sure? This is a tough time for you."

"People stepped in to help Randy and me back when we needed it. I have to step in now. It's my turn. One thing I learned all those years ago. Help is needed when it's needed, not when it's convenient."

I thought about how I'd hesitated to help Randy and felt a strong kick of shame. Maybe one of the great drawbacks to an orderly, happy life like I'd experienced was that you didn't understand immediate and desperate need. You'd never had it.

After I explained to the children that they were going to stay with Randy and his mother, they huddled together and pressed themselves against the far door. They stared silently and skeptically at Randy across the back seat. Lacey hugged her blanket more tightly and Jess pulled his bear against his chest.

Oh, Lord, please let them be okay with this plan.

Finally Jess spoke. "Aren't you big to live with your mom?"

I blinked, startled. I don't know what I expected the boy to say, but that wasn't it.

"I'm not so big," Randy said. "I still go to school."

"You do?" Clearly Jess equated size with maturity. "College? Big guys go to college."

"Not yet." Randy smiled. "Someday."

The kids continued to study him. He sat still and let them stare. Every so often he smiled at them, but their solemn little faces didn't respond.

"I used to have a father like yours," Randy blurted as we turned onto Main Street.

My eyebrows climbed nearly to my hairline in surprise as I heard that confession. I glanced at Curt and saw a similar expression on his face.

Jess looked away from Randy, watching the night speed by outside. "Yeah, right." Disbelief vibrated about him like sound waves about a tuning fork.

"I did." Randy held his hand up like he was taking an oath. "Honest." He caught his little finger under his thumb. "Pinky swear."

The kids blinked, looked at each other, and giggled. "Pinky swear," Jess whispered, like it was the funniest thing he'd ever heard. They giggled again.

"I had to call 911 for my mom too," Randy continued. "Once my father threw her down the stairs and broke her leg."

"That's bad," Lacey said, giggle gone, her intent little face pulled into a frown as she watched Randy.

Randy nodded. "Very bad."

"Did she get a cast?"

"She did. And crutches."

"Does she still got them?"

He shook his head. "She's okay now. That was a long time ago, when I was little like you."

Lacey stared, obviously overwhelmed at the idea of big Randy being little like her.

"What did you do?" Jess asked. "When he did it, I mean." He was back to looking out the window but trembling with the need to hear Randy's answer.

Randy looked out the window too. "Nothing." He swallowed. "I couldn't. I was too little."

Jess gave a great sigh. "Yeah," he said sadly. "Too little."

"But you called 911," Lacey said to Randy. "Like Jess. That was good."

Randy smiled at her. "You're right. I did. Thanks for making me feel better."

She smiled back and stuck her thumb in her mouth.

He looked at Jess. "My mom said it was okay that I didn't do anything more."

Jess glanced at Randy, then away. He nodded. "My mom too."

"But it still hurts. Even today it hurts."

Jess stared at Randy in surprise. "But you're big."

"There are some things you never forget, Jess. You just learn to live with them."

"Oh." He thought about that for a few minutes, his chin resting on the teddy's head. "Oh."

I watched and listened, amazed and impressed. I caught Randy's eye and nodded. He smiled slightly. I was not surprised to see that within a few blocks Jess and Lacey were leaning against him like they'd been leaning against the far door a few minutes ago. Carefully, cautiously, he slid his arm around them.

I welcomed Day Four sitting in the waiting room outside the emergency room, doing exactly what the room was designed for, waiting. I knew they were working on Tina. They had sent her over to x-rays because of her chest pain. How many broken ribs they found I didn't yet know.

I did, however, finally know Tina's last name. Bond.

William Bond, I read as the clerk handed me back Tina's insurance cards.

"William Bond," I said aloud. "William. Bill." My hand flew to my mouth. "Bill Bond! Curt, Bill Bond is Tina's husband!"

"I don't think I'm with you," he said as he led me to a seat.

"Bill Bond is Tom Whatley's boss at Hamblin Motors! No wonder he wouldn't talk to me when I showed up at the dealership. He thought I was there about Tina, about the phone call to Mac, about his threat, when all I wanted was to talk about Tom."

"Didn't you recognize him when you saw him at Hamblin's?"

I shook my head. "I never saw him."

As I sat leaning against Curt, my head on his shoulder, I thought about how small the world could be sometimes. While I hadn't known whom I was seeking an interview with, he had known who I was, thanks to my giving my name when I rescued Tina and the kids from him on Saturday.

But if Bill Bond was Tina's husband, then the man I had seen lecturing Joey Alberghetti as I pulled away from Hamblin's was someone else entirely. Who he was was probably as unimportant as whether Whiskers would wrap himself around my ankles three or four times when I finally got home, but it piqued my interest just the same. I thought about it for about five seconds before questions about Bill Bond took over, questions like *where was he?*

Surely he realized Tina needed medical treatment. He might be reprehensible, but he wasn't stupid. Surely he was concerned enough to seek her out here at the hospital. Even bullies understood the need to show up, to protect themselves if nothing else. But what would he say if he came?

"Sure, I beat her, but I didn't mean to hurt her."

As Randy would say, yeah, right.

No doubt Bill would fabricate some line about her falling down the stairs. He'd certainly had lots of practice. This time, I hoped, I prayed, Tina wouldn't verify his falsehoods. This time, please God, she'd press charges.

I shuddered. Enough of Bill Bond. I turned to Curt. "Tell me about your evening. In all the excitement, we haven't had a chance to talk yet."

He smiled a half smile. "Somehow it doesn't seem quite so important anymore."

"But it is important." I took his hand between mine. "At least it's important to me."

His eyes began to sparkle, and I knew I'd said exactly the right thing. No more mistakes like the other night at the gallery.

"Oh, Merry, it was great!" The joy and happy disbelief in his voice made me smile. "Delia lined up the most incredible people for me to meet."

Delia. It suddenly became harder to rejoice for him.

Oh, Lord, I'm so petty! I'm jealous!

I hated myself for being so small, so mean. I knew it wasn't Delia herself that upset me, in spite of her blond beauty and sophisticated style. I was jealous because Delia could and would do for Curt things that I couldn't. She could give him a gallery showing. She could introduce him to important people. She could open doors to the art community that I didn't even know existed.

And what could I do? Nothing. Nada. Zero. Zip. Zilch. I sighed.

Curt heard and stopped mid effusion. He looked at me, questions written in his eyes.

"Sorry," I said hastily. "It sounds like you had a wonderful time. I am truly glad for your chances to make all these professional contacts."

He grinned knowingly. "It's okay." He leaned over and kissed my temple. "I still love you the best."

I stared at him, appalled he could read me so well. I would have liked to keep my nasty feelings a secret.

"What?" He eyed me cautiously. I could see him going back over his words, looking for his mistake. When he thought he knew what was wrong, he grimaced. "*You only* is what I meant. I still love *you only*."

I nodded. "I know what you mean. It's just a sensitive subject." That seemed a safe comment.

"I know, though I don't know why. I told you she's strictly a business friend to me."

"And I told you I'm not worried about you. You're the good guy. She's the shark."

"And I'm the itty, bitty fish waiting to be devoured?"

I looked at him, all broad shoulders and athlete's body. An itty, bitty fish wasn't exactly appropriate. If indeed he had been an itty, bitty fish, I doubt Delia would have been interested, no matter how fine an artist he was.

"I'm jealous," I confessed in a rush. I never could keep a secret.

He looked at me, amazed. "Whatever for? You're ten times more appealing than she'll ever be."

Momentarily distracted, I stared at him in amazed delight. "Really?" It was obviously time for his glasses to be changed, but what joy his comment gave me.

"It's true," he said, seeing my expression. "She may be sleek and lovely in her own way, but you're real. You have a heart that cries and cares and loves."

"But she can give you so much that I can't!" There. I'd said it. My worst fear. The core of my jealousy.

Curt looked at me and nodded. "You're right. Professionally, she can open doors for me. Knowing her will save me years of trying to establish myself. Professionally, she's a gift from God."

How depressing.

He ran his finger down the side of my face. "However, for real life, for quality, character, and spunk, you win hands down. You beat Delia without even having to try."

I looked into his eyes and saw that for him this was the truth.

"Trust me on this, darlin' girl," he whispered as he bent and nibbled my ear. "I know what I'm talking about."

I shivered and giggled and nodded.

"Excuse me." It was the clerk for the emergency room.

I drew away from Curt and hoped I wasn't too red in the face. I simply wasn't used to being caught in public with a man nibbling on me. Or in private for that matter. Curt, on the other hand, merely turned and looked blandly at the woman, not a single sign of discomposure evident.

I sighed. In that wonderful catalogue of characteristics he had listed for me, he hadn't mentioned sophistication. As I tried to free my hand from his grip, I knew all too well why. I felt a spurt of reassurance when he grinned at me and refused to let go.

"Mrs. Bond is ready to go home," the woman said.

Curt and I sobered immediately, feeling slightly guilty to have forgotten Tina even for a minute or two. We hurried into the emergency treatment area and found Tina sitting in a wheelchair with a physician standing beside her. The doctor's name tag read *Sondra Blanchard, MD.*

"Are you caring for Mrs. Bond?" Dr. Blanchard asked.

"We're taking her to the home where she'll be staying." I gave Edie's name and address.

The doctor nodded. "See that she stays in bed for a couple of days. She looks worse than she is because the injuries are so visible. She has a pair of cracked ribs, but that's about it below the neck. Her face will become a veritable palette of rainbow shades over the next couple of weeks. Nothing to worry about. We stitched up the split lip on the inside, and there should be minimal scarring."

Curt and I nodded, thankful the injuries were not more serious.

Sondra Blanchard looked at Tina but spoke to us. "I told Mrs. Bond that I don't want to see her in here again." She smiled to take the sting from her words. "I want her to contact the authorities tomorrow and take steps to have a restraining order executed against her husband. One of these times he's going to do damage that isn't repairable."

Tina, full of pain medicine, gave a wobbly smile but said nothing.

The doctor patted her on the shoulder and disappeared down the hall, but not before I saw the worried expression on her face. How she must hate cases like this.

When we got Tina settled in the car, we left for Edie's house.

"Kids?" she managed to get out in spite of her damaged mouth. She must feel like she'd taken a trip to the dentist's for treatment that required lots of novocaine, her mouth all droopy and swollen and without feeling. Add to that all the aches and pains in her torso and head.

I smiled at her over the seat. "They're at Edie Whatley's. When we left, they were curled together in Randy's big bed. He was reading to them, and they were about thirty seconds from oblivion."

"Why?"

Why might be all she could say, but I knew she meant, "Why are the Whatleys willing to take us in?"

"You know Tom Whatley from Hamblin's, don't you? And his wife Edie? She works with me at *The News,* but more to the point, she was an abused wife in her first marriage. She wants to help you because people helped her."

"And Randy?"

"Her fifteen-year-old son. He's taken Jess and Lacey under his wing. He knows what they're thinking. He's been there."

At the Whatleys' we found the sleeping Jess and Lacey, teddy and blanket hugged close, cuddled together for comfort.

Randy lay asleep on the floor beside his bed, wrapped in a green sleeping bag.

"He wanted to be near in case they woke up scared," Edie whispered as we all stood in the bedroom doorway.

I looked at Tina and saw tears falling silently. Curt was holding her in his arms, her head leaning wearily on his chest as he carried her to the guest room.

We turned and entered the room across the hall. Edie had made up the bed with peach and yellow floral sheets, a cheery pattern that welcomed Tina.

"You sleep, Tina," Edie said as she stroked Tina's hair. "You're safe here, and I want you to stay here as long as you want. This is your home."

Once again, Edie's hospitality and heart humbled me.

When we turned out the lights and left the room, Tina was still crying silent tears.

Curt drove me home, kissed me at the front door, and left, as weary as I. Whiskers greeted me with enthusiasm as I stumbled to the bedroom, and we fell into bed and slept four glorious but inadequate hours before it was time to get up and face the newsroom.

I shared my breakfast with Whiskers before I left, giving him pieces of my bagel and cream cheese. He fastidiously licked the cream cheese off and abandoned the bagel as he did every morning. I wondered again why I didn't just give him cream cheese and save the bagel for me.

I could take a spoonful and slip it in his mouth, gluing the cheese to the roof of his mouth. My brother Sam used to do this to our dog when he was a kid, only he used peanut butter. He loved watching the dog try to get the stuff off with his tongue. It drove the dog crazy, but it gave Sam many a laugh.

I looked at Whiskers, grooming himself in a shaft of sun. I looked at the cream cheese tub. I looked at the spoon. I sighed. I was a softie. Whiskers and I would go on wasting tidbits of bagels for years rather than me entertaining myself at his expense.

I gathered my things together and went out to my car. I needed to call Edie and find out how the various Bonds had survived the night and make certain that Bill hadn't come near the place.

Had the police found Bill? What could they do if they did? Did they need Tina and her testimony to arrest him? Or could they do it on their own? Would Tina finally cooperate with them? Had last night truly been the last straw? Would she ask for the restraining order?

I sighed as I pulled open my car door. I climbed in and screamed.

I had found Bill Bond, and it was a cinch he was never going to bother Tina or anyone else again.

Chapter 15

Blood, now congealed, had flowed from the wound down Bill's front and onto the seat and the floor. Sitting somewhat slumped in my passenger seat, he looked remarkably similar to Barney Slocum sitting in Randy's car.

"Probably on purpose," William Poole said as the police swarmed over my car. I watched them with a churning stomach and a throbbing head. "Probably the same killer, same gun, same warped reasoning."

"But why my car?" I wailed. As I heard myself, I thought wryly how much I sounded like Randy.

William shrugged, then smiled at me slyly. "You know you're going to lose your car for a while, don't you?"

I nodded in resignation. I'd been down this road before with other cars. "Scene of the crime. But you don't have to enjoy it so much."

I wandered back to my apartment and called Mr. Hamish, the car rental man. In the short time I had lived in Amhearst, he and I had become good friends.

"Miss Kramer," he said, his voice filled with what I thought was unnecessary pleasure. "I hadn't heard from you for a while. I was afraid you found another rental dealer."

"No, no, Mr. Hamish. How could I ever leave you and your wonderful service? I just haven't had the need for a rental for a while."

"And you do now?" His voice dropped to a whisper. "What is it? A murder? A shooting? A deer?" He said the latter like he still didn't believe that story no matter how many times I tried to convince him.

I sighed. Mr. Hamish was an armchair detective, and he loved my adventures, finding them exciting and thrilling instead of frightening and unsettling like I did. I might as well tell him why the rental car was needed. He'd read about it in *The News* anyway.

"There was a body sitting in the passenger seat of my car this morning."

"How awful," he said in a thoroughly delighted voice. This was gruesome enough even for him. "Lots of blood, I'll bet. Bad for the upholstery."

Wasn't it just. "I don't have anyone here who can drive me to your garage," I said. "Can you still help me?"

"Are the police still there?" I could hear the hope in his voice.

"They are." I was sure he was trying to figure out how to rub his hands together in anticipation and still hold the phone.

"I'm sure I can get a car to you within fifteen minutes. Is that soon enough?"

By which he meant, will the cops still be there in fifteen minutes?

"That should be fine," I assured him.

"Good," he said happily. "I'll give you the nice Sable you had last time you needed a rental."

Mr. Hamish showed up in ten minutes, driving my white Sable and followed in another car by a young man he distractedly introduced as his son and partner, Liam.

"Pleased to meet you, Liam," I said, but I might as well have saved my breath. Both of them were too busy watching William and his cohorts to pay attention to something as mundane as an introduction. I had to poke Mr. Hamish in the arm to get his attention.

"The keys?" I held out my hand.

"Oh." He began absently searching his pockets with no success. He took everything out and laid the collection of change, crumpled receipts, paper clips, handkerchief, rubber bands, and Life Saver wrappers on the police car he and Liam were leaning against. He didn't even notice when his wallet fell to the ground. He was too busy looking at the ring of uniforms around my car. The body bag that lay on a low-slung gurney was much more interesting than any old keys. He wandered closer to the action.

Liam rolled his eyes and loped over to the Sable. He reached in and extracted a ring of keys.

I thanked him prettily, but I doubt he heard me. Once he'd done his duty, he had become thoroughly distracted too. Like father, like son, I thought. But at least they always gave me fast service.

As I drove to work, I called Edie.

"Everyone's fine here," she said. "In other words, they're all still asleep, including Randy."

"You would have been proud of him last night, Edie. He was wonderful with those children."

"Sort of scares you, doesn't it? You wonder when he's going to revert." I could hear the combination of hope and fear in her comment.

"Edie, bring him to church Sunday morning. He'll find a stability there that he can't find anywhere else."

Edie made a noncommittal noise.

"Come on," I coaxed. "It's Easter. And Sherrie is singing with the bell choir. He'll like that."

"I'll think about it," she said.

God, please let her do more than think!

I took a deep breath. "I've got some hard news for you. Bill Bond, Tina's husband, was found dead in my car this morning."

There was a moment of startled silence. Then, "Dead? In your car? Bill Bond? But how? Why?"

"Sort of sounds like why Randy's car, doesn't it?" I stopped for a red light. "And he was shot."

"Like the guy in Randy's car? Oh, my!"

"Tell me about it."

"Do I have to tell her when she wakes up?" Edie was fading in and out by now, but I could hear the distress in her voice. I made a mental note to recharge my phone as soon as I got to work.

"No, don't you say anything. You've got enough to deal with without having to handle announcing to someone that she's a widow. The police will come out soon to tell her."

We disconnected to static.

First things first. I called Curt as soon as I reached the newsroom and listened to his wonderfully soothing comfort. Then I brought Mac up to date on the latest death and began writing about Bill Bond. I had to stop and delete a number of times because I found I was writing editorially in what should be a straight news article. My adjectives and adverbs were noticeably negative and entirely prejudicial.

Partway through the article I called Hamblin Motors. I didn't know if they'd be in yet, or if they were, whether they'd heard about Bill, but I needed a quote from Mike Hamblin.

"What?" he shouted in my ear when I finally reached him. "Bill Bond is dead? How can that be? He was fine yesterday!"

"I'm sure the police will have more information than I do," I said primly.

"The police! Why the police? Don't tell me his crackpot wife finally did something to him!"

I thought of Tina, barely able to move last night because of what Bill had done to her, and wondered cynically what Bill had said at work about his wife. I swallowed my ire and forced myself to stick to the original reason for my call.

"I was wondering if you had any thoughts on Bill that I could include in my article on him."

"Oh." Clearly Mike was taken aback. "Like a tribute or a eulogy, you mean? Well, he was a genuinely nice guy."

Sure, I thought. That's why he used Tina as a punching bag.

"And a wonderful sales manager. The customers liked him a lot. They trusted him, you know. We will miss him terribly!" I heard a grunt, a noise of disbelief. "I still can't take in that he's dead!"

If you're surprised, I thought, imagine how I felt when I found him in my car!

And why my car? I thought again, feeling just like Randy.

"Can I come see you, Mr. Hamblin? I'm doing an article in which Mr. Bond is featured prominently. I'd like to ask you some pointed questions about him, see where he worked, that kind of thing."

Now why did I want to go to Hamblin's? Did I want to do an exposé on Bill? Make it part of the Freedom House/abused wife series?

"You were doing an article about Bill?" I could hear reticence in Mike's voice.

"Sure. You just gave me a quote for it. But I was thinking I could do something more in-depth if I could talk with you. A genuine profile rather than a standard obituary. Don't worry. It won't put Hamblin Motors in a bad light. Not at all."

"Oh." Relief. "Well, why don't you come at about six-thirty tonight? I have appointments all day that I cannot get out of, even for something this important."

He was good, I thought, making me feel he valued me even as he set me to his schedule. The trouble was Curt's opening was at seven.

"Can you make it a bit earlier?" I asked.

"I'm sorry; I can't. I would if I could." I heard the flutter of pages like he was checking his DayTimer. "Six-thirty's the best I can do."

I thought quickly. It wouldn't take long to ask my questions. I could be at Intimations well before seven-thirty. That wouldn't be too bad.

"All right. I'll see you at six-thirty."

Shortly after noon I grabbed my notebook, preparing to leave a morose Mac and the oppressive atmosphere of the newsroom to spend my lunch hour at Hibernia Park.

"If Mr. Montgomery doesn't do something soon," fumed Jolene as she yanked a dead leaf from the jade plant, "I'm going to march right up to his mansion and demand he rescue poor Mac—and all the rest of us—from rampant despair."

She stuck her finger dramatically in the air, her stance a good match for the brilliant red and black sweater made entirely of great loops of yarn at least an inch long. It should have made her look enormous, but somehow it emphasized her great figure. "There soon won't be enough St. John's Wort or Halcyon on the planet to save that idiot in the window." She glared at Mac like his job instability and resultant melancholy were by his choice.

"Do you know where Mr. Montgomery lives?" I asked, taken with the idea of Jolene, loopy sweater billowing in the breeze, ringing Mr. Montgomery's doorbell.

Jolene shook her head, unconcerned about that little detail. She was now occupied with her basket of tête-à-tête daffodils and tall narcissi. I watched her skilled hands work with the flowers and had an idea.

"Will you do me a favor?" I asked as I slid into my blue tweed blazer.

She looked at me suspiciously. Most people who asked her for favors these days wanted money. Well, so did I in a roundabout manner.

"You remember Sherrie Bauer?" I pulled my purse from my bottom drawer.

"The kid who had hysterics?"

I nodded. "I've been interviewing her and her mom and learning all about Freedom House for an article. I'm very impressed with them and what they do. Could you make Stephanie one of those wonderful baskets of flowers like you made for Mac?"

"The one he was going to give away? Sure." She waved her hand like it was no great matter. "I'm going to the garden shop over lunch. I'll get the stuff then."

"Could you do me an even bigger favor and drop it off at Freedom House? I don't know when I'll see Stephanie again, and I'd like her to have it before Easter, sort of a holiday gift, you know?"

Did that sound as much like an imposition to her as it did to me? Surely if I wanted to give someone a gift, I should take it myself.

Oh, Lord, please let her bite! And please move her heart when she sees the place and meets Stephanie!

"Sure." She shrugged. "Why not." She grinned. "I'm trying to learn to be nice."

I laughed out loud, making a noise that had been notably absent around the newsroom lately, and left before she could change her mind. I stopped at Ferretti's for a BLT, a bag of chips, and a Diet Coke, all to go. Then I drove to Hibernia Park, passing between the black lion heads set in their white pillars, and down the dirt road toward the picnic grove.

I noticed that three out of the four little whitewashed cottages along the road were occupied. Why was the fourth boarded shut, I wondered. Was it just too small for any modern family to live there, or was there some structural damage? But the sight of the mansion made the little white houses fall from my mind. The warm coppery/orange building was, quite simply, beautiful.

I found a picnic table sitting in a stream of sunlight. I tore my paper bag open and spread it on top of the table. I stood on the bench, turned, and sat on my bag. The sun felt warm and wonderful. I ate slowly and thought as I chewed. Then I just sat in the sun and thought.

Eventually I forced myself to climb out of my sunbeam. I walked slowly across the lawn to the ranger station.

"Hi," I said to the woman named Lori who sat at a desk behind the counter.

"Can I help you?" She rose and came to stand opposite me.

"I was here the other day looking for information about the mansion."

"Oh, yes," she said, quick to smile and reach across the counter to the brochure that I had gotten on Sunday. "This tells you all about it."

I took the brochure and thanked her. "When I was here over the weekend, the ranger and another man were talking about the fact that someone was staying in the park in an unauthorized manner."

She looked at me curiously.

"I'm Merry Kramer from *The News*, and I was just wondering if this person was still around. It might make a good story, you know?"

Lori's face cleared. "It would make a good story, but I haven't heard anyone talk about seeing anyone who shouldn't be here."

"No more blood in the bathroom? No more stolen lunches?"

"What?" She obviously had no idea what I was talking about.

I felt disappointed. "I guess if you don't know anything about anything, whoever it was must have moved on."

"We had someone here about ten years ago, a homeless person. We knew because we found evidence that he was using the washrooms for serious hygiene care. And some campers lost a little food." She was a kind woman. She wanted to give me something I could use in my story. "We've had summer campers who stay the fourteen days permitted, leave for a day, and come back for fourteen more days. They do this all summer because they don't have any other place to live. But I didn't know we had anyone over this past weekend."

I handed her my card. "If you hear anything from anyone, will you call me? I still think it would make a great story."

Lori nodded and I let myself out, careful to take my brochure with me. I went back to my picnic table again and thought some more. Finally, I sighed. There was no story here, just some tramp who'd been and gone.

I was driving through the exit at the far side of the park when a lightning bolt hit me. Of course! Of course!

I drove around the perimeter of the park to get back to the entrance, muttering to myself about the curse of one-way roads. After driving between the twin lions again, I pulled up to the little boarded-up cottage, edged my car off the road, and climbed out.

I looked around at the peaceful scene, the towering poplars and beeches with their branches still leafless against the blue sky, the creek tumbling and creaming over rocks behind the cottage, the slight greening of the earth as new growth pushed its way past the dead leaves of last fall. I heard the chittering of squirrels and the cawing of a crow soaring overhead.

You're crazy, Merry, crazy!

But I walked around the cottage anyway, listening, looking, trying to think like a man who needed to disappear for some reason I didn't yet comprehend. Even so, I almost missed what I was looking for. If I hadn't tripped over a stone hidden under the leaves and put out my hand to steady myself against the cottage, I wouldn't have seen the small smear of dried blood. Rusty red against snowy white.

My heart began to pound. I looked carefully at the side of the house and saw another smear. Now that I knew what I was looking for, the trail of blood smears stood out against the pristine whitewash like flares against a night sky. I followed them to the back of the cottage. There I found a window with the shutter torn free and a large rusty stain defacing the sill.

With the hairs on the back of my neck prickling in anticipation, I made my way to the window. There was no glass, and I looked directly into darkness.

Well, I shouldn't say directly, because the ground fell away behind the cottage, and the window was higher than I. But still all was darkness as I looked up.

"Tom?" I called. "Tom, are you in there?"

There was no answer, but somehow I was aware that the silence had suddenly developed a listening quality. I was also aware that I had decided the man within was Tom Whatley. It fit somehow. That is, if there was a man within.

"Tom, it's me, Merry Kramer from *The News*. I'm Edie's coworker. You remember me, don't you?"

No one answered, but I thought I heard a slight noise coming from that stygian interior.

It could be a mouse, I told myself. Or worse yet, a rat. Or a snake. There were copperheads in the park. I shuddered at the thought of tangling with one of them.

But none of those critters would make that smear of blood on the windowsill or the smears on the whitewash.

I raced around the cottage to the front door. There the padlock mocked me, but I grabbed the latch and tried anyway. The door didn't even rattle under my assault, let alone open. I ran around back again.

"Tom! Can you hear me? Tom!"

I was feeling unhappy about the lack of response from inside when, very distinctly, I heard a weak moan. Then a hand appeared, gripping the windowsill. Dried blood stained the fingernails and light denim shirt cuff.

"Tom!"

As quickly as it had appeared, the hand disappeared, followed by a groan. Then nothing.

Heart pounding, I reached in my bag and pulled out my cell phone. I jabbed 911 but nothing happened. Then I saw the flashing notice: low battery. I felt like screaming in frustration when I realized that with the confusion over Bill Bond this morning, I'd forgotten to recharge.

Muttering all kinds of invectives at myself, I searched madly for some way to raise myself to window height. Tom, if that was Tom, needed help and immediately.

I started for the road. I'd drive my car back, park it under the window, and stand on the trunk. That'd give me plenty of height. I'd only taken a few steps when I dodged a poplar and realized with keen disappointment that the trees were too close to allow for the passage of the car.

The shutter! I swung around hopefully. It wasn't a shutter like I usually thought of them, two pieces that met over a window. This shutter was one large piece of wood painted green, boards nailed across it in a Z pattern to make it sturdy.

My shoulders slumped as I stared at it. It lay on the ground, flat as the proverbial pancake. It would raise me all of two or three inches.

But, I thought, becoming twitchy with excitement, I could turn it on its side and rest it against the house. I grabbed the closest edge and pulled, all set to drag the thing to the cottage and prop it against the wall. Surprise sped through me as my hands slipped. I staggered backwards and fell right on my rump, overset by the unexpected weight.

"It's okay, Tom," I called like he knew or cared about what was happening. "I'm coming. It'll just be a minute."

I pulled myself to my feet and eyed the shutter with a new respect. I took a deep breath and tried again. This time I only tried to lift the heavy wood a couple of inches. While I managed to do so, I couldn't get any purchase to pull. No matter how hard I gripped, my hands slid.

I stepped back and studied the shutter again. I reached my arms as wide as I could, stepped close, and gripped the far edges. I could just grasp them. I lifted.

Again all I could manage was a couple of inches, and my back was not happy about either the weight or the awkward angle. I took a baby step backwards and dragged. The shutter followed. I would have cheered if I weren't panting from the exertion. Step. Drag. Step. Drag. The blood rushed to my head from the downward angle and my hands ached. My back kept complaining with unkind little jabs like electrical shocks and my calves threatened spasms. I gritted my teeth and reminded myself of the absurd folk truth *no pain, no gain*.

After forever, my backside finally bumped into the cottage. I stood, each vertebrae creaking.

"I'm here, Tom. I'm here."

Not that it did Tom much good. The shutter was still flat on the ground, only now it was flat next to the cottage instead of halfway across the yard. How was I to get it against the cottage? Inch by inch, I thought sadly. There was no other way.

So I moved it inch by inch. Lift it a bit on one side and prop it against the house, run around to the other side, lift it a bit, prop, run back to the first side. Lift. Prop. Lift. Prop. All the while, between the oofs and the out-of-breath puffs, I kept up a commentary for the sake of the wounded man inside.

"Hang on, Tom. I'm coming. I'm moving the shutter into place. How did you get hurt? Have you been taking care of yourself? What have you been eating and drinking? Edie's been mad with worry. You should have called her, you know. But she never lost faith in you. Even Randy has confidence in you. Can you believe it? Oh, Tom, I'm almost there!"

Finally the shutter rested against the side of the house at an angle that wasn't too steep for me to run up, yet should be high enough to let me at least see into the cottage. That is, if the shutter didn't slip and collapse onto the ground as soon as I tried to mount it.

I ran to the creek and looked for a couple of rocks that were both good sized and carryable, not an easy combination. After trying several that were simply too heavy, I managed to carry three back to the shutter and space them against the edge digging into the ground. I tried to make them wedge tightly, like putting something in front of a car's tires to prevent the car from rolling.

I stepped back and took a deep breath. I put a foot on the shutter and waited to see what happened. Nothing moved. I slowly put my full weight on that foot. Still nothing moved. I started to walk up the incline and felt the shutter slip. My stomach flipped and I screamed, "Please, God!"

The sliding shutter hit a bump in the stones beneath the whitewash and stopped its downward movement. I stood still, arms outstretched like that would hold the shutter steady. When there appeared to be no further slippage, I took another step and another. Soon I was at the window, and it was waist high.

"Yes, Lord!"

I grabbed the windowsill and peered into the room. Everything was so dark after the light of the wonderful spring day that I could see nothing. I threw a leg over the sill and waited an agonizing couple of minutes until I could distinguish shadows. It was a good thing I waited that long because Tom was huddled at the bottom of the window. If I had climbed in immediately, I would have fallen or stepped on him. As it was, I had to push myself off to the side to avoid him.

As soon as I was inside, I fell to my knees beside him. He hadn't reacted in any way when I had jumped down, and that fact frightened me not a little bit. I reached out and touched him. No response, not even a moan.

He couldn't be dead! Not in the last ten minutes! Please, God!

I felt carefully until I found his face. Immediately my hand stilled as I caught my breath in dismay. He was burning with fever. But that was a good sign, wasn't it? He wouldn't still be hot if he were dead.

I slid my hand to his neck and felt for his pulse. Beneath the hot flesh I felt the shallow but steady beating of his heart.

I slumped with relief.

"Tom, can you hear me? When was the last time you had anything to drink?"

I didn't want to probe to find his wound. I was afraid I might make it bleed or something. I also didn't know what to do if I did find it. Instead I placed my hand on his forehead and smoothed back his hair.

"How long have you been hiding in here? Since Thursday? It must be a while because you stink, but who cares about that? You're breathing!"

I nearly jumped out of my skin when Tom moved his head. He groaned softly and said, "Edie."

"No, Merry."

"Edie, don't leave me."

"Just for a couple of minutes to get help."

"Edie!" He became agitated and began clutching at me.

"Easy, Tom. Be still."

"Edie, don't leave. Don't leave!" He could barely speak, but the anguish in his voice broke my heart.

"It's Merry and I won't." Though how I'd get help and keep that promise I didn't know.

"I love you," he whispered. "I love you."

I gave up on the Merry business and said simply, "I know."

He quieted and I wondered again how I was going to get help.

In the distance I heard a car and wished I had a means of communicating with it. I'd just have to wait until Tom fell asleep again and then go for help. Hopefully that amount of time wouldn't do him any more harm than the time he'd been here already.

Loud bumps sounded from immediately outside and the light from the window overhead was blocked.

"No," I cried, visions of the shutter being replaced dancing like a nightmare through my head. "We're in here."

I lay Tom's head gently on the floor and stood. I sagged with relief when I saw not a shutter but a large man in a tan uniform at the window.

"Who's we and why are you here?" The voice was full of authority and no sympathy. "These windows are boarded shut to keep people out."

"We need an ambulance," I said. "There's a seriously injured man in here."

A flashlight shone in my face. I closed my eyes against the assault and stood still, letting the man look at me. In a short time the beam moved away and focused on Tom.

"Are you Merrileigh Kramer?" The man's voice was abrupt but no longer unkind.

"Yes. How did you know?"

"Your purse is out here."

I remembered dropping it when I started working on the shutter. "Get an ambulance, will you?" I asked. "He's been hurt somehow, but I can't see how in the dark. He's burning with fever. And call the police. Ask for William Poole. Tell him it's about Tom Whatley."

He hesitated, then grunted and disappeared. While I was sorry to lose his presence, I welcomed the sunlight that flowed again into Tom's little cell.

It wasn't too long before the front door of the cottage was opened, admitting more light, and shortly thereafter the police arrived in the comforting person of William Poole, then the ambulance for Tom.

"Have you called Edie?" I asked William as the EMTs worked on Tom. We stood outside in the fragrant fresh air.

"I'm just about to."

"When you're finished, can I talk to her for a minute? I need to know what she wants to do about Tina and the kids."

"What kids?"

"The ones she and Randy took in for the night."

"Randy's home?" He looked none too pleased.

"He went home with the kids. He had to. He slept with them. Oh, William, you'd have been so proud of him last night!"

He didn't look convinced. "I don't think I want to know about this now." He reached for his phone. Edie was crying with relief and joy when he finally passed it to me "for one minute only."

"What about Tina and the kids?" I asked, cutting through her thanks. "Are they all right? Should I come over so you can go to the hospital?"

"Tina's mom picked them up about fifteen minutes ago. Merry, how is he?"

"I don't know, Edie. He's unconscious."

"He's truly alive? You're not just telling me that, and then I'll get to the hospital and they'll tell me the truth?"

"Edie! You've been reading too many novels."

William held out his hand in front of me.

"I've got to go. William wants me off the phone. And he's fine. Well, not fine maybe, but certainly not dead."

And with those happy words, William took the phone. I waited until Tom left for the hospital, never regaining consciousness, then turned to walk to my car.

"Where's she going?" the ranger asked William. "Don't you need to question her?"

"Don't worry about her," William Poole said. "We know where to find her."

I frowned at him. "You make me sound like I'm one of your regular troublemakers."

He grinned, the furrows on his brow undergoing a seismic shift. "You get yourself in enough predicaments to be one."

Chapter 16

I walked into the newsroom feeling as weary as I'd ever felt. The poor night's sleep and the fatigue following the adrenaline high of finding Tom combined to make me crave nothing more than sleep.

I was shocked awake by the great rainbow bouquet of balloons soaring above my chair and the huge vase of velvety red roses sitting in the middle of my desk.

"What's all this?" I asked Jolene who was intent on her computer screen.

She glanced at me blankly for a minute, then leaped from her chair. "Oh, Merry! Congratulations!" She threw herself into my arms.

"Thanks," I said somewhat breathlessly as she squeezed me tightly. "But what for?"

In answer, she stepped back and giggled.

I watched a grinning Mac striding toward me. Grinning. Mac. Those words rarely went together. "You're happy," I told him. "What's wrong?"

"Nothing's wrong. You're just a pessimist."

I rolled my eyes. Talk about the pot talking to the kettle!

He grabbed me in a bear hug and shouted in my ear, "You did it, girl!"

When he released me and I could hear again, I put my hands on my hips and demanded, "Okay, what is going on here?"

He held out a Web site printout.

I grabbed the paper and read. I read it again. I looked up in shock. "Me?"

"You."

Me.

Mac grabbed me again, dancing me around my desk. Any residual fatigue vanished as it hit home. I'd won a Keystone Press Award! Me, Merrileigh Kramer! I'd won for the articles I did last winter on His House and the pregnant girls who lived there.

I began to giggle just like Jolene and doubted I'd ever be able to stop.

"We're saved!" Mac hugged me again. "You saved us!"

"From what?" I asked around a giggle. I sounded like a bleating lamb.

He didn't answer, just grabbed the printout back, and reread it with a satisfied smile.

Jolene took pity on me and explained. "Mr. Montgomery can't very well fire a reporter who has just won such a prestigious journalism award or the editor who came up with the assignment, now can he?"

A small burst of skeptical air escaped me.

"Now, come on, you know he can't," Jo said.

"You're making the assumption that Mr. Montgomery cares about public opinion."

Jo waved that comment away as unworthy. "Everyone cares about public opinion."

There was enough truth there that I decided not to comment. "Are these from him?" I indicated the balloons and flowers.

Mac shook his head. "He doesn't know yet. At least I don't think he does."

"We thought we'd tell him tonight at Curt's show," Jolene said. "Nice and publicly."

I wasn't sure about that idea. "But it's Curt's show. We can't distract from him."

"Yeah, we can." Jo waved that consideration away just like she did everything she didn't want to think about or agree with. "He's so nice he won't care."

She was undoubtedly right, but still . . .

Mac grabbed my arm. "You can tell Monty what a wonderful editor I am—"

"Monty?" Jo and I said together.

He ignored us. "—to think up the series you won for, and I can tell him what a sterling reporter you are, a veritable paragon of prose, a princess of perspicacity, a woman of wondrous wisdom."

Jolene nodded. "And everyone will be impressed beyond all and overwhelm Mr. M. with praise and congratulate him for being wise enough to buy a paper staffed by such clever people."

"And he can't possibly fire any of us!" Mac finished triumphantly.

The coconspirators stood before me, smiling broadly, pleased as punch with themselves and their strategy.

I pointed my finger at them. "You guys are too much."

Jolene batted her eyes. "We try."

I shook my head at them. They were both clever to a fault, unbelievably frustrating more times than not, and incredibly dear to my heart. What if I'd chosen to stay safe in Pittsburgh instead of risking a life in Amhearst? I'd have missed these two wonderful, nutty people, to say nothing of Curt.

"Curt!" I said. "I have to call Curt!"

I grabbed my phone and called his home number, his cell phone, and finally Intimations. No answer anywhere. As I waited through all the empty rings and answering machines, I swallowed my inclination to ask Mac and Jolene what we'd do if their plan didn't work and Mr. Montgomery was still unimpressed with his staff. I shrugged mentally. If their plan didn't work, at least I would have a very impressive resumé.

I grinned as I hung up the phone, undoubtedly looking every bit as demented as Jolene and Mac. A Keystone! It was all I could do not to hug myself.

"The balloons are from me," Mac said, unable to keep the news of his thoughtfulness quiet any longer.

"Balloons," sniffed Jolene, adjusting one of the beautiful crimson roses. She bent to sniff. "Flowers are the proper gift, you idiot."

Mac refused to be chastised as he dragged down a Mylar balloon with a big CONGRATULATIONS imprinted on it and waved it in Jo's face. She in turn pushed the whole bouquet under his nose.

"Flowers," she declared.

"Flowers wither."

"Balloons deflate."

"Flowers die."

"Balloons crawl on their bellies on the floor."

By now they stood toe to toe, and I expected hostilities to escalate momentarily. I thought about stepping between them before they annihilated my gifts but decided against it. They were crazy, both of them, but my life would be so flat without them. I grabbed them about their necks, one in each arm, and hugged.

"By the way," Jo said, rubbing her neck after I released her. "I took your basket to Freedom House." She looked at me sternly. "That place is falling down."

"True," I said, "but you don't need to frown at me. It's not my fault."

"Um." She studied me cynically. "You sent me there on purpose, didn't you?"

"Sure," I said. "I needed the flowers delivered."

She snorted. I grinned.

"Don't think you can charm me." She glowered. "I know a setup when I see one."

"And?" I waited expectantly. *Oh, Lord, let her help! Please let her help!*

"The least I can do is buy decent furniture for her office."

It wasn't what I'd hoped for at twenty-five thousand dollars a month for twenty years, but it was a start.

I hugged her. "Thanks, Jolene. That's kind of you."

"And maybe see that the place gets painted and fixed up."

I grinned. "That's even better!"

"And maybe pay the rent for the first year so they can get Like New up and running."

"Jolene!" I was overcome.

She raised an eyebrow. "Is that enough?"

I pulled a rose out of my bouquet and handed it to her. "You are wonderful."

She leaned over and put the rose back in the vase, smirking all the while. "That's what Reilly always says."

My phone rang as I tried to think of a comeback.

"Thought you'd like to know," William Poole barked in my ear. "Whatley's main problems are blood loss and dehydration. He should be fine in spite of a nasty shoulder wound."

"Thanks, William. That's wonderful news."

At the name *William*, both Mac and Jolene stiffened like a pair of spaniels on point.

"The doctors said that if you hadn't found him when you did, he'd have been in big trouble." William grunted what passed for a laugh. "Not that he's not hurting anyway, but at least it's not life threatening."

"How's Edie doing?"

"She hasn't stopped crying since she got here."

I was laughing when I hung up. So many wonderful things happening all at once!

"What does Poole want? And what's it have to do with Edie?" Mac demanded.

"You know how Tom's been missing?" I began.

"He's been found?" Jolene clapped her hands.

"Where? How? By whom?" Mac demanded, ever the newspaperman hot on the scent of a good story.

"Hibernia. By following a blood trail. Me."

"You? You found him?"

I glared at my editor. "You don't have to act so surprised."

"I'm not surprised. I just can't believe you didn't say anything sooner."

I glanced at the flowers and balloons. "I got sidetracked."

Mac barely gave my gifts a flick of a glance. They were fluff. The story was all. "So give, woman. Tell me every single detail."

So I did, ending with the news that Tom was in the hospital, still unconscious, with Edie at his side.

"But he's going to be okay?" Jolene asked.

"So William said."

"Flowers," she said, completely in character. "We'll send a huge colorful bouquet of spring flowers, including irises and lilies and daffodils."

"Throw in some baby's breath," I said as I shifted the roses to the side of my desk. I had work to do. "I like baby's breath."

Mac nodded approval. "Good, Jolene. Tell them to put a balloon or two in the arrangement. Merry, you get that story written. I've got to call Dawn. She's been praying."

Jolene and I looked at each other. He was going to call Dawn? Because she'd been praying?

He saw our look and quickly turned to stomp back to his desk, but not before I saw the blush suffuse his face. Poor Mac. He was well and truly smitten. And he certainly had good taste, finally, after years of chasing everything in skirts. But I still had reservations.

I made quick notes about my adventure with Tom, then turned off my computer and gathered my belongings. My brain was mush. It was time to go home, regroup for a few minutes before going to see Mike Hamblin, and then moving on to Intimations. I gathered my balloons and roses.

"Don't worry. I'll bring them back," I assured Mac, who frowned as he watched me try to shepherd the uncooperative floaters through the door.

Whiskers loved my flowers.

"Get away from them!" I shouted, shoving him to the floor from the bureau where he sat trying to eat them. "Go bat a balloon."

In fact the balloons scared him as they hovered and shifted and twisted in the drafts. He eyed them fearfully and wouldn't go near them. With an eye to saving my roses, I wrapped the balloon strings about my jewelry box and pushed it next to the roses.

Whiskers sat on the bed and looked longingly at the fragrant flowers, then fearfully at the balloons. He made no move to approach either. Safe for the night.

I pulled on my little black dress, nothing as classy or expensive as the one Delia, Miss Black Dress herself, was certain to be wearing. Still, as I checked myself in the mirror for cat hair, I didn't think I'd shame myself or Curt. I thought I looked as sophisticated as I'd ever get with my black hose and shoes and my one piece of good jewelry—a miniature portrait on ceramic that my great-great-grandmother had painted—pinned to the shoulder of my black dress.

As I pulled into Hamblin Motors at 6:23, I was listening to KYW, the all-news station out of Philadelphia. I wanted to know if there were any reports about Tom Whatley being found. I didn't think the news had leaked yet, but I wanted to know before I talked with Mike Hamblin. One thing for sure: I wasn't going to be the one to tell prematurely. There was too much at stake, like finding the bad guys.

I found an empty parking slot near the front door of the Hamblin showroom, no mean feat with the limited open space on the lot where cars, vans, and pickups sat cheek by jowl. Maneuvering called for an excellent eye and nerves of steel, and I was delighted when I slid into the rare parking slot without dinging Mr. Hamish's car or anyone else's.

Hamblin's sat on Route 30 just east of Amhearst, and the four-lane highway passed mere feet from the showroom. Across the street was a small dying strip mall with a bookstore, a dollar store, and a few other miscellaneous businesses.

I shoved the gear into park just as a knock came on my window. Howard the salesman peered in at me.

I rolled down my window. "Hello, Howard."

He smiled with what he thought was charm. Today he was wearing a cream twill shirt with Hamblin Motors over the heart.

"I'm sorry, but we're closed," he said. "Our colleague died this morning, and we're closing early in memory of him."

I nodded. "Bill Bond."

Howard seemed surprised. "Yes."

I pushed my car door open and stepped out. I flipped the lock switch and closed the door, feeling virtuous about how well I was caring for Mr. Hamish's car. "Mr. Hamblin is expecting me. It's all right."

Howard didn't look convinced and followed me to the glass doors. I pulled the doors open and walked into the showroom. Howard followed.

"It's okay, Howard. Truly. I promise not to steal any of the cars, toy or real."

He frowned at me. Obviously humor wasn't one of his strong points.

"Say." I paused. "Do you guys wear denim shirts one day a week?" I pointed to the Hamblin Motors logo on his cream shirt.

Howard looked disconcerted by the change of topic. "Yes," he said hesitantly. "On Thursday. We have a different shirt for each day of the week. Today's is cream twill, and everyone wears that, even Mike. All except Bill. He likes ..." He swallowed convulsively and looked suddenly sad. "*Liked* to wear a dress shirt and tie. Mike let him since he was sales manager. It set him apart."

"Was Bill good to work for?" I asked gently.

Howard nodded. "I liked him a lot. Every so often he'd get temperamental, but mostly he was fun. He was good at his job." He sighed deeply. "It's so sad!"

I made a noncommittal noise. How could a man be one kind of person at work and another at home? I made a mental note to ask Stephanie if this was a common phenomenon.

Howard led me inside and to a handsome man with dark curly hair standing by the toy showcase against the outside wall of the showroom. The front of the showcase was open, and he had been rearranging the contents, trying to make room for something else by the looks of it.

He smiled warmly when he saw me. "Merry Kramer? I'm Mike Hamblin."

We shook hands while Howard stood watching.

"It's all right, Howard," Mike said, dismissing his salesman. "She and I have an appointment."

Howard nodded, though he still looked at me suspiciously. "Then I'll see you tomorrow, Mike." He turned and walked away.

Mike watched him go. "He's a nice enough guy," he said like he had to explain Howard. "Lots of our customers like his slow, thorough service. He makes them feel safe."

I nodded, not really interested in what the customers thought of Howard. "What did your customers think of Bill Bond?"

"Come on back to my office where we can talk more comfortably," Mike said.

I nodded and followed him across the showroom to the door that Howard had been forced to take me through on my last visit.

When we entered Mike's office, I was immediately taken with a large toy car sitting on his desk. It was about two feet high and three feet long, much larger than any of the toys out in the showcases. It had a long hood, a flat roof, and a rumble seat. Spare tires were mounted on the running boards on both sides just behind the hood . The door to the driver's side was open, and I could see the seats had upholstery that looked as good as new.

"That's one big toy," I said.

Mike laughed. "It's not a toy. It's a showroom sample. I found it at an antique show over the weekend. Some guy sold it to me for a thousand dollars." Mike laughed. "Poor chump."

I looked at the scarred metal of the car. "A thousand dollars sounds pretty pricey to me."

He shook his head. "A model this size is probably worth between twenty-five and thirty grand."

I looked from him to the car in disbelief.

He grinned. "Amazing, isn't it? But I know what I'm talking about when it comes to cars, whether toys, models, or the real thing."

"Do you have any life-sized antique cars like Model Ts or anything?" If he did and Mac thought it would make a good story, I'd give it to Larry, the sports guy. He actually knew one model of car from another, unlike a certain charming journalist who shall remain nameless.

We talked about his antique car collection and the huge garage he'd had built at home to house all ten of them. Rather, he talked and I listened. He told me about the shelves that circled his garage for the huge toy car collection he had, everything from a Stutz Bearcat to the latest Matchbox.

"What you see out there are not necessarily my finer pieces." He waved toward the showroom. "They're the ones my customers like and recognize. The bulk of the collection is at home." He grinned. "I love cars of any size!"

Then he described his security system in much more detail than I wanted to know. As he talked, I thought that the retail car business must be more lucrative than I'd ever imagined. We were talking a big bucks hobby.

Finally we got around to Bill Bond.

"Wonderful, wonderful man," Mike assured me. "Such a tragedy."

"Have you any idea why someone would shoot him?"

He gravely shook his head. "I can't begin to imagine. What is it they always say? *Cherchez la femme?*"

Sure, I thought cynically. Blame it on some poor woman.

I sat forward. "Do you think Bill had a woman tucked away somewhere?" *And did he beat her too?* I wanted to ask.

Mike quickly held up his hands in denial. "No, no. Bill was not the kind of man to have a girlfriend on the side. I was referring obliquely to his wife."

"His wife?"

Mike looked uncomfortable. "She's . . ." He paused. "Let's just say she's unusual."

"How?" I asked bluntly.

He shook his head. "I'm sorry. I shouldn't have said anything. It's all speculation."

I waited a minute, but it was obvious he wasn't going to talk about Tina anymore. Had he just suffered a slip of the tongue, or had he meant to cast doubt on her character, to turn the eyes of people to her as a probable culprit? I wondered what he'd say if I told him that at the time of Bill's death she was almost unconscious from the battering given by the man everyone at Hamblin's seemed to consider so wonderful.

We talked some more about Mike's best buddy Bill, and Mike took me into Bill's office. A picture of his family sat prominently on his desk. Tina smiled warmly at the camera, Jess and Lacey leaned against her legs, and Bill sat behind her, arm lovingly about her shoulder.

A picture's worth a thousand words, they say. Sometimes pictures lie.

"He was a dependable man, always here when I needed him," Mike said, staring at the picture. "We're going to miss him!"

"Did he ever lose his temper with your salesmen?"

"Never. Now why do you ask that?"

"With the customers?"

"Absolutely not."

"So you don't think he had a temper problem?"

"I'm not sure what you're insinuating, but I don't think I like it."

I smiled and changed the topic. "Tell me some Bill stories so I can get a feel for him."

"The customers liked him because he told them jokes and made them laugh."

I waited expectantly, but that was it.

I tried again. "I understand he liked to wear a shirt and tie instead of the staff shirts."

"He had good taste in clothes and liked to dress formally."

I hated interviews like this one where the person appeared polite and cooperative but gave me nothing. The question I had to ask myself was whether the stonewalling was on purpose or not. I made another leap in subject matter.

"How did Bill get along with Tom Whatley?"

Mike blinked. "They got along fine. Why wouldn't they?"

"Bill was sales manager, but Tom was top salesman."

"Bill was proud of Tom."

"No resentment? No jealousy?"

"Bill was a wonderful, wonderful man."

Yeah, yeah, so you've said. "Do you think Bill's shooting has anything to do with Tom's disappearance?"

Mike looked surprised. "I hope not. I do. If they're linked, I'm going to start thinking that Hamblin Motors is the object of some strange vendetta."

I tucked that highly speculative comment away for later thought. "Have you heard from Tom since he went missing?"

Mike shook his handsome head. "Of course not."

That line at least had the ring of truth.

"Why do you think Tom Whatley has disappeared?"

"Men run away for all sorts of reasons." Mike smiled hesitantly. "I'd say *cherchez la femme* again, but this time I wouldn't mean the wife."

I forced myself to smile back, thinking of Edie and her pain. Another woman, ha!

After a half an hour, I bid Mike adieu and walked thoughtfully to my car. I thought of the various things he had told me about Bill, bothered by the fact that none of them had substance, none of them had body. Everything was generalized and nebulous. Where were the "I'll never forget the day that Bill ..." stories?

I turned as I walked across the macadam lot and looked back. Mike had returned to his toy showcase as soon as I walked out the door. As I watched, a big man came from the back of the building and joined him in front of the showcase. I realized I was watching the same two men talk as I had on my previous visit. Mike Hamblin, owner, and Joey Alberghetti, head repair guy.

Something was definitely off-kilter here at Hamblin's. I knew it. I just didn't know what it was yet. Was it Mike? Was it Joey? Was it Bill and his meanness still polluting the air? My great hope was that when Tom regained consciousness, he could tell us things that were now unclear.

I put my hand on my car door handle and pulled. Nothing happened.

Oops, I thought. It's locked.

I reached into my purse and began rummaging for my keys. I couldn't find them. I dumped the bag onto my trunk lid and swished things around, searching. Among the usual detritus of wallet, lipstick, and sunglasses, I found the list I had been looking for last week at the grocery store and three quarters that had escaped my change holder, a pen I had inadvertently snitched from the bank, and several peppermint Life Savers that had liberated themselves from the wrapper, but no keys. I returned the items to my purse one at a time. Still no keys. I felt in my coat pockets. Nothing but crumpled tissues and an ATM receipt for an amount that I didn't think I'd entered in my checkbook.

I thought back to my arrival at Hamblin's. Pull into the lot. Park. Turn off the motor. Jump like an idiot at a knock on the window. Smile sweetly at Howard. Get out. Push down door lock. Go inside.

A chill slid up my back. I peered into the car and there, dully reflecting the parking lot lights, hung my keys in the ignition. When Howard knocked on the window and I began talking to him, my pattern was disrupted.

I'd climbed out without the keys.

Chapter 17

Without much hope, I tried my other car doors. All locked. Why did I have to pick this evening to become responsible?

I sighed deeply. I was already later than I wanted to be for Curt's shindig. Now I'd be later still.

I walked back to the showroom. Surely Mike had one of those long pieces of metal that slid down into a door and popped the lock. I thought nostalgically of old-style locks and straightened clothes hangers. I sighed deeply again and pulled the showroom door open.

Mike and Joey, their backs to me and their attention on the showcase, didn't hear me. I paused as I tried to think of how I might ask for help without sounding like an idiot.

"You found a good deal this time, Mikey." Joey was patting the showroom model that Mike had brought from his office. "Where you going to put it?"

"I'm not sure, but I think it'll fit in here if I take a couple of the toys over to the other case."

"Is there a shelf that's deep enough for it? It's one big baby. You know we're going to have to kill her."

"The shelves are all adjustable. We can make one deep enough with no trouble. Why should we kill her?"

"Because she's going to figure it all out any minute now."

"Her? She's just a cute little chickie. Nothing to worry about."

Joey shook his head. "Don't you read? She's that reporter who already solved a couple of crimes."

"Her?" Mike was aghast. "That little thing?"

"Her." Joey polished the front fender of the model. "So she's got to go. Before she blows the whistle."

"Don't you think someone's going to start noticing that all these dead people have a connection to Hamblin Motors? If she can figure it out, so can the cops."

"All the bodies have to do with *The News*, Mike! Except for Barney, but he don't count. Besides he was found in a *News* reporter's house. With the girl dead too, that's where the cops'll look."

"You hope."

"She goes, Mikey." Joey's voice was steel.

Mike stared at Joey. "You like killing, don't you?"

Joey thought about the idea for a second. "I don't think I like it so much as I don't mind it."

"You're sick."

Joey grinned. "If you say so."

"I still wish you hadn't done Barney Slocum. He was the best courier we ever had. Dumb and dependable is a hard combination to find."

"He was trying to get out, Mikey."

"Why would he want out? He made a bundle driving a car a couple of hundred miles a couple of times a week. The only danger was if he dinged the car, for crying out loud! Then I had to have it fixed before we could sell it."

"He kept muttering something about how his kid was doing drugs. He couldn't deliver them anymore now he saw what they did. All his wife did was cry. Garbage like that. He was even starting to go to church!"

"Church?" There was horror in Mike's voice. "Barney?"

Joey nodded. "To pray for the kid, he said."

"Pray." Mike's voice was full of disgust. "I hate it when a good man gets a guilty conscience."

Joey nodded. "I put him in Tom's garage as a warning, you know? I mean, I had to put him somewhere, right? And no one knew he ran for us. It's not like anyone'd think aha! Barney, Tom, Hamblin's, drugs."

"You'd better be right about that." Mike looked at Joey. "But explain to me how you ever saw a warning in dumping the body."

"The body said this is what happens to people who mess with us. People who start to think about talking." He ran a gentle finger over the roof of the model car. "Are you going to have it restored?"

"I haven't decided. I kind of like it like this, but collectors are used to restored pieces."

"So restore it then. Not that you'll ever sell it." They both laughed.

"Just be careful, Joey. It's dangerous playing games with oblique threats."

"She knew what the threat meant," Joey said softly.

Mike looked up from his showcase. "She?"

"Tom's wife."

"And just how did she know?"

Joey shrugged. "I called her."

"What?" Mike stared openmouthed. "You're crazy! What did you say?"

"I told her that she shouldn't say anything to the cops or else."

"Or else what?"

"She'd get what her old man got."

Mike continued to stare until Joey began to fidget.

"Don't worry." Joey's manner was defensive. "She didn't know it was me."

"You're an idiot!"

"I'm not!"

The men glared at each other, and I could feel the waves of their animosity wash over me. If politics made strange bedfellows, apparently crime made stranger ones still.

Drugs! Hamblin Motors was somehow a center for drug trafficking. And the dead man in Randy's car was a courier, a dumb but dependable courier who'd developed a conscience. Unbelievable!

Taking a deep breath as if to calm himself, Mike turned back to his cars. "Look at the detailing on the interior of this baby. That's why it's so valuable. Be careful, Joey. I don't want to be taken down because you decided to play games."

Once again Joey's gentle hands played with the model. He gave a short laugh of pleasure. "Look! The front seat tilts forward! And the floor brake catches and releases." He laughed again, then glanced at Mike. "Don't worry, Mikey. I'm careful. And we're still going to have to kill her."

Mike sighed. "It's a shame. She's sort of cute, you know? So serious when she asks her questions."

A terrible chill swept over my body, freezing me to my core.

"We wouldn't have to do her if you hadn't gotten carried away last night." Mike rubbed the roof of his model with a soft cloth.

"Well, you should have seen him last night. He was a madman. You'd have killed him too."

"He came here?"

"He wanted to score, and he was in bad shape. He must have gone after his wife again. His knuckles were all bloody and he had blood stains on his shirt. But it was the gun he was waving that made me sort of nervous."

"Bill had a gun?" Mike was incredulous.

"He said it was to keep that Tina witch in line. She wanted to leave him and take the kids and he wasn't going to let her."

"So why'd he want to stop her? All he did was beat her. He should have let her go and gotten someone he liked."

"Mikey, for a smart man, you're dumb. It was the beating he liked."

Mike shuddered. "That's sick."

"Maybe, but it's power. And so was the gun. He was going to use it to threaten her and the kids."

"The man was a miracle at selling cars, but he couldn't keep his hands off his wife. And that wasn't enough. He was going to shoot her? It's a good thing he's dead. I'd have had to fire him."

"He didn't know what he was saying. He was falling apart before my eyes, needing a fix so bad he was shaking and sweating. Ugly." Joey snorted. "He threatened to do to me what he did to Tina, all the time waving the gun at me. I didn't know if he meant he'd beat me or shoot me. Like he'd ever lay a finger on me. But the gun. Any fool can pull a trigger. It was me or him, let me tell you. The guy was going to shoot m—Hey, the trunk opens too!"

"That's a rumble seat, buddy, not a trunk."

I listened, unable to believe what I was hearing. Models and murders—and my murder!—discussed in the same casual tone of voice.

"Rumble, schmumble," Joey said. "If you move that Model T and that Oldsmobile on the second shelf to the other case, you could lower that shelf and have plenty of room for the model. Our weak link, besides that girl and she's easy to fix, is Tom. If he shows up, we're in deep trouble, and I mean deep!"

"Grab the Olds, will you? And the Model T? And I don't think he's going to show, not after all this time. He's dead somewhere."

"You wish." Joey reached into the case and pulled out two of the cast-metal cars. "I know I hit him; I just don't know how bad."

"Next time you'll shut your office door before you hand out any bags."

"How was I supposed to know he was still here? He should have been long gone. Instead he drives that car off the lot and into the garage as cool as you please. He pulls up right next to my office. 'Hey, Joey,' he calls out the window. 'This car's got a knock like you wouldn't believe. You'd better fix it before we show—' Then he realizes what he's seeing. Me and Bill and him stare at each other for a minute, sort of frozen like. Then he hits the gas. I run after him and take a shot at him. I know I got him because the car swerves into that light post out there." He jerked his head toward the lot.

Mike grunted as he wrestled with the metal supports that held the shelves in place in his case. "He'd better be dead, Joey. I'm not taking the fall for your stupidity."

Joey straightened to his full height and glared at Mike.

"Don't try and threaten me with your size, Joey." The last of the metal supports came free and Mike placed them in a position that would allow room for his new model. "I'm in charge here, and don't you ever forget it. You're a rich man because of me."

"If it hadn't been for me, you'd never have made the original contacts, and don't you forget that," Joey said.

Mike grunted as he set the glass shelf on the newly positioned supports, then took his prize and slipped it into the case. "Nice." He nodded with satisfaction.

"Nice," Joey agreed. He handed one of the toys to Mike and they started to turn.

Suddenly reality slapped me across the face, and I dropped to the floor, hugging a sports utility vehicle of some kind. If they found me, I knew all too clearly what would happen to me. The only question was whose car they would put my corpse in.

I could hear the men walking across the showroom to the other toy showcase. Under cover of their footsteps, I slipped under the SUV, thankful for the high-slung chassis. I crouched against the inside of the front passenger tire, making certain that nothing like a foot or the hem of my new red coat stuck out. All I had to do was stay here as quiet as a mouse until they left. Then I could get out of here, call William, and report what I'd heard.

It seemed such a good plan when I made it.

"Hey, Mikey," Joey called in an excited voice. "She's still here."

My heart stopped midbeat.

"What do you mean, she's still here." Mike's voice had a chill that froze my blood.

"That white Sable out there?" I could just imagine him pointing. "That's the car she came in. I saw her climb out, talking to that imbecile Howard."

"Then where is she?"

I pressed myself against the tire and prayed. I heard the two of them moving around the showroom, looking in all the sales cubicles, opening the door back to Bill Bond's office.

"We've got to check the garage area," Joey called as he went through the door to the offices.

I strained to hear whether both of them had left the showroom or if it was just Joey. I didn't have to wait long before I heard the *click, click, click* of Mike's feet as he slowly circled the showroom once again.

As he moved away from me down the inside wall, I dared turn and study the distance between my hiding place and the door to the outside. Surely I could make it to and through the door when he was at the far end of the room. All I had to do was make the parking lot and run screaming into the street. There was enough traffic that I would be safe.

I rolled to my knees, preparatory to making my mad dash. I shook off my coat on the theory that in my black dress I'd be harder to spot as I ran. I glanced back over my shoulder to see where Mike's feet were.

And looked directly into Joey's eyes.

He was crouched on the far side of the SUV, looking directly at me with a smirk that made my skin crawl. As fast as a striking snake, his hand reached out and fastened about my ankle.

I screamed. I hate screaming women. I read about them in novels all the time, and they always sound so wimpy. I joined their ranks without a second thought.

Not that the scream did me any good. It was purely a reflex response, the result of feeling that huge, callused hand wrap itself about my leg. And when he began to pull me inexorably toward him, I screamed again. I also began kicking at his hand with my free foot, landing more blows on my own ankle than his hand. Once he hissed in pain, and I felt a surge of victory. Then I missed and the heel of my dress pump rasped over my ankle, shredding my stockings and drawing blood. He saw and smiled nastily.

Suddenly both ankles were imprisoned by those cold hands and I was pulled ignominiously from beneath the car on my stomach, my little black dress rutching up to my thighs, getting all wrinkled and dusty, certain to make Curt feel less than proud when he saw me. Not that it probably mattered. I was in grave danger of not making it to Intimations or anywhere else ever again.

As Joey dragged me inexorably into the space between the SUV and the sports number parked next to it, I grabbed frantically at the front tire of the SUV as I slid past.

Oh, dear Lord, help!

I dug my nails into the rubber or whatever it is that tires are made of these days, wrapping my hands about the back of the tire where it met the hub. I managed to slow Joey down, and then, to my surprise and relief, bring him—or rather me—to a stop.

He released my legs, and I began to scramble back under the car, hope burgeoning. How premature. With daunting ease, he stood, leaned over, and grabbed me about the waist.

My body jackknifed as he tucked me under one arm. The air rushed out of my lungs like I was a leaky balloon. My fingers lost their precarious hold on the tire, and I tore several nails as I scrabbled for another grip. I slammed my head against the lower edge of the driver's door, striking hard enough to paint a field of stars and red flashes behind my eyelids.

Joey walked across the showroom with me dangling at his side like Raggedy Ann. He dropped me unceremoniously in a heap beside the showcase where Mike was waiting.

"It worked, Mike. Dumb woman thought I'd left the showroom. She fell for my little trick just like we knew she would." He sneered down at me. "She was so easy."

Joey was obnoxious even when he wasn't filled with overweening pride, but I found him particularly repulsive at that moment. I shook my head to clear it and pushed myself to my knees, refusing to lie at his feet like an overcome Victorian maiden. My head ached fiercely, but I wasn't going to go gently into that good night. No, sir, I was not.

Mike looked down at me with disdain. "She's yours, Joey. Kill her. Just don't put her in my car. I don't want the cleanup bill."

They both laughed at Mike's clever repartee while I dragged myself to my feet by holding onto the shelves of the showcase.

"And, Joey." Mike's voice became steely, reminding both Joey and me that he was the man in charge. "I don't want any possible connection to the dealership."

Joey nodded. "Not to worry, Mikey. Not to worry."

I stood, swaying gently. My hand closed around the roof of one of the toy cast-iron cars as I grabbed for a handhold to keep from falling. My shoulders slumped and my head hung.

"Get rid of her," Mike ordered again and turned his back, his contempt for me written boldly in every line of his body.

Joey reached a hand in my direction as I swayed yet again, carefully leaning away from him. He was grinning broadly at what easy prey I was when I swung the cast-iron toy clasped in my hand full at him. The collision with the side of his head startled and rocked both of us. Shards of pain raced up my arm and across my shoulder, but Joey fared worse. His eyes went vacant and he slid silently to the floor, unconscious.

Mike turned at the sound of the blow, and I felt a thrill of satisfaction at the disbelieving expression on his face. Then his eyes narrowed, and I felt a jolt of fear.

OhLordohLordohLordohLord!

I turned and raced for the door. I pushed it open and ran into the parking lot, his footfalls pounding behind me. I sped toward the street and the traffic with the drivers and the passengers who would be there to save me.

But there was no traffic. Not one single car. I raced straight down the middle of the lefthand lane in stunned disbelief. Where was a traffic jam when you needed one?

I knew I couldn't outrun Mike. After all, I had on dress shoes and my legs were much shorter than his. But I ran for all I was worth as my side began cramping and my lungs felt filled with fire as they gasped for oxygen.

What if he has a gun?

That thought ratcheted up my panic several notches. Suddenly my shoulder blades itched like a flotilla of mosquitoes had picnicked on them. Telling myself that he'd been unarmed when we talked and that he hadn't had time to get a gun before chasing me did nothing to ease the feeling of a bull's eye painted smack-dab in the center of my back.

I tried to judge how close behind me Mike was, to hear his footsteps slapping the street, but I was breathing so harshly that I could hear nothing. I fought the urge to glance back, knowing it would only slow me down and frighten me further.

When I heard a car, I wanted to sing with relief. Rescue was at hand! I turned and stood still, waving my hands and shouting, "Help! Help!"

My relief turned to terror when I realized that the car was driving in the wrong lane. It wasn't slowing but driving full speed straight at me. The headlights grew and grew until they merged into one cyclopean eye leading the roaring monster to devour me.

I raced for the side of the road and the great sycamore that stood there, desperate for its protection. I dived behind it, my pulse pounding, my blood thundering in my ears. I screamed as the car roared past, inches from the boll of the tree, inches from me.

My hands ground painfully across the gravel at the base of the tree until I slid to a halt spitting dirt. My knees fared no better, but I didn't care. He'd missed me!

As I lay there gasping and thanking God I was still alive, a deep rending noise filled the night, setting up gooseflesh all over my body. I rolled onto my side and saw that while Mike had missed me and the sycamore, he hadn't been able to avoid a large rock just beyond. He had driven right over it, and it had promptly ripped the undercarriage of the car to shreds. He was going nowhere, at least not on his wheels.

I pushed myself unsteadily to my feet and stood weaving as I waited to see if the car burst into flames or self-destructed in some other way, a probable sign I watched too much TV. Nothing happened, unless you count a swearing and apparently uninjured Mike climbing from the ruined car. He balanced himself against the side of the car and began searching the darkness for me.

I didn't wait until he spotted me. Once again I began to run, fear licking at my heels. As I raced across the still deserted highway, this time I heard his footfalls loudly and clearly as he chased me. I took a perverse satisfaction from the fact that his breathing quickly sounded as labored and gasping as mine. I refused to think about how close he must be if I could tell so accurately how out of condition he was.

I forced myself to keep running. My goal was the large shopping mall a quarter of a mile away. People and safety!

OhLordohLordohLordohLord!

After a seeming eternity I dashed down the grassy swale that separated the road from the mall parking lot. The bright lights of the stores beckoned to me, offering hope and protection. I ran straight toward them, but they were still so far away, at least the length of a football field. I despaired reaching them before Mike reached me.

Some distance ahead at about the twenty-five yard line two cars pulled out of their parking spots.

"Help!" I shouted, waving my hands like a madwoman. "Help!"

Both cars turned away from me and pulled onto the drive that ran beside the mall sidewalk.

"Back here!" I yelled, "Help! Please!"

They drove away as I groaned my disappointment. I risked a glance over my shoulder and screamed. Mike was mere feet behind me.

I had been running down the wide lane between the parking rows. At about the fifty-yard line I came upon the first two parked cars. I swerved suddenly, running between them. I could hear Mike immediately behind me, his hand slapping against one of the cars as he attempted to make the same abrupt turn I had.

I danced around a shopping cart abandoned between the cars, then stopped. I whirled, grabbed the cart, and shoved with all my might. It careened down its narrow alley right into Mike, catching him in the stomach. He and it were tangled and falling when I raced away.

The stores drew ever nearer, but still no moving cars, no people. Directly ahead was the Chester County Book Company, its lights ablaze, and I could see a clerk at the sales counter. I raced the last few yards with my skin twitching in expectation of a hand falling heavily on my shoulder at any second. I yanked open the store door and raced inside, so out of breath I could barely speak.

"Help!" I managed between gasps as I all but fell onto the sales counter. "Call the police! Help me!"

The clerk, a middle-aged woman with a soft jawline and wary brown eyes, stared at me.

"Police! Please," I begged as I glanced over my shoulder. I gave a little scream. Mike was standing on the sidewalk just outside the store, staring at me through the great storefront window, his expression a mixture of malevolence and uncertainty. I bolted instinctively, driven by fear of him, dodging between bookshelves until I got as far from the front of the store as I could. I ended up in the last aisle, crouching in Inspirational/Religion. There was no one there except me.

As I tried to slow my breathing so I could hear what was happening in the front of the store, I noticed I was stooping in front of a shelf of Bibles. I wanted to grab an armful, all different translations, and hold them in front of me to ward off the evil that was Mike, sort of like using garlic or the sign of the cross to ward off a vampire. But even in my fear, I knew the Bible wasn't merely a talisman to be used as a good luck charm. It was the very Word of God, and as such I respected it.

And the God about whom it taught.

I felt my fear lessen as I thought about the Lord.

Help me think clearly, Lord. You said that if I walked through the flood, you would be there and the waters wouldn't overwhelm me. You said that if I went through the fire, you'd protect me. Well, I'm pretty wet, and the flame's awfully close! Be with me now.

Feeling much calmer, I moved to the end of my aisle and peeked out. I couldn't see Mike, and I didn't think he'd followed me into the store. Now that I was reasoning instead of reacting, I knew he wouldn't dare come in. Too many people, too much light. I was safe as long as I stayed here.

I looked behind me. I knew there was another door somewhere back there. There had to be, fire regulations being what they were, to say nothing of delivery men needing access. If I could get to that door and out, I could disappear into the darkness. I could escape completely.

But could I? It was dark and deserted behind the store at this time of day. No deliveries or delivery men. What if Mike was waiting for me out there? I shivered at the thought, rubbing my arms to take away the chill. Forget the back door.

I took a deep breath and walked purposefully toward the front of the store with its lights and counter and customers.

I reached the counter just as the sales clerk replaced the phone in its cradle. "The police?" I asked.

She nodded and looked at me cautiously, I can only assume to judge if she'd done right. Like most people, she probably didn't want to think she'd called in a false alarm.

"Thanks." I smiled and hoped I looked saner than I had a few minutes ago when I rushed in screaming.

"They said they'd be here as soon as they could, and you should remain in the store until they got here." She folded her hands on the counter in front of her.

I nodded. "Do you mind if I call them again? I could explain my problem better." In truth, I felt an overwhelming need to talk to William Poole. I held out a hand toward the phone.

I saw for the first time the scrapes and cuts on my palms, the blood and broken nails. I was stunned. I hadn't realized I'd been hurt so badly. Also for the first time, I became aware of the burning pain.

I glanced down my body and grimaced at my dress, dirty and wrinkled, a trip to the dry cleaners its only salvation if I discounted the three-corner tear near the hem. I stared silently at the ruins of my hose and the bloody abrasions on my knees which had suddenly begun hurting too. My ankle, swollen and bruised, throbbed where I had kicked myself as I tried to get away from Joey.

But I was alive, safe here in the store, and I had a story that would jolt Amhearst. Hands, knees, and ankles would heal, and compared to what Tom Whatley had been through, my plight was nothing.

I was smiling at how fortunate I'd been when it suddenly occurred to me that standing here in front of huge plate-glass windows was not the wisest thing I could do. Who knew how desperate Mike felt and what he might do. He stood to lose both his legitimate business and his illegitimate one, his reputation and his much-loved cars, both big and little, when I told my tale. In exchange he'd gain an orange jumpsuit with a number stenciled on its back and a compact little room without a seat on its toilet.

That well might be enough to drive a man to shoot. I didn't think he'd been the one to do any of the killing thus far; that had been Joey. Mike hadn't dirtied his hands that way. Apparently he saw himself as a businessman, carefully overlooking all the ruined lives that resulted from the drugs he'd been supplying.

But he was no longer a secret success. He was about to become a well-known criminal, a situation that might drive him to atypical behavior. Desperate men in desperate straits did desperate things, like shooting witnesses.

A large support pillar reaching from floor to ceiling stood nearby. After an apprehensive glance out the front window, I quickly moved behind it. The sales clerk watched me much like an animal trainer might watch an escaped lion.

"Please," I called across the space between us. "The phone? You dial this number for me, okay?" I gave her William Poole's office line. "Then hand me the receiver."

The sales clerk nodded, dialed, and passed me the phone. Apparently she decided I was all right in spite of my appearance because she said, "I'm going to get you a damp cloth and some Bactine."

I smiled my thanks and leaned against the pillar. Of course I got William's voice mail. I pushed the proper numbers for a transfer to a dispatcher.

"Sergeant Poole is currently in the field," the dispatcher told me. "Would you like to speak to someone else?"

"This is an emergency. Please forward my call to him. Tell him it's Merry Kramer and it's about the Tom Whatley case. I know who shot him and why."

Chapter 18

The police cruiser pulled up in front of Intimations and I climbed wearily out. I'd spent the last hour with William, telling him what I knew and watching as the police swarmed Hamblin Motors, establishing a crime scene that took in the whole property and everything on it, including my car. Or rather Mr. Hamish's car. Hence the need for a lift.

"Thanks, Jeb," I said just before I slammed the door.

Jeb Lammey smiled at me. "Don't you worry, Merry. We'll have him in no time."

I nodded. "Of course you will. You guys are the greatest."

Still, I didn't like the idea that Mike Hamblin was on the loose. When the police arrived at Hamblin Motors, they found Joey sitting on the showroom floor holding his head. He was sent to the hospital where they determined he had a concussion. Tomorrow morning he would be on his way to jail.

"You did good, Merry," William told me as he watched the ambulance drive away with Joey and a patrolman. "You're one feisty lady."

"That's me," I said wearily. "Can I please go to Curt's showing? I need to be there for him. If you need to talk to me more, you can do it later, can't you?"

"Do you want to stop home first to change or something?"

"William, are you telling me I don't look lovely?"

"Uh." He thought for a moment, his furrowed face becoming a veritable landscape of hills and valleys. "Yeah. That's what I'm saying."

I gave a little laugh. "An honest cop, just when you don't want one." I patted his arm. "Thanks for the offer, but there's not time. I've got to go as I am, or it'll all be over before I arrive."

I'd almost fallen asleep on the way to Intimations.

"Remember, Merry," Jeb cautioned as I slammed my door. "No dark alleys."

He pulled away and I turned to the gallery. I had almost reached the front door when an arm slid around my waist and a desperate voice hissed in my left ear, "Don't make a sound or I'll hurt someone."

Even as I tensed, a smart-mouthed response echoed inside my head: "Gee, I wonder who that someone would be?"

Oh, Lord, it's flood and fire time again. Protect me.

"Don't do this, Mike." I twisted to look over my shoulder at him, thinking that looking him in the eye might make killing me much harder for him. "You haven't killed anyone yet. Don't start now. You don't want to be tried for murder. Drug trafficking's bad enough."

He made an indecipherable noise that could have meant anything.

"It's all over, Mike. The police are at Hamblin Motors. Joey's in custody. You know as well as I do that he'll say anything to try and get off. Turn yourself in. Cooperate. Tell your side of things. Make it easy for yourself."

"Shut up! Don't tell me what to do." His voice shook and he refused to look at me, staring over my shoulder at the dark street. "I've got a gun in your back." He poked me to be certain I felt it. I did.

"Don't do it, Mike, for your sake as well as mine."

"Move," he commanded. "Into that alley over there."

"Over there?" I asked, pointing.

"Yes." He released the pressure about my waist and gestured with the gun. "Move."

Instead I turned to face him full on.

Years ago my mother had a cleaning lady named Lillian, highly undereducated but absolutely obsessed with every crime that ever happened. The more violent the crime, the more she was fascinated/repulsed by it. She was a devoted watcher of the reality shows about police chases and accidents and tragedies. She followed lurid cases with an intensity usually reserved for commodities traders toward the stock market. The gorier the crime, the more involved she became, and the more she had to say. Some of her opinions were even logical.

"If somebody ever tells me to get in a car at gunpoint," she said many a time, waving her arms for emphasis, "I'm going to say, 'Do I look like an idiot to you? You want to shoot me, shoot me here where there's people around. I ain't going with you, no, sir.'" And she'd shake her head with finality.

Lillian's wisdom roared through my mind like a freight train.

"Move," Mike ordered again.

"No," I said. "I'm not going with you."

He blinked and raised the gun.

I squared my shoulders and stared at him defiantly. "If you want to shoot me, you're going to have to shoot me right here with me looking you straight in the eye and where all the people at Intimations will hear the shot and come running."

Mike waved the gun in my face. "I mean it when I say I'll kill you."

"Maybe you do, maybe you don't. But why should I make it any easier by going down a dark alley?" And I quoted Lillian. "Do I look like an idiot to you?"

Behind me the door to Intimations opened and a burst of noise filled the street. The owner of a local real-estate business and his wife exited the gallery amid vociferous good-byes.

"Turn yourself in, Mike," I breathed even as I turned my back on him.

"Hello, Mr. Ellis, Mrs. Ellis," I said loudly and made a run for them, my back twitching once again. It occurred to me that if I developed a nervous tic as a result of tonight's happenings, I should send the doctor's bills to Mike. Not that he'd have the means of paying them when William got finished with him. "You know Mike Hamblin, don't you?" I turned and pointed in Mike's direction.

"Who?" Mr. Ellis asked.

Mike was gone.

My hands stung as the cool metal of the Intimations front door bumped my abraded palms as it closed behind me. My knees hurt every time I took a step. I was limping on my swollen ankle, and I ached from head to toe.

But this was Curt's night, and I was going to share it with him if it killed me.

I was thankful for the milling crowd that hid me. If I could get to the ladies' room before anyone noticed me, I knew I could repair much of the damage that had been done to my person. I could wash my hands and knees and get rid of the blood. I could comb my hair, brush the dirt off my dress, and take off my stockings. Bare-legged would be better than laddered as I was now. I looked for the rest room sign.

I spotted Curt near the back of the room, his dark curls gleaming in the state-of-the-art lighting the gallery boasted. He looked wonderful, his handsome face alight with vitality and life, his intelligent eyes behind their glasses intent on the person to whom he was speaking. The intervening crowd prevented even a glimpse of the person beside him, but I would have been willing to wager that I knew who it was. And I knew she was lapping the attention up like a thirsty pup did water.

Not that she was as awkward as a pup. Or as uninhibited. Or as cute.

I grimaced as I heard myself. *I'm sorry, Lord. That wasn't particularly nice.*

I found the rest room sign and was about to sneak off in that direction when the crowd between Curt and me suddenly separated as neatly as a block of butter when someone draws a warm knife through it. He lifted his head and looked directly at me.

And smiled. Full wattage.

My stomach did a somersault, and I smiled back with all my heart.

He gave a little come-here jerk with his head, and I began walking toward him.

I had been right. It was Delia standing beside Curt. He stood with his hands in his pockets, and she stood pressed close, her arm laced through one of his. The two of them were talking to her father and another man who stood at Curt's right, but I hardly noticed them. For a minute all I saw was her hand resting possessively on Curt's arm.

I sighed. She looked beautiful in a sleek black floor-length dress whose simple lines screamed big bucks. Her blond hair was pulled back in a slick knot at her nape, not an escaped wisp in sight. Marvelous golden earrings danced at her ears, her only jewelry. She was her own best ornament.

But Curt was smiling at me.

I knew the moment Delia realized she no longer had his attention. She went still, and I could see her eyes narrow. Slowly, gracefully, she turned to follow his line of sight. When she saw me, she blinked in disbelief, in distaste, in scorn. Halfway across the gallery I could hear the sharp click of her tongue, a definite sound of disgust.

And still Curt smiled. And I continued smiling back, steadfastly ignoring Delia.

It was an act of faith, that walk across the gallery. I was choosing to believe he had meant it when he told me, "You beat Delia without even having to try."

The contrast between the two of us women would never be greater than right now, I thought. If his love were at all wobbly, all of us would know it shortly.

By the time I reached Curt, the pleasure in his eyes had been replaced by concern. I realized he hadn't been able to see how disreputable I looked when I'd been back by the door. Now I stood before him in all my wretched glory.

Delia shuddered gently and did her best to ignore me. She pulled at Curt's arm and indicated the man across from her. "Curt, Mr. Whitsun has a point about . . ."

But Curt wasn't listening to her. He was still smiling at me. He took a step in my direction, pulled his hand from his pocket, and reached for me.

"Are you all right?" he asked in a gentle voice.

Nodding, I put my hand in his. My heart pounded with joy. He had spoken truly about loving me. He had chosen me. I couldn't stop grinning.

Then he gave my hand a squeeze.

I gasped and tried to pull away.

"Merry!" He lessened his grip but didn't release me. He turned my hand palm up and looked at the dirty, bloody mess.

"I took a dive behind a tree and skinned my hands and knees," I said before he could say anything more. "But I'm okay."

"Are you sure?" It was Mr. Whitsun looking unconvinced. He was staring not at my hands but at my legs with the ruined hose, brush burns, and blood. I looked down and grimaced.

"If this were New York," he continued, "I'd say you'd been mugged but good."

"It's just surface injuries," I said. "You should see the other guys." And I grinned.

Mr. Whitsun laughed companionably.

Curt pulled me against him and wrapped an arm about my shoulders. He seemed oblivious to Delia hanging on his other arm. Even she was finally struck with the obvious: Curt had chosen. She pulled her hand free, and immediately Curt wrapped his other arm around me too.

I rested my head against his shoulder and thought how utterly weary I was and how wonderfully sturdy he felt. I began to relax, a dangerous thing when you're as beaten up as I was. I ordered starch back into my spine and hoped I could continue to stand upright.

I smiled prettily as Curt introduced me to Mr. Whitsun, the man from the Broughley Gallery in New York.

"Mr. Whitsun is going to take four of my paintings," Curt said, pride and satisfaction filling his voice.

"Oh, Curt, how wonderful!" I hugged him about the waist, taking care to turn my hands palm out. "I'm so glad for you. You've made a wise decision, Mr. Whitsun."

Curt turned to the fourth member of the group. "Mr. Montgomery, you remember Merry, don't you?"

Mr. M was looking at me with as much favor as his daughter.

"Good to see you again, Mr. Montgomery," I said. "I didn't get a chance to speak with you at *The News* when you stopped in for that brief visit the other day."

I heard myself and flinched at the indiscretion. Referring to his turn-tail visit wasn't the wisest thing I'd ever done. It must be post-trauma stress. Rather that than that I was just too dumb to keep my mouth shut.

Mr. Montgomery looked at me, appalled. "You work for *The News?*"

I nodded.

"I thought you were just a friend of Curt's," he said, his tone making it obvious that "just a friend of Curt's" could be ignored. If I worked at *The News*, he'd have to pay attention to me, if only to decide to fire me.

Curt heard the insult and gave my shoulders a squeeze. "Merry's a lot more than just a friend, Mr. Montgomery. She's the love of my life."

His easy statement took my breath away and sent color flooding my face. Mr. Whitsun smiled indulgently at me while Mr. Montgomery looked sharply at Delia. Poor Delia.

"Merry! Where have you been?" Jolene rushed up to me, took one close look, and said again in horror, "Where *have* you been? You look terrible!"

"Jo, ever tactful." Reilly, Jolene's husband, stepped up and gave me a quick hug. "You know Merry always looks wonderful."

"I know." Jo was still staring at me aghast. "She's one of those cute-as-a-bug's-ear girls who is so adorable it makes your teeth ache. Usually."

"But not tonight." Mac had appeared behind Jolene and was peering at me through narrowed eyes. "What happened? Who did this to you?"

I grinned at him. "Have I got a story for you!" I said at the same time Curt said, "She fell."

Curt looked at me with one eyebrow raised. "Didn't you?" He hated it when I got myself in danger because of my job.

Before I could explain, the front door to Intimations flew open, and William Poole stalked in, looking as official and authoritative as I'd ever seen him. People stepped quickly out of his way as he moved purposefully toward us.

He stopped in front of me and said, "He turned himself in."

"Good." Satisfaction coursed through me.

"He said you told him to."

"I did."

"When he had a gun in your face."

I heard several gasps, but Curt's "Merry!" was the loudest by far.

"Who had a gun in your face?" he demanded.

"Mike Hamblin," I said.

Jolene gave a little scream. "You went there to do an interview and he stuck a gun in your face and you got him arrested? Nobody's going to want to talk to you after this."

I ignored her and said to Curt, "But he didn't want to use it."

"And just how did you know that?"

"He hadn't killed anyone. It was Joey that murdered Barney Slocum and Bill Bond."

Curt glared. "But there's always a first time."

I waved away his concern. "I'm fine."

"But Mike Hamblin?" Mac wasn't about to lose the main story over concern for me.

"Mike had a drug ring working out of his business," I said.

"And he's down at headquarters singing away, telling us all kinds of interesting things," William said with satisfaction.

"What's he saying, William?" I knew I'd get a fuller explanation at a later date, but for now I wanted to get some holes filled in. "I know they were trafficking in drugs, but I haven't the vaguest idea how. I know they used Barney Slocum—"

"Who?" Jolene demanded.

"Barney Slocum. You know. The guy found dead in Randy's car."

Everyone nodded except Mr. Montgomery and Delia, even Mr. Whitsun who was hanging on every word. Both Mr. M and Delia looked like they'd eaten a very sour grape.

"Yeah," said William. "Barney Slocum was the courier." And he stopped.

"More," I demanded.

"Lots more," said Mac.

"You know they inventory the lot monthly." William looked at us to be certain we were with him. We all nodded. "Well, between inventories, Barney Slocum would take a car off the lot with a temporary tag and drive the drugs wherever he was told. The car would appear back on the lot a day or two later, no one the wiser. They would use a different car for every run, so there was never a pattern or particular vehicle the authorities should look for."

"Is that what happened to the missing car that you thought Tom might have stolen? This Slocum character had it, and when he was murdered, it disappeared somehow?" Mac asked.

William shook his head. "No. Tom did steal that one."

I nodded. "Steal might be a bit strong, but he did take it. He was shot driving away in it, but he only took it because Joey was coming after him."

William nodded. "So Tom told us."

A surge of joy shot through me. "Tom's awake?"

"And well," William added. "A bit weak and beat up, but all things considered, he's fine."

"What did he say about the missing money?" I asked.

"He didn't say anything, but Mike admitted it was all a hoax to pin suspicion on Tom so that if he ever was found, his word would be doubted."

"So you're saying Tom Whatley stumbled on this drug ring, and that's why he was shot," Mac clarified. "He never took the money and he's completely innocent of any wrongdoing."

William nodded.

"Well, I just knew he hadn't walked out on Edie." Jolene's tone of voice said that being shot wasn't nearly as surprising as the other would have been.

"So why didn't he just go to the hospital or the cops?"

Mac had just asked the big question. We all looked at William for the answer.

"He said that he was afraid for Edie and Randy. They weren't in danger unless he was near them. He felt he had to stay away, had to hide. He said all he could think about was Tom Whatley's death. He said he panicked. He drove to Hibernia, hid the car very well, then hid himself. Then before he knew it, he was too weak to do anything."

"So how did you find him?" Curt asked.

"Merry found him," William said.

Curt turned over one of my hands and ran a finger gently over the scrapes. "That's how you did this?"

I shook my head. "I did this when I was being chased by Mike after I knocked out Joey. He tried to run me down with his car."

"Joey?" asked Mr. Whitsun, still trying to sort everything out.

"Mike." I smiled. "It's confusing."

"But it won't be when you finish writing the story," Mac said. "I can see it now. Another Keystone Press Award to Merry Kramer!"

"That's right," Jolene said, throwing herself back into the conversation with renewed enthusiasm. "Mr. Montgomery, did you know that Merry Kramer, *your* reporter, just won a Keystone Press Award for an outstanding series she did last winter? Isn't *The News* fortunate to have a reporter like her on its staff?" She beamed at me. I beamed back.

Congratulations swirled around my head, and I basked in them. It took some time before I became aware of Mac clearing his throat and looking pointedly at me.

"Oh!" I turned to Mr. Montgomery. "I couldn't have won the award without Mac," I said. "The story idea was his and he's such a great editor and he's done such a good job at *The News* and—"

"What she's trying to say," cut in Jolene, "is that *The News* has a wonderful staff starting right at the top with Mac. He's a terrific editor. And Edie with features and the family page is great, and so is Larry, the sports guy. And of course there's our award-winning Merry Kramer, Amhearst's own Brenda Starr. And then there's me. I'm the best administrative assistant or whatever you want to call me that the paper's ever had. We're a unit, Mr. Montgomery, and together we'll give you the best newspaper in Chester County, maybe in Pennsylvania."

Sometimes Jolene really got it right.

Chapter 19

Easter Sunday was a beautiful day, warm and sunshiny, just the way it's supposed to be. Curt and I walked hand in hand beside Chambers Lake at Hibernia Park, enjoying being together after the chaos of the past week. Our companionable silence was rich with satisfaction and tenderness. Any man and woman could make conversation. Only a special few couples are able to keep silence.

We rounded a bend and came upon a pair of Canada geese nesting in the high grass at the water's edge. As we approached, the male began hissing at us while the female continued to sit on her eggs.

"We won't hurt her, Papa," I said softly. "Don't worry."

He didn't believe us, but he did settle down after we were past.

A big boulder by the water beckoned, and we sat side by side, shoulders touching. Curt had on his dress slacks and shirt, collar open and sleeves rolled back. I still wore my dress but had changed to walking shoes. I'd done enough fancy footwork in dress shoes to last for years.

I lay my head on Curt's shoulder, content just to be sitting next to him. He slid his arm around my shoulders and gave a gentle hug.

"Imagine," I said. "Randy and Edie both came to church this morning."

"I think they were impressed too," Curt said. "I watched them while Sherrie sang and the bell choir played. They were sitting at attention the whole time."

"Yeah?" With my minimal musical abilities, I had to concentrate so hard on my chimes that the whole congregation could have risen and walked out, and I wouldn't have noticed. "Especially Randy, I bet."

Curt laughed. "You should have seen his face. The boy has it bad."

"Poor kid. I think he's doomed to failure with Sherrie. But it's probably a good thing. Fifteen is too young to be that involved with someone."

"If he had any ideas about trying to talk with Sherrie after the service, Jess and Lacey cut him off at the pass. They were climbing all over him."

"It's good for him to be loved like that by the little ones. And it's good for their mother to be loved by Edie."

"Tina was pretty brave coming today with her face still so damaged. She's one courageous lady."

"I hope they all come again. I hope they come all the time."

"I wouldn't be surprised, especially if you ask them." He smiled down at me. "They owe you big time."

I frowned. "I don't want them to come because they owe me. I want them to come because of the Lord Jesus."

"Maybe eventually that's why they'll come." Curt reached for my hand. "In the meantime, who cares why they come. Just so they're there to hear the Gospel."

"You're right." I laced my fingers through his. "I mean, Mac comes strictly because of Dawn, but maybe some day he'll fall in love with the Lord too. At least that's what I keep praying."

A pair of mallards floated by, the male's deep green head iridescent in the bright sun.

Apparently Curt was looking at those marvelously tinted feathers too. "God makes colors that I'll never be able to reproduce, no matter how hard I try." His voice had a fatalistic ring to it.

"But that's what keeps it interesting," I said. "The trying. If you could automatically do it perfectly, where would be the challenge?"

"And I need challenge?"

"Sure. We all do."

"Speaking of challenge, is Mac going to accept Mr. Montgomery's offer to remain as editor at *The News*?"

"He already has." I grinned. "It was all he could do not to shout, 'Yes! Yes! Yes!' in the man's ear when he called, but he acted very maturely, just like a responsible editor should. 'I'll give you my answer within a week,' he said, all quiet and controlled. Like the answer was ever in doubt!"

"So the whole staff stays intact."

"Every last one of us, right down to Jolene, who probably saved us all with her impassioned speech the other night."

Curt ran his thumb across my palm. It tickled in a wonderful way. "She'd make a great politician. She could sell anyone on anything."

The thought of Jolene running even our town, let alone the county, state, or country, was daunting, especially since she could probably organize us better than anyone had in years. I wondered what party she was registered under, assuming she'd ever gotten around to registering, which was doubtful.

"I saw her and Reilly talking with Stephanie Bauer this morning," Curt said. "They were very intent. What's going on there?"

"Jolene's going to give Freedom House some much needed funding." I tried not to sound too smug.

"And who planted that little seed in Jolene's mind, I wonder?"

"I wonder." I giggled.

We fell silent, and I watched a glorious billowing cloud sail across the sky, entranced as wisps spun off to trail behind, then slowly disappear completely.

"What color is the sky?" I asked. "Azure? Indigo? Sapphire? Lapis? Delft? Cobalt? Ultramarine?"

Curt looked up and studied it with his artist's eye. "Blue," he said emphatically. "Very definitely blue."

I laughed. "I love you."

"Mmm. Me too." He bent down and kissed the top of my head. "Did I thank you yet for coming to my show the other night?" His voice was surprisingly serious.

I straightened and looked at him. "Well, of course I came. It was a very important night for you."

"But you'd just been through a terrible ordeal, and if that weren't enough, you had one of the biggest stories of your career to write. And still you cared enough to come. That meant a lot to me."

I was at a loss for words, a rare occurrence. I finally managed, "I'm glad it pleased you."

"I also want you to know that I'm very proud of you."

I probably glowed. "You are?"

He nodded. "Winning your award, helping Edie and Tina, taking in Randy, finding Tom, getting Mike and Joey. You had a pretty full week."

"I'm proud of you too," I said. "Your show went wonderfully well, you sold several paintings, and Mr. Whitsun is taking your pictures. And of course Delia will continue to hang you in Intimations as well as in Philadelphia."

"You're not worried about her anymore, are you?" He eyed me curiously.

I shook my head. "Not anymore. I believe you when you say you made your choice."

"You shouldn't sound so amazed."

"It's just hard to believe. Delia's absolutely beautiful."

"But you're real. And you're just what I need and want."

I hugged his arm. "I'm just glad you weren't embarrassed by how I looked when I showed up at the gallery. I was afraid that you would make believe you didn't know me."

"Never, love. You're mine, and I want the world to know it."

I felt like my smile would crack my face, it was so broad. "Thank you," I managed to whisper.

Curt reached into his pants pocket and pulled out a purple plastic egg with a pink ribbon tied around it. He put it in my hand. "Happy Easter, sweetheart."

I held it for a minute, then shook it. Something inside thunked.

"A miniature chocolate bunny? Or maybe a Hershey's Hug and Kiss?" I raised an eyebrow at him. "Personally I'd prefer one of yours."

Next thing I knew he had his arms about me and was very thoroughly kissing me. When we broke for breath, I rested my head on his chest.

"Mmm. I knew yours would be better. Sweeter too."

I felt the rumble of his laugh against my cheek.

"Open the egg, Merry," he said.

I sat up and made a big production out of untying the ribbon. Then I pretended the two halves of the egg were stuck and I couldn't pull them apart.

"Open it," Curt hissed in my ear.

I grinned unrepentantly at him, but I opened it. My curiosity couldn't stand the suspense any longer.

The facets of the diamond reflected sunlight in a myriad of sparkling rainbows as the ring fell into my skirt.

"Oh, Curt!" I could barely breathe.

He picked up the ring and took my left hand in his large hand. "Marry me, Merry?"

"Oh, yes!" It came out in a whisper, but inside I was shouting. "Oh, yes!"

Also check out these books in the Amhearst Mystery Series!

Caught in the Middle

Gayle Roper

A murder lands reporter Merry Kramer the biggest story of her life. But will she become the next victim?

A corpse was not what Merry was looking for when she opened the car trunk. *Things like this just don't happen to real people*, she thought. But Merry Kramer is new in town--and has yet to discover what hides behind the smiling faces of the residents of Amhearst, Pennsylvania.

As a staff reporter for a local newspaper, Merry finds the job contrasts incredible: as shocking as finding a body one night … as routine as writing a human interest story on a local artist the next day. But when another death is discovered, suspicion begins to dawn … and seemingly inconsequential choices forge a link that makes Merry the next target.

Caught in the Middle is the first in the Amhearst series of mysteries featuring feisty reporter Merry Kramer. Gayle Roper has written over seventeen books and is a member of Mystery Writers of America.

Pick up your copy today at your local Christian bookstore!

Softcover 0-310-20995-1

Caught in the Act
Gayle Roper

Two romances. One murder. Who ever thought life could be so complicated?

Every time Merry goes somewhere with Jolene, something bad happens. This time it's murder. Can Merry clear her friend of the crime without getting killed herself?

Perpetual bad-hair days, not one but two romantic entanglements, a selfish coworker—life is already complex for reporter Merrileigh Kramer. But when she finds her coworker's ex-husband dead at the couple's home, Merry realizes that the complications are just beginning.

Who would want to kill a nice guy like Arnie Meister? It turns out the list is long and getting longer. Meanwhile, the rest of her life isn't exactly on hold—particularly since it includes a new, potential Mr. Right. Merry finds herself smack in the middle of a bewildering maze of romance, personal choices, and murder. Only faith in God and her own instincts can help her solve not just the mystery of Arnie Meister's death, but of her own heart.

Softcover 0-310-21909-4

ZondervanPublishingHouse
Grand Rapids, Michigan

A Division of HarperCollins*Publishers*

We want to hear from you. Please send your comments about this book to us in care of the address below. Thank you.

ZondervanPublishingHouse
Grand Rapids, Michigan 49530
http://www.zondervan.com